WHERE THERE'S A WHISK

SARAH J. SCHMITT

RP|TEENS
PHILADELPHIA

Running Press Teens
Hachette Book Group
1290 Avenue of the Americas, New York, NY 10104
www.runningpress.com/rpkids
@RP_Kids

Printed in the United States of America

First Edition: October 2021

Published by Running Press Teens, an imprint of Perseus Books, LLC, a subsidiary of Hachette Book Group, Inc. The Running Press Teens name and logo is a trademark of the Hachette Book Group.

The Hachette Speakers Bureau provides a wide range of authors for speaking events. To find out more, go to www.hachettespeakersbureau.com or call (866) 376-6591.

The publisher is not responsible for websites (or their content) that are not owned by the publisher.

Print book cover and interior design by Frances J. Soo Ping Chow
Whisk illustration copyright Getty Images/Panom73

Library of Congress Cataloging-in-Publication Data
Names: Schmitt, Sarah J., author. Title: Where there's a whisk / Sarah J. Schmitt. Other titles: Where there is a whisk Description: First edition. | New York, NY : Running Press Teens, 2021. | Summary: Eighteen-year-old Peyton Sinclaire believes winning the "Top Teen Chef" culinary scholarship is the only way to secure her future, but with nine other cooks in the kitchen and a meddling producer only interested in stirring the pot Peyton may have bit off more than she can chew. Identifiers: LCCN 2020047163 | ISBN 9780762496815 (hardcover) | ISBN 9780762496822 (ebook) Subjects: CYAC: Reality television programs—Fiction. | Cooking—Fiction. | Friendship—Fiction. Classification: LCC PZ7.1.S3363 Wh 2021 | DDC [Fic]—dc23 LC record available at https://lccn.loc.gov/2020047163

ISBNs: 978-0-7624-9681-5 (hardcover), 978-0-7624-9682-2 (ebook)

LSC-C

Printing 1, 2021

TO LOUIS.

I never knew what was missing from my life
until the moment we met.

OLIVE JUICE.

CHAPTER
ONE

CRACKING MY KNUCKLES, I STAND MOTIONLESS as everyone else races around me, whispering frantically into their headsets. The thumping of my heart blends with the hum of electrical current coursing through the jungle of wires and cords. Anticipation and dread collide in this time and place. In a few minutes, my life is going to change forever.

"Peyton Sinclaire," a woman says, her voice slicing through the din of production.

I jump at the sound of her voice.

She scans something on the tablet in her hand. "They're almost ready for you."

"Uh, yeah. Whenever." I'm trying to be cool and relaxed, but what few nerves that have managed, up until now, to remain calm are starting to rev into high gear.

The production assistant, or PA as everyone around here calls them, nods but doesn't bother to look up. "I'll walk you through what's going to happen. Don't worry. You'll do great."

"Thanks." I'm not sure how she could know whether I'll be great or not. Especially since I've only been able to manage a total of four words in her presence. In a few minutes, the cameras will begin rolling, and they won't stop for an entire month. Everything I say and do will be fodder for the editing room. How can anyone be sure how *great* someone will be under those conditions?

The PA continues giving her instructions, eye contact not required. "You're going to be the first person to enter the set."

When I don't say anything, she looks up. This tiny gesture grants her my full attention. "Aren't you excited?" she asks, her eyes narrowing. "Do you have any idea how many people auditioned for *Top Teen Chef*?"

"Um, yeah. I'm super excited." I'm also about to throw up all over her shoes.

"You should be," she huffs in a way that makes me wonder if she auditioned but didn't make the cut. That would be awkward.

Top Teen Chef. Personally, I think the name lacks pizzazz for a teen reality cooking competition. I mean, we're going to be battling for a full-ride scholarship to any one of the four American Culinary Institute campuses. I feel like the name of the show should include the words *epic*, *smackdown*, or maybe *cage match*. I grin at the thought of a round cage filled with every cooking gadget I can imagine. We would come armed with graters, strainers, and mandolines. The crowd would chant our names, and when we win they would shower us with marshmallows—flambé style. I don't realize that I let out a little chuckle until the PA clears her throat and I quickly force myself to stand at attention.

I don't think she would enjoy my reimagining of the show as much as I do.

"It will be just you and the camera crew on set when you go through the doors," she continues. "Take your time. You just need to walk in, look around, be impressed—that kind of stuff."

I know exactly what she means because I've watched every episode of every cooking competition show that has ever aired on Food TV. Every show starts off with these confident cooks who are ready to take home the prize, but when they enter the hallowed grounds of the kitchen, they turn into four-year-olds on Christmas morning. It's cute. Now I'm about to find out if those reactions are real or staged. I close my fist and open it, repeating the process until the tingling in my hands goes away.

The PA listens intently to something being said on her headset; then, after a moment, she raises her eyes from her tablet and turns her attention back to me. "You ready?"

"One question."

She stares at me for what seems like forever before saying "What?" in what I can only assume is her trademark impatient voice.

"What am I supposed to do after I look around?"

"What do you mean?"

"Like, once I've seen everything and the next person comes in? Should I get out of their way?"

"Just stay on the set, looking around until the next person comes in. We'll space out everyone's arrival. It will probably take an hour or less."

"Right, but what do I *do* when they come in?"

"I guess that's up to you," she says, still looking at me like she can't tell whether I'm joking or serious. "But if I were you, I would talk to everyone you can. No one wants to watch a group of newly graduated high schoolers standing around, staring at each other."

"Not even if you play that old-time western showdown music? Maybe the camera guy could zoom in real close on our eyes. I can squint really well."

I thought my attempt at a joke was rather good, but she is not impressed.

Or she doesn't have time to answer because whoever is whispering in her ear must be saying something important, as her face is stern with concentration.

"They're ready for you." She raises her hand and motions to the double doors in front of us. "These are swinging doors, so don't pause when you enter, or they might swing back and hit you."

"And that would be bad."

"Yes, and it'll also make it into the blooper reel we're planning for the end of the season."

"Good to know," I mutter, staring at the door and trying to shake off the sudden feeling that the walls are starting to close in around me.

Get it together, Pey, I tell myself. Exhaling, I place both palms on the doors and push hard enough to make a memorable entrance. The doors don't budge, but unfortunately I keep moving. Right up until the moment my nose slams into the door and my brain rattles inside my skull.

The entire backstage crew stares at me as a hot red flush sweeps across my face. I can already feel the lump forming on my lip where I bit it.

"What happened?" the PA yells as she races over to my side. "Are you okay?" she asks, putting her hand under my chin and lifting my face up. She uses the flashlight app on her phone to blind me while she inspects the damage.

"Ow," I say, twitching my nose and blinking as fast as I can to hold back the tears. "That wasn't the entrance I was going for."

She studies my face, turning it from one side to the other. "No blood. You think you're ready to try again?" I see her sneak a peek at her phone. Probably checking the time.

"Is it swollen?" I ask, running my tongue along the inside of my mouth, wincing.

"Nope. You look great."

I'm pretty sure she's lying. But on the other hand, she's not shrinking back in horror, so that's a good sign.

She presses the button on her walkie-talkie. "Can someone check on the swinging doors?"

"Tell them they're not swinging," I mutter, still touching my lip. "Can I have a mirror?"

She ignores me and checks the locks on the door. "No, we're good on this side." A moment later I hear a click from the bottom of the door. "Thanks," the PA says into her walkie.

She turns to me, her smile wide. "I think we're ready now."

"Can I have a mirror?" I repeat.

"No time. Are you ready?"

"If I say no, will it make a difference?"

"Nope."

"Then I guess I'm ready."

She pushes me back into place before fading away into the shadows.

I inhale and count to three before exhaling, trying to forget my stinging lip and damp palms. It's now or, well, I guess it's just now. I give the doors a gentle nudge, just to be sure, before pushing my way into the biggest opportunity of my life.

Standing at the edge of the set, I am overly aware of the cameras as they follow me like some magic eye in a fantasy movie. Then there are the lights—the very bright, extremely hot lights—and the boom mic waiting to catch anything that the mic on my shirt might miss. Of course, I only know it's called a boom mic because a disembodied voice keeps yelling, "The boom mic is in the shot," and "Hold it higher." However, everything fades away as I walk, for the first time, onto the set. All I can see are the shiny chrome appliances and the neon letters spelling out the words "Top Teen Chef" in fancy script.

If I could design the most incredible kitchen, somehow this setup would still be better than that. Spanning the middle of the room are eight brightly colored cooking stations neatly organized into four rows for the contestants. At the back, behind the stations and a large table, are the state-of-the-art appliances— everything from an ice cream machine with flash freeze to a salamander broiler, and even some equipment I've never seen before. I pinch the flesh between my thumb and index finger slightly, just to make sure I'm not dreaming. Nope, not dreaming.

Taking up one entire side of the room is the true shining jewel of the set: the pantry. As I walk between the shelves and peer into the fridges, I swear it has got to be bigger than our grocery store back home, and it must have some kind of special lighting because I have never seen such vibrant red tomatoes or bright yellow peppers. Even when it's not overrun with weeds, which is most of the time, the vegetables growing in the trailer park's community garden definitely have never looked this good. I pick up a package of spinach so green it looks fake. Then, before I can check out anything else, the doors swing open and in walks the first of my competitors, a tall, muscular Black guy who looks as gobsmacked as I feel. When our eyes meet, we both break out into giddy grins.

"Can you believe this place?" he asks in a thick drawl as he turns, taking it all in.

I shake my head. "It's so unreal. Can you believe we are going to get to spend every day here?"

He laughs, and there's something about his charisma or the way he seems enthralled by everything in the room that puts me at ease. "I hear you. My whole family thinks I'm ridiculous for wanting to spend my summer sweating in a kitchen, but I think it's going to be incredible. By the way, I'm Malik."

"Peyton," I say. I'm not sure whether we're supposed to shake hands or not, so I wait a second to see what he does.

A half beat passes before he extends his hand toward me. Handshake it is. "I'm from Alabama."

"Oh my God, we're practically neighbors," I say, taking his hand and giving it a firm shake.

"Really? Where's home?"

"Florida."

He tilts his head. "You know Florida isn't really the South, right?"

"I'm from northern Florida. Fifteen miles from the Georgia line."

"Well, in that case you're Southern enough for me."

An awkward silence falls between us as Malik looks up at the microphones hanging from the ceiling and then glances at the camera. I remember what the PA said about no one wanting to watch people stare at each other.

"It's kind of weird, right?" I ask, hoping to break the silence.

"Like we're being spied on?"

"Yeah. Which, if you think about it, we kind of are."

He gives one more look at the camera and then back at me. "I'm a pretty good judge of character, and I like you, Florida. I think we should make a pact," he says, leaning in close.

"You want to form an alliance? You know we don't get to vote who stays and goes, right?"

"I know the rules," he says, shaking his head as if he can't believe I would think he didn't. "We need to make a pact to have each other's back."

The image of the cage match competitions worms its way back into my mind, and I smile. "I think that sounds like a plan. Who are we watching out for?"

Malik straightens, looking very serious. "You know they had to have brought someone on the show to be the troublemaker. *That's* the person we've got to watch out for."

"What makes you think the producer would do that?"

"Because I know reality TV, and somebody in this cast is going to bring the *drama*." He practically sings the last word.

"But how do I know you're not the troublemaker?" I ask

with a grin. "Your first move would probably be to get inside my head, so that way I don't suspect you when you start pointing fingers at someone else."

He starts to answer me, then stops.

I continue to smile, willing to wait him out.

"You know," he says, "you don't. But the way your mind works makes me wonder if I can trust you." He pauses for the briefest of moments before continuing. "Still, we're neighbors, so we should stick together."

"A regional alliance is good enough for me. Besides, if you are the troublemaker, I'd make an *excellent* sidekick. Just saying."

"Really?" he says, one eyebrow perking up.

I nod. "I have been known to create quite the diversion when the moment calls for it."

He laughs again, and I smile. It's easy to see that this is a guy who knows how to lighten the mood and make people feel comfortable—my nerves have even settled a little after our short conversation.

"I can't wait to hear about your exploits."

I pretend to wince. "I would, but it's one of those things where if I tell you—"

"You'd have to kill me?" he finishes.

I shake my head. "You'd have to clean my kitchen for the rest of the show." Then I give him my most innocent face. "And I'm very messy."

"You know what? Never mind. And I am definitely going to keep my eye on you."

I just grin at him as a friendly silence settles between us. I like Malik, and I'm glad the first person I meet is friendly and funny. If he's right about the show bringing someone in just to stir up trouble, it'll be nice to have an ally with a sense of humor.

CHAPTER
TWO

JUST AS I FINISH MY THOUGHT, A GIRL WITH LONG, curly black hair enters the studio. She doesn't walk as much as float through the door and over to us like a wingless pixie. I swear her eyes practically glow and seem to shift between green and brown under the set lights, creating a stunning contrast with her light brown skin. Her wide smile welcomes us in, but there is a glint in her eyes that makes one thing very clear—she isn't someone to be underestimated.

"Hey," she says, drawing the word out. "I'm Lola from Vegas."

She walks straight toward me with her arms open. Does she expect me to hug to her? Because I am not a hugger. With the camera's all-seeing lens on us, I awkwardly accept the embrace, patting her on the back while still trying to keep some distance between us.

Personal space may be an issue with her.

She seems unfazed as she moves on to Malik, who opens his arms and matches her enthusiasm.

"Check this place out," she says as she steps back. "It's amazing." Her gaze lands on the pantry and stops. "I think I might die right here and now." She turns to us, her eyes wider than humanly possible as the camera moves in, loving every minute of her performance.

"I'm pretty sure the health department would consider dying on set a health code violation," I say, laughing.

Like Malik, Lola is animated and friendly, and as I listen to her and Malik chat with each other, I can't help but like her. I also can't help but be a little intimidated. I come from a town where reputations are passed down from one generation to the next. When your dad is the town crook, you get used to trying to blend in. How am I going to have any chance of catching the attention of the judges if everyone on the show is as charismatic as these two? I glance back at the door just as it begins to swing open again.

"Hey, guys," I say, nodding toward the movement.

The new arrival saunters in with gelled-up black hair and a leather jacket. His eyes are bluebird blue and his jawline looks as sharp as a kitchen knife. If not for the slight scar on his forehead, directly between his eyebrows, he would look perfect.

"A boy," Lola whispers to me, grabbing my arm and giving it a series of squeezes. "A *cute* boy."

She is so close I can smell her, and it's like powdered sugar and lemons. Great, the only other girl here so far is basically sunshine on legs.

"I see him," I say as I try to gently reclaim my arm.

After a quick glance at my three castmates, I can't help but wonder where Food TV found all these people. Is there a talent agency nearby that specializes in super cool teen chefs?

"What's up? I'm Paulie from Jersey City."

Lola is the first to speak up. "Hi, Paulie. I'm Lola from Vegas, and this is Malik from Alabama and Peyton from somewhere in Florida."

"The panhandle," I say quickly. "So inland, but not too far from the ocean." It's more for the camera than the new arrival because if I'm going to fight my inner wallflower, I have to start sometime, right?

Paulie nods. "Cool."

With the introductions complete, Lola slides right over to Paulie and links her arm with his. She really is one of those touchy-feely people.

"Vegas, huh?" Paulie says, giving her arm a playful nudge. "My uncles go there twice a year."

"You should go with them next time and I'll give you the tour."

"I'm not really the gambling type," he says.

"And yet you're here gambling for a future like the rest of us," I say.

"Nah," he says, his grin never faltering. "I'm the odds-on favorite."

"You think so, huh?" Lola says.

She unlinks her arm from Paulie's and comes to stand next to me in feminine solidarity. "Well, I think Peyton and I might have something to say about that."

"Good," Paulie says. "I like cute girls who can cook."

I roll my eyes and pretend to answer a vintage rotary phone. "Hello?" I pause before covering the imaginary mouthpiece. "The 1950s are calling. It's for you."

I expect him to throw some shade, but to my surprise he laughs, and his bravado melts into something more relaxed. "Nice. I thought you were the girl-next-door type, but I might have been wrong."

I almost laugh. No one has ever thought of me as "the girl next door." Most of the time they whisper to each other and then laugh. Malik and Lola continue chatting with Paulie as I slip to the edge of the conversation circle. Watching them, I look for what the casting people must have seen. Paulie is the player of the group, and while Lola may look like a character from a fantasy novel, she doesn't strike me as someone who is afraid of going after what she wants. Malik is a little harder to figure out, but if I had to make a bet, I'd say he's never met a stranger. He has charisma in spades.

"If you had one showstopper dish, what would it be?" Paulie asks Malik.

The question snaps me back to the present.

"Oh, we don't know each other well enough for me to share all my secrets," Malik says, raising his chin just enough to look down on Paulie. "But let's just say that if barbeque is involved, you're going down." Malik pauses just a second before relaxing into a grin and then slapping Paulie on the back.

For his part, Paulie looks like he's not sure which side of Malik is the real one. I think they both are—and I would like to stay on the nice side. Paulie holds out his hand for a low five and Malik slaps it, grinning.

"Got to respect the sauces," Paulie says. "I've lived in Jersey my entire life, and I thought I knew what barbeque was, but a couple of years ago my family went to Texas, and man oh man."

"And what did you learn?" Malik asks.

"Turns out, I did not."

"And you think you know what it's all about after one trip to Texas?"

"Nope. So I'm more than willing to try whatever you want to share."

Listening to the two of them is like being a spectator at a tennis match. "So," I interrupt, "if Malik is the barbeque king, and I'm the baker—" I throw that in, realizing that I haven't yet established my domain in this competition "—what does that make you?"

Paulie gives me a stunned look. "Are you serious?"

"Um, yeah?"

He chuckles and gives me a little shake of his head. "I'm Italian and from New Jersey—I'm literally a walking stereotype."

"Aren't we all?" Malik asks with a knowing grin, before a disembodied voice quietly tells us to limit our conversation to basic biographical facts, food, and the kitchen, and all four of us instantly look like we've just been caught cheating on a test.

"Well, I should warn you all," Paulie says after clearing his throat, "if there is any challenge where we are using pasta, I'm going to wipe the floor with you."

"Don't be so sure," Lola says, rising to his challenge. "My abuela might have taught me everything I know about Cuban cooking, but I've got a style that's all my own."

The confidence in this room is enough to suffocate me. I hope the mics are picking up everything, because these taglines are priceless. I feel like I should say something about cupcakes and icing, but I have nothing.

"What? Are you some kind of plating junkie?" Paulie says, waggling his eyebrows playfully.

I glance between the two of them. "Was that supposed to be some kind of kitchen insult? If it was, it was weak."

Lola grins at me and gives a little nod of appreciation. "Presentation is part of the game. Right, Peyton?"

"Part of it," I agree

Her brows furrow at me. "Are you telling me that as 'the

17

baker,' you don't think presentation is important? No one wants a wedding cake that's slapped together, do they?"

"Well, no, but if it looks good and tastes horrible, no one's going to ask you to bake anything for them again."

Lola looks at me like I've broken our silent bond of sisterhood.

"It's a fair point," Paulie says. "This is a cooking show, right? So no matter how pretty it looks, if the food on the plate tastes gross, then you'll be back in Sin City before you know it."

If I were to say something like that, I'd probably get a death stare in return. But somehow Paulie makes it sound playful and not at all like a betrayal.

Lola gives him a smile and flips her hair over her shoulder. "Oh, *I'm* not going anywhere."

Any reply Paulie might want to say is cut off when the doors swing open again and in walks a guy with bleached blond hair and tattoos on one arm.

"The bad boy," Lola says to me out of the corner of her mouth. "Things just got interesting."

I turn to agree that he looks like he should be shredding onstage at a punk rock concert after a long day of surfing, not sweating it out in a culinary competition, when I realize that she is already off, giving the new guy a big hug and taking charge. She does know this isn't a dating show, right?

After a brief exchange, Lola drags the new arrival over to us. "Okay, everyone, this is Adam, and he's from California."

"What part?" I ask, trying to sound open and friendly.

"Oceanside. It's between LA and San Diego."

"We were just talking about our specialties, so what do you cook?" Paulie asks, throwing a lifeline to Adam, who looks like he's drowning under Lola's gaze. "I'm Paulie, the Italian guy," he adds and then rattles off everyone else's names and what we like to cook, or in my case, bake.

"I guess that makes me the locally sourced vegetarian?" he answers, and I can read the silent "thank you" in his eyes when he looks at Paulie.

Of course he is, I think as panic starts to bubble in my chest. A bad boy with an environmental streak. Casting nailed it again. I glance quickly at the door and hope that the next person to come through isn't another picture-perfect competitor, because otherwise I'm not going to stand a chance.

"Are you vegetarian or vegan?" I ask.

"I'm vegan, but in order to become a more well-rounded chef, I'll use dairy and eggs if I need to. I prefer to stick with plant-based foods, though."

"Huh," Malik says. "Aren't you worried that it could make this competition more challenging for you?"

Adam shrugs. "Maybe, but I like to think I'm pretty versatile. I'm the only vegan in my family, so it was either learn to cook or grow up eating raw vegetables for dinner every night. Wait until you see what I can do with a spaghetti squash."

The conversation turns to Adam's preference for meat substitutes, and when Paulie starts asking Adam about how he would make the perfect meatless meatball, I mentally start taking notes. Everyone is so caught up in the discussion that we don't realize another competitor has entered the room until he is standing next to me.

"Aloha," he says, giving a quick wave of his hand. "I'm Hakulani."

"Oh, hi. We didn't see you come in," I say quickly.

"Yeah. You guys were having a pretty intense conversation."

"Well, we should introduce ourselves," Lola says.

Paulie points toward her. "This is Lola. She's going to be the entertainment director for our duration. I'm Paulie," he adds, holding out his hand for Hakulani to shake.

Hakulani accepts it enthusiastically and the introductions begin again. When he turns his back to me to talk to Adam, I make eye contact with Lola, who nods in Hakulani's direction and mocks fainting. She's not wrong. He is definitely swoon-worthy.

For the first time since our arrival, the conversation drifts away from cooking as Hakulani and Adam compare West Coast surfing with the waves in Hawaii. They both have very strong opinions on where to catch the best waves.

As they agree to disagree, Hakulani turns around and asks where I'm from.

I somehow manage to say, "I'm from Florida."

"Oh, cool. Do you surf?"

What would you do if a ridiculously handsome guy was standing in front of you, asking if you surf?

"Um, sometimes." Yeah, you lie. By *sometimes*, I mean I have been out on the water, on a board, and have caught exactly one wave that ended with me wiping out hard. And for my effort, I ended up with a nasty case of coral rash. "But it sounds like you surf a lot."

"Yeah," he says, "but most of my friends are better than me."

"Same," I agree, and that is not a lie. "But the beach is kind of far away; and between work and school, it's hard to get out there."

"Have you ever used a longboard?" His eyes light up with excitement, and I feel my stomach do a little flip. "I'm still learning how to control the beast. My buddies think I'm ridiculous, but I saw this picture of my grandfather when he was my age and—" He stops suddenly.

"What?"

"Never mind. It's stupid."

"No, seriously. What were you going to say?"

He hesitates, then continues. "It's just that, when I'm out in the ocean, sitting on the board, waiting for a set, I feel closer to him—like he's still around." Hakulani pauses before adding, "He died a few years ago."

My heart jolts. "I know what you mean," I say quietly, aware each word is being picked up by my mic. "My Grams was the one who taught me to bake. When I miss her, I head to the kitchen and pull out her recipes. It's not the same, but it helps."

"Yeah," he says, but there is a sadness that is settling between us as we both think about the person we've lost.

Before I can think of anything to say to break the silence, Hakulani turns with everyone else toward the doors to watch the latest contestant enter. I spin around and swallow a groan. By the way she stops and poses for the camera, I'm pretty sure this is the bringer of drama from Malik's prophecy.

CHAPTER THREE

UNLIKE THE REST OF US WHO ENTERED THROUGH
those swinging doors with varying degrees of nerves, or in my case, slightly overwhelmed with a bruised lip, this well-dressed blonde is standing in front of the doors like she has all the time in the world. She is not even trying to hide the fact that she's sizing all of us up as if she is our judge and jury in determining who among us is worthy of her attention—and the cameras are eating it up. I recognize the look she gives me as she scans the room. It's the same one I got from the girls at school: dismissive and unimpressed. As far as she is concerned, I am irrelevant. We both know we're not playing in the same league, and in a way, it's comforting. I'm used to people underestimating me— and I'm more than willing to use that to my advantage.

Her gaze darts back and forth between Lola and Hakulani, and with her marks found, she saunters over to them, a practiced smile perfectly in place. I'm not sure how they're going to edit this for broadcast, but I'm envisioning some dramatic telenovela cuts that would be perfect. The newcomer stops next to Lola, who beams at her. And in that instant, the queen has chosen her princess.

"Hi," Lola says, continuing the tradition of starting the introductions. But this time, her words tumble out of her mouth, and the pitch of her voice is a little higher than before. I'm surprised at how quickly the cool Vegas girl falls under the spell of this glamorous influencer.

"Hey," the blonde bombshell says. Her voice is as cool as her outfit, which probably costs more than my aunt's lot rent. For the year. "I'm Dani."

"We were just talking about what everyone likes to cook, like vegetarian or baking . . . oh, and where we're from," Lola says, finally stopping to take a breath. "Where are you from?"

I look back at the new arrival, trying to figure out what has turned Lola into a bundle of bumbling energy.

"Bet she's from Manhattan," Paulie whispers as he maneuvers in to stand close to me. For a second, I'm acutely aware of the warmth of his body, but then again, it could just be the lights.

"How can you tell?" I ask, still looking at Dani. There's an air about her that screams posh, but beyond that, I don't see anything more special about her than the rest of us.

He nods in her direction. "The walk, the attitude, the clothes. I don't even think that skirt has made it to the boutiques yet. She's got connections."

"Wow, you're an expert on pasta and women's fashion? So impressive."

"Hey, I have seven sisters. Six older and one younger. One works in the Garment District as an assistant to a fashion photographer, and another has been making her own clothes since she was like ten. They talk a lot of fashion over Sunday dinner."

"Seven sisters?" I ask, my eyes wide. "It's amazing that you even learned to talk."

"Very funny," he says, nudging me with his elbow. "It just meant that there was a lot of time for listening."

"SoHo," Dani says, answering Lola's question.

I'm stunned at how one word can seem so flat and bored. I mean, how can Dani not find all this even just a little bit exciting?

"Ha," I whisper back to Paulie. "You were wrong. She's not from Manhattan."

He just grins.

"What?" I ask.

"SoHo," he says, the smile growing even wider, "means south of Houston Street. In Manhattan."

Dani is answering Lola's questions about the best places to eat in the city, and all the other contestants are hanging on her every word. "Oh," I say, trying not to look at Paulie. "This is my first trip to New York. Everything I know about the city either comes from history class or the *Hamilton* soundtrack."

He chuckles. "You know when they sing, 'They're battering down the Battery'?"

I nod.

"That's the south end of Manhattan. SoHo is north of that, on Broadway."

"And you're into theater?"

"It's *Hamilton*," he says as though that explains everything. Which it kinda does. "If I were you, Peyton, I'd keep an eye on her. She's basically NYC culinary royalty."

"You know who she is?"

"Yeah, and if she's here, there's a pretty good chance the whole competition is rigged in her favor."

"So, who is she?" I say, looking back at Dani just as she flips her hair over her shoulder and lays a possessive hand on Hakulani.

He looks down at me. "You're joking, right? You really don't know who she is?"

I shake my head.

"That's Daniela Moretti," he says, staring at me and waiting for a light-bulb moment to happen.

It doesn't.

"Moretti?" he repeats. "As in the daughter of Chef Moretti, world-renowned chef to the stars? Owner of the Moretti's empire? You can buy his pasta sauce at the grocery store."

I glance back at Dani. "No way."

"Believe me or don't. It doesn't change the facts. That girl was born with a wooden spoon in her hand."

"Why would someone like her be on the show?" I ask, watching her as she gracefully laughs at a joke or something Hakulani said.

"Good question. Her godfather is Jimmy 'Hot Sauce' Hooper."

"The burger guy?"

"That's the one."

My stomach clenches. How am I supposed to compete with someone who was probably perfecting her béarnaise sauce while I was trying not to overcook the mac and cheese? "But that still doesn't answer my question: Why is she here?"

Paulie shrugs. "She doesn't need money for culinary school. I'm pretty sure her dad can afford the tuition. Unless . . ."

"What?"

"Maybe he was the victim of a Ponzi scheme and lost his entire fortune."

"Be serious," I say.

"It's an explanation."

"Not a very good one."

"True, but there's another explanation."

"What?

"She's a *ringer.*"

I turn to watch as Dani begins talking to Malik and Adam.

"They wouldn't do that, would they? Not with someone with a pedigree like hers. It would be too obvious." I glance over at Paulie. "Wouldn't it?"

I don't have long to dwell on this because the doors swing open, revealing the last member of our cast.

Even from this distance, I can see this girl possesses the same level of style that Dani has, but instead of the flashy designer outfit, she's wearing a magenta and dusty rose sari. The cuffs have a delicate design embroidered in gold thread, and the fabric drapes neatly over her left arm. Her makeup and hair are perfectly done. As stunning as she looks, the first thing that I think, once some of my awe has worn off, is: How the heck is she going to cook dressed in such a beautiful outfit? I imagine what I would look like if I had to bake in the nicest outfit I owned—and shudder.

As she walks up, smiling at the small group closest to the door, I am acutely aware that if we were in a segment about which of these eight people doesn't belong, the obvious answer is me. I feel so plain and unremarkable standing next to everyone that I'm even more shocked when she stops in front of me first and says gently, "Hi, I'm Inaaya."

Even her name is elegant. "Peyton," I say before everyone else moves in to introduce themselves.

A few minutes later, a disembodied voice yells, "Cut."

Then, from the shadows, the entire crew emerges to reset

the stage for whatever comes next. The disembodied voice begins barking orders for us to line up, and the PAs race around, moving everyone to different-colored marks on the floor.

"This is your assigned color," a crew member says, grabbing my arms and moving me less than a foot to a turquoise X on the floor.

"Look at the color of the mark you are standing on," the disembodied voice commands. "If we are lined up for filming and you are standing anywhere other than on your mark, you are wrong."

Paulie takes his place next to me and nudges my arm. "You ready for this?"

"Sure," I say. I am absolutely lying.

"Quiet on the set," the disembodied voice says. "Action."

CHAPTER FOUR

"HEY, EVERYONE," A CHEERFUL VOICE SAYS FROM behind us. Surprised, we all turn to see Jessica Evans sweeping into the room.

"Are you kidding?" I whisper, barely containing my excitement.

I love Jessica Evans. Two years ago, she was a stay-at-home mom who made and sold cakes from her kitchen to help her family make ends meet. Now, she's the network's newest rising star all because she won a cooking competition just like this. She is funny and sweet and all the other gushy words someone can say about another person. I turn to Paulie. "I can't believe *Jessica Evans* is going to be the host."

"I can tell," he says, laughing at my fan girl moment.

Jessica waits as the cameras catch our reactions and get some footage of her beaming at us before she continues, "I'm Jessica Evans."

Everyone breaks out in applause. It's very possible that I start it and everyone else is instinctively joining in.

"Welcome to *Top Teen Chef.* You are some of the best cooks in your generation. And this competition is going to give you a chance to show the judges—and America—your talent and passion for food for the opportunity to win a culinary scholarship to the American Culinary Institute."

We all cheer and clap. Somewhere in the back of my mind, I'm acutely aware that our excitement is genuine. No matter how chill anyone had been when we first got here, it's not lost on us now that the competition has begun.

Jessica waits for us to settle down before adding, "Are you guys ready to meet the judges?"

"Yeah!" we say in unison.

"Then meet restaurateur A. J. Yang and Food TV's favorite cooking couple, Angelica Meyers and Billy Caine."

Again, we all go wild as the judges walk in, waving to us and the cameras before taking their seats at the judges' table. I try not to look directly into the cameras, which I'm starting to realize is basically impossible. I mean, they are right there, in front of us, panning our faces to get up-close reactions. We stop cheering after a few seconds, but then the disembodied voice tells us to keep going. Apparently, they didn't get enough excitement footage from all of us. We all try to make our smiles and applause appear genuine, but there is an air of awkwardness now. I hope this isn't something we'll have to do often.

They must have gotten what they wanted because, as if by some unspoken cue, Jessica straightens, turns a little more to face us, and continues on like nothing happened. "You've all got talent; you wouldn't be here if you didn't. But now it's time to see which of you has the fire to go for what you want and whose dreams will be put on ice."

"What is she talking about?" I whisper to Paulie, but he is looking at Jessica with an unreadable face. I turn to Lola, who just shrugs.

"Today is your *first* challenge," Jessica says.

This time the reactions the cameras pick up are a combination of disbelief, confusion, and, in my case, petrification.

"But don't worry," Jessica says quickly. "No one is going home."

Relief ripples down the line, and a few of us break out into uneasy smiles, the unspoken *yet* hanging in the air around us.

"She could have led with that," I grumble, forgetting about my mic.

"First, we're going to hand out your official chef attire, and you'll find that your jackets match your kitchen station." She pauses, eyeing each of us. "Want to find out where you'll be cooking while you're here?"

I nod my head and clasp my hands together. I feel like I'm

in a dream, but this is all real—the competition, the opportunity, everything. It's not happening to someone on a screen but to me, right now. I take a deep breath and try to listen to Jessica, but my brain isn't cooperating. A couple months ago I was nothing but the daughter of the town criminal, with no chance of going to community college—much less the best culinary school in the country. I'd spent my whole life believing that things like this happened to other people—not to me. But here I am.

Jessica turns to A. J., Billy, and Angelica, who have moved next to a table with a kaleidoscope of colored chef's jackets. "Would you do the honors?" she asks them.

The set lights are already hot, but in this moment, it is like someone has cranked up the heat even more, and I feel my heart skip a beat. I discreetly reach for Paulie's arm to steady myself, just in case, and other than a slight shift as he leans a fraction closer, he doesn't draw attention to us.

"You okay?" he whispers through his wide smile.

"Yeah," I whisper back.

I'm so caught up in the moment and in my own thoughts that I don't see A. J. pick up the turquoise jacket and whip it open. I also don't hear him call my name.

Thankfully, Paulie nudges me slightly with the arm I'm holding on to and I quickly jump out of line. I hear a giggle from somewhere to my left and try to laugh it off with a quick smile over my shoulder. As I approach the steps leading up to the judges, I remind myself to breathe and not trip up the stairs.

"Thank you," I say, sure that my voice is shaking. I reach out and take the jacket, the fabric much softer than I expect. Then, not sure what to do next, I stand there, waiting.

"Peyton," Angelica says, gesturing toward the rows of work kitchens. "Take your place at the station that matches your uniform."

I smile and walk as steady as I can to my kitchen, which is in the far-right corner of the back row. Everything in it is the same color as my jacket, from the towels to the utensils. Even the oven is turquoise. I'm sure I'm supposed to stand and watch everyone else get their jackets, but I can't help running my hand over the cool metal of the mixer. The one I have at home is held together by electrical tape and prayers, but this one is top of the line and I bet it even has all the fancy attachments.

"Hey, neighbor," a voice whispers to me, and I snap my head up to find Paulie buttoning his own jacket, which is the shade of a ripe pomegranate. He takes his spot in the corresponding kitchen, located in the same row as me.

"Hey," I whisper back as I watch Dani get her salmon-colored jacket from Angelica. She basically skips to her station, which is in the front row, right in front of the judges' table. I take a moment to be grateful at how lucky I am to not be under the constant eye of the judges. Then I sneak a peek in the drawer labeled "mixer." Sure enough, every attachment you can imagine is neatly organized. I'm wondering how long it will take me to utterly destroy this system when the drawer slips from my hand and springs shut with a *thunk* loud enough for the entire room to hear.

All heads turn in my direction.

"Sorry," I say sheepishly.

The procession of handing out the jackets continues, and the yellow jacket, which matches the station directly in front of me, is in Angelica's hands. "Hakulani Iosua, please come forward."

With his back to me, I can't see his face as he accepts it, but, when he turns around, and grins in my direction, I wonder if someone in the editing crew is going to insert a little light flash and ping sound effect every time he shows his perfectly straight smile.

As Hakulani walks toward his station, I catch a glimpse of Dani's face.

Paulie must see it as well because he moves closer and whispers, "What's her deal? She's got a primo spot and she looks disappointed."

"Don't know," I say with a shrug.

"It's probably because you're surrounded by the two most awesome guys in the competition," he says, flexing his arm.

"You think that's it?" I ask, laughing into my hand.

As Hakulani steps into his kitchen, he turns, and he and Paulie high-five over my counter.

After another minute or so, the final jacket is given out, and the judges take their places at the table.

"Cut," the disembodied voice calls out. "Get ready for the first challenge."

The studio erupts with noise and motion as everyone scurries around to get the set ready for our first challenge.

Malik, whose station is next to Hakulani's and in front of Paulie's, walks around to the center of our stations. "How's it going, Florida? Nice color."

"You too," I say, admiring the dark pumpkin color of his jacket.

Paulie and Hakulani move in closer, too.

"I can't believe they're making us do a challenge on our first day," Hakulani says.

Paulie raises a brow at him. "What did you think we were going to do? This is television. Every day we're here costs them more money."

"That's probably why they are cramming an entire season into three weeks," I add.

Before anyone can say anything else, the disembodied voice directs us to follow the PA, who is waving his hands in the air, trying to catch our attention. As the whole cast gathers around, I hear him say, "Wardrobe has a selection of pants and shirts that you'll be wearing today, which are over there on the rack with your names pinned to them. Get your pants and a shirt, and then you can follow me so you can change."

Inaaya looks relieved. "I was hoping I wouldn't have to cook in this," she says, lifting her skirt up slightly. "I don't know why they had me wear this in the first place."

"Probably to highlight your Indian heritage," Dani says as she sorts through a pile of pants, looking for hers. We all fall silent as she pulls out a pair of soft gray leggings before looking at all of us. "What?"

"You know, there is more to me and my cooking than where my family comes from," Inaaya says, looking a little annoyed.

Dani laughs. "Right, and I'm sure Paulie is more than slicked-back hair and leather jackets."

"Wow," Paulie says, grabbing a pair of black jeans.

"Oh please," Dani says as she accepts the shirt that's handed to her. "This is television. We may not have a script, but don't forget that we're all still characters." Then she saunters off the set without another word.

"She's not wrong," mutters the wardrobe person as they hand me a shirt. "We've got entire sets of clothes for you at your apartment, and everyone has a particular style and look."

"Five minutes," the disembodied voice calls over the speaker. "Set the stations."

I wish I could ask them more about the look they chose for

me, but I don't have the time, so I race in the direction the PA sends me and find the nearest bathroom. Dani is already in one stall, and Inaaya and Lola are right behind me, the doors clanging shut as they step into their own stalls. In three minutes, I return to the set, my original outfit folded in my arms and pressed gently against my chest.

"What do I do with these?" I ask the woman in wardrobe.

She reaches for them. "I'll take them. You'll get them back later tonight."

"Thanks."

"Of course."

"One minute," the disembodied voice calls.

"Peyton," Jessica calls, motioning me to the front where she is gathering the rest of my competition. "We're going to line up here to get started. Do you remember where your mark is?"

I scan the ground and find my turquoise X between Hakulani and Malik. Thank goodness I'm going to be with people I'm comfortable with.

Inaaya is the last to return from changing, and the wardrobe assistant meets her at the door, draping her outfit gently over an arm before heading somewhere into the bowels of the studio with the rest of our clothes in tow.

Before the cameras start rolling again, Jessica turns to us and takes a deep breath. "How are you all doing?"

A few people say they're doing fine, but most of us just stand there. "Overwhelmed?" she suggests.

"Is there something that's more than overwhelmed?" I ask.

"Like *super* overwhelmed?" Paulie suggests.

"At least," I say, tilting my body slightly so I can make eye contact with him farther down the line.

"It's day one," Jessica says. "Completely normal. You'll get used to it."

"If we last that long," Lola says.

I think that's the first time she has been anything less than confident.

"Quiet on the set," the disembodied voice calls.

Everyone straightens up as the judges return to their seats.

Once we're ready, Jessica begins her introduction. "Today, the judges are going to get a little taste of who you are. And your introduction will be in the form of a meal that tells us who you are, not just as a chef or baker, but as a person." She pauses before adding, "Just to make sure you heard me, I said meal. And by meal, I mean make an appetizer, entrée *with* a side, and, of course, dessert."

My mind starts racing. Three courses, made from scratch, with no prep time to plan. I've watched every episode of every cooking show on the network, and this is the part I never understood. How do they come up with their ideas on the fly? Just thinking about it makes my stomach flip-flop. I look straight into the camera and I swear the red light is mocking me.

Jessica turns toward the judges. "Any words of wisdom for our young chefs?"

Angelica smiles at us. "You'll be judged on how your dishes taste as well as presentation. Use your food to introduce yourself to us and the world. Today, the pantry will be open for the entire round."

"And don't be afraid to ask Jessica for help or advice," Billy adds. "She's been where you are. She's probably the best tool you have access to."

"Aw, thanks, Billy," Jessica says before looking at A. J. "Anything to add?"

"Yeah. It's simple: have fun. Yes, this is a competition and, yes, the stakes are pretty high, but don't hold back. What's the worst that could happen?"

"Food poisoning," I mutter.

A split second later, I hear stifled laughter from the dark part of the studio. *Damn, the mic.*

"I'm sure you're all ready to get cooking," Jessica says and we all cheer in agreement.

I glance at Paulie, who is staring at the judges' table and rubbing his hands together in anticipation.

"ACI, here I come," Hakulani says.

Jessica raises her hands to get our attention. "All right

chefs, you have three hours to come up with your menu and prepare it." She stands there, waiting as the cameras circle around us, capturing our hand-wringing and nervous bouncing on the balls of our feet. "There's only one thing left to do."

Another dramatic pause.

"Let's get cookin'!"

CHAPTER FIVE

THE ROOM ERUPTS IN CHAOTIC MOTION. EVERY-
one rushes the pantry, trying to get whatever essential ingredient
they'll need before someone else gets it first. Everyone else looks
so sure of what they're going to make, while I feel like a squirrel
drunk off rotten crab apples. I reach blindly for spices and rice
and vegetables.

The fruit is next, and I load up on oranges. Nothing like leaning into the Sunshine State's most famous export. I'm about to
turn around to search the refrigerator for supplies when I spy
small green limes hidden behind a bushel of pears. A slow smile
spreads across my face. I take the entire bag and rush back to my
station to drop off my haul before making a return trip to grab
dairy and meat. The menu is slowly unfolding in my mind, and it
screams Florida panhandle.

After preheating the oven, I look over my supplies to make
sure I have everything I need. I still have no idea what I'm going
to do for an appetizer, but I really need to get the pie crust baking

and the filling ready. I open the box of graham crackers and, out of habit, start crushing enough to make two pie crusts.

"Crap," I say as quietly as I can.

Paulie hears me. "What's the problem?"

I look over at his station, where he is opening can after can of tomatoes, splashing a little from each as he puts it aside. "It looks like somebody died over there."

He grins, using his arm to swipe all the empty cans into the trash at the end of the counter. "I'm here to cook. No one said I had to keep it clean." He points with his chin. "What mischief are you up to?"

"I wasn't thinking and doubled the recipe."

He pauses for a moment. "And?"

"I only need one."

"Big deal. Make two," he says. "You never know."

I nod and go back to finishing the crust and pressing it into two tart pans before popping them in the oven. Normally, I don't need a timer to know when a pie crust is done. I can tell by the smell. It's that sweet spot just as the crust becomes golden brown but before it's overcooked. Even thirty seconds can make the difference between good and perfection. And a graham cracker crust is even less forgiving than dough when it comes to overcooking. But today, it's probably a good idea to pay attention to the clock. I grab the turquoise kitchen timer and twist to ten minutes.

Since I now have two pie crusts, I go ahead and whip up a double batch of filling, careful to keep an eye on the oven. I know the timer is ticking down the seconds, but it's hard not to peek inside. Not all ovens bake the same and I haven't had time to figure out this one's quirks.

"Hey, Peyton," Jessica says, standing on her tiptoes to look at my station. The camera is right behind her.

"Hey, Jessica," I answer, trying not to be nervous. "Congratulations on winning your show."

"You're so sweet," she says with a smile. "As a fellow baker, I just had to come and see what you're up to. What's in the oven?"

"Pie crust," I say. "For key lime pie."

Her eyes widen. "I think that might be my favorite pie."

"Mine too," I admit with a grin. "The sweetened condensed milk really highlights the tartness of the lime."

"Agreed," she says. "What are you working on here?"

"I'm cutting strips of steak for citrus asada fajitas with fresh pico and guac," I say quickly, slicing through the skirt steak. I pause my cutting and glance up to flash a quick smile to the camera. With a knife in my hand and a mental to-do list running through my head, I feel more confident.

"What kind of citrus are you using?"

"Oranges, of course," I say, zesting the peel.

"Right. You're from Florida," Jessica says with a gentle laugh. "Well, I can't wait to see what you do with all this citrus."

"Thanks, Jessica," I say, keeping my eyes on my knife instead of the camera. Nothing says amateur like cutting off a fingertip.

When she finally leads the camera away from my station, I rush to the sink to wash my hands before moving the crust from the oven to the blast chiller.

On my way back to my station, I check out some of my competition. Inaaya is de-boning a full fish with a pair of fish tweezers. I can't believe how quickly she pulls out the tiny bones. I'm going to have to ask her for some pointers.

Lola is stacking various sizes of foam disks until she has a cone shape that must be at least three feet tall. And on Adam's station, I'm pretty sure he's got every spice on the rack organized into four groups.

Everyone is rushing around to get their dishes done, and I still don't have an appetizer. No matter how good my pie is, I can't win this round if I'm missing an entire course.

Going back into the walk-in cooler, I survey what's left of the supplies, and I have to give it to my castmates: there's not much.

Seafood is a no-brainer for a Florida girl. Even where I live, the fresh catch of the day is only a couple of hours old when you get it. But all I see are a few scallops and a broken crab leg. Not enough to make a complete dish for the judges. On the top shelf, far in the back, are two containers filled with something that is slimy enough to suggest it came from the ocean. I reach for them, but my arms are too short. I duck my head and try again, this time reaching under the wire rack and using my fingers to nudge one of the containers toward the edge. Once it's within reach, I grab it and read the label.

"Yes!" I shout, causing those around me to turn, including all three judges, who are keeping a running commentary from their elevated vantage point at their table. A. J. stands to crane his neck to see what I'm up to. "Sorry," I say, but I don't mean it. I make quick work of getting the other container and am rewarded with a second helping of my magical ingredient. I race back to my station and resist the urge to start chopping now. I still need to finish the marinade for the steak.

"Peyton," Jessica says once she finishes interviewing Lola. "I noticed you were pretty excited about something in the cooler."

I look up and my eyes zoom in on the red light. With each blink, the words in my brain disappear.

"Uh, yeah," I stammer. "I found my inspiration for my appetizer."

"That's great," she says, peeking over the countertop of my station. "Can't wait to see what you do with it. Smells fishy."

She laughs at her own joke, and I know I'm probably supposed to do the same, but I just freeze up.

As she pushes away from my counter and walks behind me on her way to spy on another cast member, she whispers, "Breathe and relax."

46

I take a deep breath as the cameras follow Jessica, then begin to mix up a batter for my appetizer. Hakulani glances over his shoulder. "Batter?" he asks. "You're going to serve fried food to Angelica?"

I don't know if his words are meant to get under my skin, but they do. Angelica is known for her clean, fresh, grilled-never-fried cooking. Number one rule of feeding people is to know your audience. My face falls and then he quickly adds, "I mean, if you can catch her attention with something outside her culinary lane, that would be epic."

He's not doing a good job of digging himself out of his hole, but he looks so earnest that I go against my gut and decide to give him the benefit of the doubt.

"That's what I'm hoping for," I say, pointing at the tails of his shirt peeking out from the bottom of his chef's jacket. "Nice shirt, by the way."

He glances down, almost embarrassed. "My aloha shirt? Normally I wouldn't wear one. Too touristy for me, but the wardrobe person was insistent that I wear them as part of my brand. I'm eighteen. Do I really need a brand?"

"What?" I ask in mock horror. "You don't have a brand? I'm not sure I can be seen with you." I smile at him and start cutting the tomatoes for the pico.

"Oh yeah?" he asks, glancing over his shoulder. "What's your brand?"

"Lard and butter, baby," I answer quickly. "Or butter and lard. I'm not sure which order will resonate with the focus groups."

"I don't think you can go wrong leading with butter," Malik says as he turns and races to grab something in the pantry.

"He has a point," I say.

Hakulani smiles before stepping back from his counter and looking into my station. "Key lime pie, huh?"

"Yeah. It's kinda my signature back home." I take my hand juicer and pop the limes in before squeezing all the juice into a measuring cup.

"Best key lime pie I ever had was from a food truck on Kamehameha Highway," he says as he steps back and picks up a knife to slice something.

"What was so great about it?" I ask.

"It was dipped in chocolate."

"Watch out. I might steal that idea," I warn him. "You don't want to help out the enemy, do you?"

He laughs, and then we both turn our attention back to our dishes.

A few minutes later he heads to the pantry and returns with two cans of Spam.

I wrinkle my nose. "What can you make with that?"

He pops the top. "I think you mean: What can't I make?"

"I said what I meant."

"Have you ever tried it?" he asks, shaking the can in my direction.

I shake my head and lift the measuring cup to see how much juice I have. "I wouldn't even know what to do with it."

"Well, maybe I can teach you," he says, popping the top off the can and giving me a wink.

I pause, mid-cut. Is Hakulani just being naturally friendly, or is he flirting with me? I look down so he can't see my face turn red. Of course, we've only just met, so it's probably more likely that he is being nice. I mean, we're on a television show and going to be working next to each other for as long as we're here. That's it. He's just being neighborly. Plus, when you're surrounded by people who love food, offering to make dinner for someone doesn't mean they're interested in you. Does it?

A roving camera crew parks in front of Hakulani before I have a chance to respond to him, then Jessica begins to pepper him with questions about what he is working on. Apparently, I'm not the only person surprised to see Spam being used in today's competition.

I glance up at the giant red timer hanging over the middle of the room. Each second that ticks by feels like a thud in my head. Once the crusts are cool enough, I fill both with the pie filling and stick one in the oven and put the other one in my tiny fridge for later. I glance at the timer again, making a mental note to check it in twelve minutes. Grabbing the rest of the ingredients for the pico and guacamole, I begin chopping, my mind racing through the things I still have to do. I put the pico in the cooler before getting to work on the avocados. After a few minutes, I check the time, taking my eyes off my blade long enough to slice open the tip of my finger.

"Ow," I cry out. Every head on the set and probably most of the ones sheltered by the dark turn to look at me. Some, like Hakulani and Paulie, are staring in concern. Dani has an amused smile on her face.

"What happened?" Paulie asks.

"Cut myself," I say, grabbing a paper towel and wrapping it around my fingertip as I step back from my station. The medic arrives like a bloodhound on the hunt.

"Let's get you bandaged up," he says, steering me over to the corner with a Red Cross emblem taped to the wall.

"But my pie," I say, trying to pull away.

"Sorry, Peyton," the medic says. "We have to follow the blood-borne pathogen protocol. I'll get you patched up as quickly as I can, but you can't go back to your station until I'm done."

"Just give me a bandage," I argue. "It's not that bad. It's practically stopped bleeding already."

The medic ignores me and sits me down on a stool. He doesn't give me a bandage so I can get back to my pie. At any minute the timer is going to go off and if I'm not around to pull it out, the custard will burn. Not that this guy cares. He cleans the cut for several minutes, flushing it with sterile saline over and over with a plastic syringe, during which time I definitely hear my timer ring. When he is convinced I don't need stitches, he smears salve over my finger before putting a waterproof bandage over the cut. The bleeding has slowed, but he wraps it up in gauze anyway. With each step and minute that goes by, I can smell the damage being done. By the time I get back to my station, my pie is beyond saving.

"I tried to get your pie out," Paulie says. "But Jessica stopped me. Apparently, they're more afraid of you accusing me of sabotage than burning the whole studio down."

I yank open the oven and smoke pours out as the smell of burned graham crackers wafts across the room. I pull out the pan, dropping it on the stainless-steel counter. The entire kitchen is silent. Well, almost silent.

"Look," I hear Dani say in a stage whisper, "the baker burned her pie. Guess we know who *not* to worry about."

My entire body feels hot and my face sizzles with humiliation. I want to tell her off, but she's right. I am the baker who burned her first baked dessert.

"Oh no, Peyton, what happened?" Jessica asks, more for the people viewing at home than out of real concern for me. So much for baker solidarity.

"I guess I burned my pie."

Wanting to be rid of the smell of burned graham cracker, I grab the pan off my station counter and dump the blackened goo in the trash before quickly walking to the dirty dish area. It's the only place the cameras don't seem to go. Maybe it's because the piles of dirty dishes don't make for good optics. I flip the tart pan into a mostly empty sink and turn on the cold water. After letting it run a little bit, I splash my face and dry it off with the cuff of my jacket. After two deep breaths, I turn and walk back into the brightly lit studio and plaster a smile on my face. I won't give anyone the satisfaction of seeing me cry. When I arrive, all remnants of the burned pie have been carried away by some unlucky crew member.

Paulie gives me a thumbs-up and whispers, "You got this," as I walk by.

Jessica is still waiting at my station. She nudges the camera guy and he zeroes in on me. "Everything okay?" she asks.

I force myself to look up and smile, trying not to be mad at her. She was just doing her job. "Yeah. Luckily, I've got a backup." I pull the second tartlet pan from the fridge and set it on the table to come to room temperature.

Jessica claps her hands together. "That's great news. I'm so glad we're still going to get to taste your key lime pie."

"Absolutely," I say, forcing myself to sound calm. I go through my mental checklist. As much as I need to get the pie in the oven, I still have two other courses to prepare. I preheat the grill burner and toss the skirt steak on before turning back to Jessica.

"Take two," I say, smiling as big as I can. That's what the camera wants, right? Happy teens having a good time in the kitchen. Wholesome entertainment for the whole family. When I glance at the clock, however, my smile fades. Back home it takes me the better part of an hour to finish a key lime pie from baking to plating. That's all that's left in the competition. It's going to be close.

Jessica nods her head toward the stations across from us, and the camera turns away from me. "We should let Peyton get back to work," she says and gives me a wink.

Once she's out of earshot, Paulie gives me a head nod and a grin. "Aren't you glad you made that second crust now?"

I shoot him a quick smile before turning back to finish the guacamole and pull my steak off the grill, trying to work around my overly bandaged finger. "I suppose you're going to say I owe it all to you. It's like you knew something was going to go wrong."

"Actually, I was hoping there'd be an extra one to eat later tonight."

I don't say anything, and Paulie must sense that I'm not in the mood for banter because he focuses on his sauce as I take one of the containers I found in the cooler and dump the contents out on my station.

Thankfully, the rest of my cooking time is uneventful, because I don't think my heart could handle one more disaster. As the minutes tick down, I fill a whipped cream canister with whipping cream, vanilla extract, and powdered sugar. Once the lid is on, I give it a good shake to mix the sweet concoction together before loading the nitrous oxide cartridge into the holder and make quick work of squeezing out a ring of perfectly sized rosettes onto my pie slices.

Finally, I turn my attention to the part of the competition that I was dreading—plating. At the diner where I work, we keep it pretty simple. Most of the time you just add a slice of orange or maybe a parsley leaf, and then send it out. But I doubt that will impress the judges, so I grab a key lime and slice five thin wedges, clipping them in the middle so I can twist them on top of the cream rosette. Just as I set the final one down, the buzzer goes off and we all throw our hands in the air like every show I've ever seen. If I wasn't so stressed, it would be funny.

The first challenge is over, and I accept a group hug from both Paulie and Hakulani, who has come over from his station. Malik gives me a fist bump over the counter.

"Tough luck about the pie," he says, and I can tell he means it.

I thought this was going to be a competition where people were prepared to stab each other in the back to win, and I'm pleasantly surprised that I might have been wrong.

"Thanks," I say. "I had a backup, so fingers crossed."

"That was smart," he says, giving me two thumbs-up.

Hakulani looks over his shoulder as the PAs prep the dais for our presentations and the judges take their seats. "We're not through yet," he says, and all of us stop smiling.

CHAPTER
SIX

I TRY TO REMAIN CALM AS, ONE BY ONE, MY COM-
petition steps forward to present their dishes to the judges, but
I am totally freaking out. Not only do I have to explain what I
made and how I made it, but now everyone is telling these personal, moving stories that are winning over the judges. The
problem is that I don't have a good story.

I mean, I could talk about my fried conch fritters and how
the first time I had them was during a tailgate party before
homecoming. I could tell them about how we go from car to
car, tasting whatever dish each family made. Of course, I'm not
going to mention the part about how my family never brought a
dish or had a spot for themselves—usually we didn't even go to
the game afterward. I also *cannot* say that, some years, that was
the only thing I'd have to eat that day.

Even though I was the first to get my jacket, I'm the last to
present my food. Thankfully, the prop crew has a way to keep
the dishes warm. Not hot, but hopefully edible. Unfortunately,

I'm following Lola, who has not only created this culinary masterpiece, but also charms the judges with her dream of elevating buffet food from the casino floor to high society by adding glamour, glitz, and style. Apparently, it also tastes as amazing as it looks, because I'm pretty sure I saw Billy's eyes roll to the back of his head.

I watch as the production crew carries in my beveled blue metal plates piled high with conch fritters and places a serving in front of each judge, next to a clear glass condiment container of citrus mustard. I can hear Angelica still raving about Lola's presentation as I approach the judges' table. When I picked these plates from the stacks, the blue beveled texture looked like the shimmery blue of the ocean, but under the lights of the judging area, they just look like old, banged up, blue plates. Compared with Lola's glitz, they look like junk. Taking a deep breath, I start my presentation.

"There's a saying in Florida that the farther north you go, the more Southern you feel." This gets a smile from Billy and A. J. Nothing from Angelica. She just stares between the plate and me, her lips turning down like she smells something rancid. And just like that, everything I plan to say dribbles out of my brain like early morning drool. "Um, this is what I like to call Florida Gulf cuisine."

What am I saying? I've never uttered those words in my life. I panic and look at Jessica, who gives me a smile and nods encouragingly. Angelica looks unimpressed as she picks up her fork and begins to poke at the fried ball. I feel like I'm drowning up here.

Clearing my throat, I try to salvage my presentation. "For the appetizer, you have a deep-fried conch fritter with a citrus dipping sauce." And that's how I describe the dish that's supposed to have happy memories for me. Deep fried and a sauce. I swallow and try to think of any clever comments. After a beat of uncomfortable silence, the judges realize that I am not going to say anything else, so they pick up the fritter and dip it into the sauce.

It's funny how, when you're panicking, you notice the most random things. Like how Angelica picks up her fritter and daintily dips it in the sauce. A. J., on the other hand, picks up the largest chunk and dunks it. Then, as Angelica nibbles on her bite, Billy pops it into his mouth and chews thoughtfully. Both A. J. and Billy pick up a second fritter. Angelica doesn't even finish her first, which gives her a chance to speak before anyone else.

"My biggest issue was the grease. It overshadowed the sauce, which I found to be bland."

I nod, but in my head I'm yelling that she barely tasted the food. How would she know?

A. J. looks sideways at her. "I don't know what you're talking about. Mine were perfect. And this sauce. What did you put in it?"

My mind goes totally blank before it starts screaming *ORANGE*, which is the only reason I say anything. "The base is orange marmalade and some creole seasoning and lemon. Oh, and mayo."

"I'm getting a hint of horseradish," Billy says before taking another bite.

"You're right," I answer, smiling at him like I didn't mention it on purpose, like it was a test. "Just a pinch." I can't believe I forgot to mention the horseradish.

A. J. wipes his mouth with a napkin. "It's not the prettiest thing I've seen, but what fritter is? The taste, however, is the epitome of down-home Southern comfort."

"I agree," Billy says. "It definitely captures life on the Gulf." His comment triggers some distant trivia I know about him being born in Mississippi. "I'm looking forward to what you have in store for us next," he says, wiping his face with his napkin.

For the moment, I feel pretty good. Angelica pushes her plate away as if the mere viewing of the dish makes her sick, but I try to ignore her.

"Next course," she says. I expect her to snap her fingers so someone will come rushing over to clear the plates from her sight.

"Right," I say, before the production crew clears the remnants of my appetizer and replaces it with the entrée. "Keeping with the orange theme, this is asada fajitas with a citrus marinade, pico de gallo and homemade guacamole, and a side of Spanish rice."

"Is this a special dish for your family?" Angelica asks.

"Not really," I say with a shake of my head. "I was trying to bring a Florida flare to the dish by carrying the orange from the sauce into this course."

I watch helplessly as they eat each element of the meal, their eyes focused on the plate as they push the food around, inspecting it like a crime scene investigator, looking for any clue that something is wrong with it. Or maybe I watch too many reruns of crime shows.

"The rice is a little undercooked," Billy says as he spreads the food out on the plate with his fork. "And the steak is slightly overcooked. Have you ever used a sous vide?"

I'm struggling to understand the words coming out of his mouth. *Sous what?*

"Uh, no."

"Look into it. Your steak will cook perfectly next time, and it won't flatten out like these strips have."

"I agree," A. J. says. "The flavor is really tasty, though, and the orange really comes through."

"I felt the rice lacked flavor," Angelica says, looking pleased that her fellow judges agree with her this time. "Did you make the tortillas from scratch?"

I shake my head. "I ran out of time," I admit.

She smiles, but there is a hint of pity in it. When I was planning, I should have thought about what my audience would want to eat. But I was so worried I would run out of time, and then there was the pie.

As if reading my mind, Angelica sits up a little straighter and says, "Because of the pie?" She smiles innocently.

There's no way the producers aren't going to show the burned pie, because it's now become a conversation point of the judging. Which means my sliced finger is going to be shown, too. Why did I have to label myself as the baker when we were introducing each other? What does it say about my skills when I cut my finger and burn my pie during the first challenge?

I force a laugh and smile brightly, hoping anyone watching will think she and I are sharing a private joke. "That certainly didn't help."

"Next time, make your tortillas from scratch—these taste commercial. And you really need to work on your time management if you ever hope to run a kitchen." She doesn't even look at me as she delivers her last critique. Instead she makes a note on the pad of paper by her plate and underlines it. Three times. "If everyone is done, please bring out the dessert."

Even though the first pie had been disastrous, I know the second one is perfect. I glance over my shoulder at Paulie, who gives me the thumbs-up. Of course he can be supportive. His meatballs with a Mediterranean flare were a hit, but I'll take any encouragement I can get.

I nod, respectfully, as production places the crisp, white plates down before beginning my final presentation. "The key lime pie *is* Florida. The zing from the limes and the cool, creamy texture is like the ocean breeze at night. This was the first pie my Grams taught me to make when I was a little girl." I struggle to contain the tears that want to slip down my face. I could use a Grams pep talk right now.

"This was the pie that made me fall in love with baking," I add, folding my hands in front of me to let them know I am done. I suck in a quick breath and wait. My presentation started out rough, but I think I redeemed myself. At least I hope I did. Sure, no one is going home tonight, but in this group, you still don't want to be the one to come in last.

All three take a bite. And then a second. And a third, and so on, until each entire piece is devoured. Unlike A. J. and Billy, Angelica doesn't lower herself to use her fork to smooch the crumbs down to get every last bite. But she does finish it. Satisfaction rises from the pit of desperation I'm in. She liked it. I mean, I'm not expecting great raves about the pie, but she can't chow down like that and then say she didn't like it.

"This," Billy says, "is sheer perfection."

A. J. goes even further. "The crust has the perfect level of crunch, but the filling is unbelievable. It tastes like you picked the limes off the tree today. But even more than that, when you talked about this pie, for the first time since you've stepped up to present, I felt like I actually got to know a little bit about you. And it shows in your cooking."

"Thank you, Chef," I say, resisting the urge to use the edge of my sleeve to wipe away a tear that is threatening to slide down my face. I will not be that person who cries all the time.

"It's good," Angelica says. Billy turns his head, giving her a look of confusion. Her lips are pursed together, and she doesn't offer any other critique.

Just as Jessica is about to speak, Angelica leans forward. "You were lucky to have the supplies ready after burning the first pie."

My face is aflame with embarrassment. Of course she would mention the pie again.

"I think we were the lucky ones," A. J. says, giving Angelica a side glance. "True, your entrée was a little shaky, but the fritter and this glorious specimen of a pie tell me there's more than meets the eye with your cooking ability. You have a talent for bringing out each flavor and elevating simple dishes."

I resist the urge to drop to my knees in relief. I didn't completely bomb out. Several other people had overcooked or undercooked food. And only Paulie's cannoli got better comments in the dessert category, and that's mainly because of Angelica. I might not win this round, but I think I should land somewhere in the middle of the pack.

After presentation, we're all corralled into a large room that is staged to look like a game room. There are two large bar top tables shoved together with eight chairs crowded around. Off to the side is a pool table with a selection of pool cues on the wall. Adam heads straight for the table as soon as we enter.

"Anyone want to rack 'em?" he asks.

"Sure," Paulie says.

After a moment, Lola joins them.

"You're going to play pool?" Inaaya asks.

"Why not?" Lola asks. "It's better than chewing on my nails around the table."

"Yeah," Paulie says, rolling a cue stick back and forth across the table. "This is going to be the worst part," he adds.

"Worse than the elimination?" Adam asks.

Paulie nods. "The waiting is *always* worse."

The rest of us settle in around the table. Hakulani sidles up next to me, and, as fate would have it, Dani sits directly across from me, while Inaaya and Malik sit together by the corner. Other than the sound of resin orbs smacking into each other and the occasional "Nice shot," the room is silent.

"I've been in more barbeque competitions than I can count," Malik says, breaking the silence. "And I've always hated sitting around while people judge my cooking. But at least in those situations, you just find out if you won or not. No one makes you stand in front of them as they pick your stuff apart."

"Judging doesn't have to be bad," Dani pipes up. "My father is always constructive when it comes to my cooking. He just wants me to be the best."

I roll my eyes, too tired to hide it, which means that, unfortunately, Dani is looking right at me when I do. Her eyes narrow and she starts to say something.

Inaaya saves me before Dani can say whatever is on her mind. "Did anyone else think Angelica was particularly brutal?"

I send her a look of gratitude. I don't have the energy to deal with Dani right now.

"She said the bread of my curried asparagus and peppers bruschetta was soggy," she continues. "Of course it was. They kept it under the warmer for thirty minutes. What did she expect?"

"I loved how Billy told her to blink twice if her taste buds had been kidnapped by aliens when she said Adam's stuffed habanero peppers didn't have enough heat," Hakulani says, laughing, and the whole table, including Dani, joins in.

"What made it better was A. J. asking for a glass of milk and then guzzling it down," Malik said.

Lola slaps her knee and says, "The milk was sliding out of both corners of his mouth."

Before the laughter has a chance to die down, the door opens and a PA pokes in his head. "They're ready."

The room is instantly quiet, and I suddenly think I'm going to be sick.

CHAPTER SEVEN

AS WE WAIT FOR THE DISEMBODIED VOICE TO tell us to find our marks and line up, Jessica walks over to us. "Hey, guys," she says. "I just wanted to let you know what's going to happen next."

A wave of relief washes over me. "Thank you," I say to no one in particular.

Jessica just laughs, before continuing. "During an elimination round, I'll announce the winner of the challenge, and then, in no particular order, I'll let the contestants who are safe from elimination know and have them return to their stations until there are only two people remaining."

"Will it only be one person per elimination round?" Malik asks.

She shakes her head. "I know there are one or two double eliminations, but I don't know which ones. The producer makes that decision."

"Who is the producer?" I ask.

"You should have all met her during your final casting interviews," she says. "Her name is Caitlin Merriweather, and I'm sure if you haven't seen her around, you will before the day is over."

I do remember Caitlin. She came down with a film crew a few weeks ago to get some footage for my introduction package. I was never able to get a good read on her, but she seemed pretty cool. She asked a lot of questions. Not just of me, but of everyone she met while she was in town.

The disembodied voice tells everyone we're going to start in one minute. Jessica gives us a thumbs-up and hurries to her place to wait. When the red light flips on, she smiles brightly into the lens. "Are you ready to find out whose food blew the judges' minds and who needs to go back to the cutting board?"

We all clap our hands, but no one cheers. I think we're all too nervous.

"You all did a great job!" she says, her eyes roving down the line. "I did a similar challenge during my competition, and I know how hard it is. You should all be proud of yourselves." She pauses for a moment before continuing. "It's time to announce the winner of today's competition and those who, if this were an elimination round, would be safe and moving on to the next challenge.

"Sadly, if you are the last chef remaining, you will have a five-minute penalty during tomorrow's competition. But on the plus side, since this is not an elimination round, you'll still have a chance of being named the Top Teen Chef."

I glance down the line at all the nervous faces and take in a slow, measured breath, hoping the mic doesn't pick up how fast my heart is beating. Five minutes is a huge penalty. I sneak a glance at the pantry, which has miraculously been cleaned up after today's pillaging. A late start could mean the difference between creating a killer dish that wins the challenge or being stuck with everyone else's leftovers.

Jessica's smile flickers, and her eyes dart in the direction of the cameras, then back to all of us. "Relax," she says, forcing her smile even brighter. "Remember, no one's going home. This was a practice run."

Her words are completely lost on us—no one relaxes.

"Okay," she says, drawing out the word. "If you can't do any of that, then breathe. We don't need anyone passing out. It will guarantee you'll get screen time, but you do not want the internet trolls to make you a meme."

That breaks the tension and everyone laughs.

As the camera focuses on the judges, Jessica smiles at us one last time, pointing to the corner of her mouth to remind us to do the same. As the cameraman pans back toward her, Jessica beams at the television audience before continuing. My hands are folded in front of me, and I pinch the fleshy part between my thumb and pointer finger as a reminder to make some sort of expression. I give what I hope is an excited smile, but my lips feel awkward and strained. I glance at Hakulani on my right and Lola on my left. They both look so relaxed and at ease. How do they do that?

Suddenly, Lola takes my hand and holds on to it, squeezing it like she's trying to cut off the circulation. Okay, so maybe I'm not the only one freaking out.

"Breathe," I think to myself and my lungs comply. At least I think I said it in my head, but I'm not sure because at that same moment Lola lets out a low, slow breath, too. We glance at each other and exchange strained smiles.

One by one, in what feels like a glacial pace, Jessica lists off the top seven chefs, starting with the winner of today's challenge.

Paulie. No surprise. The judges love him.

Lola.

Dani. Of course.

Hakulani.

Inaaya.

Malik.

Adam.

That leaves me.

Despite my amazing key lime pie, I'm in last place.

I feel the weight of everyone's pity as they all turn and look at me, but I know, secretly, they're heaving a sigh of relief that it's not them. I can't blame them, either, because even though I'm not leaving the show, I would give anything for it to have been someone else's name that was called last.

I take a deep breath, holding it for a second until Jessica says, "Peyton, I'm sorry, but you will have a five-minute delay during the first Landmark Challenge."

I let out the breath. I knew there was a penalty, but hearing it directed at me undercuts any confidence I had left after judging. I thought I had what it took to keep up with everyone here, but now I'm not so sure.

Jessica is looking back at me, her eyes wide. *Say something,* she mouths.

Oh, right. "Thank you for this second chance," I say to the judges and Jessica. "I won't let you down."

At least I am not going home, and I still have a chance to prove I belong here. I just need to take this one step at a time. Tomorrow is the Landmark Challenge. If I keep my mind focused on that, maybe I won't get caught up worrying about elimination. As long as I'm here, I still have a chance. But if I don't up my game, I'll be heading back to Florida for a lifetime of making pies for family reunions and truckers who stop in at the diner.

When the red light on the camera clicks off, everyone—cast and crew alike—lets out a collective breath and, just like that, the first day is over. Paulie, Hakulani, and Inaaya are at my side in a heartbeat.

"Are you okay?" Inaaya asks. "I was freaking out."

I nod and grin. "I'm still here, right?"

"Yes, you are," Paulie says, and he knocks his shoulder gently into mine.

Just then, a PA strides onto the set, looking over something on her clipboard. "I have your dressing-room assignments. Also, all your luggage has already been taken over to the apartment. You'll need to be ready to leave the apartment at eight in the morning for the challenge tomorrow."

Her eyes scan the page one last time. "That's it. Let's go."

We follow the PA down a long hall as she points each of us to different dressing rooms. When I hear my name, I peel off from the rest and enter a small room with a couch, a small table, a makeup mirror, and a temporary wardrobe. On the table is a letter with everything I need to know about getting ready for the show and what to do with my clothes when we're done filming.

I find a pair of black pants that will become part of my chef uniform when we're in the studio. Dropping my jacket in the laundry basket as instructed, I tug at the bottom of my shirt to straighten it out. In the corner of the room is a mini-fridge packed with water bottles. Parched from the day of cooking, I grab one and gulp it down.

A knock at the door breaks the silence.

"We're leaving," the voice on the other side says.

When I open the door, the rest of the cast is marching by.

"Hey," Paulie says, pausing so I can catch up with him. "You okay?"

I shrug. "I am officially the worst cook here, Angelica thinks my food is bland and insignificant, and I'm probably not even going to last the week."

"Yeah, but other than that, are you okay?" he asks with a grin.

I look at him for a moment before letting out a sigh and then a small laugh. "Yeah. I guess I am."

"Good," he says as we march out of the building and into the roar of New York City at rush hour.

CHAPTER
EIGHT

I DON'T THINK I REALIZE HOW EXHAUSTED I AM until we load into the bus and head to the apartment. Judging by the yawns and weary expressions on everyone's faces, I'm not the only one.

As he stares out the window, Hakulani absentmindedly begins singing under his breath, and I am totally enchanted by his voice. The cameraman sitting in the front seat catches every note. I don't know about anyone else, but if this world was capable of magic, then his singing would turn the streetlights into palm trees and honking horns into crashing waves.

When he finishes, Lola is the first to speak, waking from her trance before turning around to get a good look at him. "I have no idea what any of that meant, but if you play the ukulele, I will marry you right here on the spot."

Hakulani makes a strumming motion in front of his chest and gives her a smile. "I won't hold you to that."

"Well, could you at least sing me to sleep every night for the rest of my life?" she asks, draping one arm over the seat back and resting her chin on the ledge. "Or is that asking too much considering we just met?"

"Maybe a little too soon," Hakulani says, laughing and running his hand through his hair, his elbow lightly brushing my shoulder.

Lola lets out an acerbated breath and flops down against the seat. "Fine. I guess I understand."

"Hang in there, Lola," I say, reaching over the back of her seat to pat her on the shoulder. "We're young. There's still time to find someone who can sing and play the ukulele."

"Now you're just being mean," she says with a faux huff as she turns and looks out the window.

"What's the name of that song?" I ask.

"*Kawaupuahele*," Hakulani replies.

"Lola's right. You have an incredible voice."

He smiles at me, but before he can say anything, the bus slows to a stop in front of a tall apartment building complete with a doorman. It's hard enough to believe people really live like this, and it's even harder to believe that I'm living like this—even if it is for less than a month.

The PA ushers us to the elevator and swipes a card in front of a round black sensor. She doesn't even push a button. The elevator just knows what floor to take us to and starts to rise with surprising speed. With each floor we pass, my stomach gets a little tighter. It's not like I'm afraid of heights or anything, but I don't know if I've ever been this high before. I mean, other than the plane ride here.

The elevator doors open into what I think is a long hallway, but as soon as I step out and look to my right, I see a living room and I realize that I am completely wrong.

"Is this entire floor one apartment?" I ask, looking from one end of the hallway to another. The mirror hanging from the wall across from me shows me that I'm not the only one grasping for how to respond.

"It's a penthouse, technically," Dani says, correcting me. "But we're not even on the Upper East Side, so it hardly counts," she continues, loud enough for me to hear the disdain in her voice, but I'm too overwhelmed to care.

"Follow me," the PA says, leading us out of the elevator and into the apartment. She points to the right. "Living and dining room are that way, kitchen is around the corner, and I'll show you the bedrooms, and you'll find out who your roommate will be."

Inaaya and I fall in step with each other, grinning with excitement. I've heard about fancy New York apartments, and by "heard about," I mean I've seen them on TV. But never in my wildest dreams would I have thought I would ever have the chance to live in one. "Can you believe this?" I say to no one in particular.

"What?" Inaaya asks. "That as part of our being on a reality cooking show we also get to live in a multimillion-dollar apartment—I mean, penthouse? Oh sure. It's no big deal." We look at each other before bursting out in giggles. Everyone turns to look at us, and the PA raises one eyebrow but doesn't say anything.

We stop at a hallway with four doors branching off, and the PA turns around. "There's one master and three regular bedrooms. The producer has already assigned you to your room, so if you have any questions, you can bring it up with Caitlin. She'll be here in a little while to do some interviews and talk with each of you about the season." The PA taps her phone a couple of times. "Roommates are Dani and Lola, Peyton and Inaaya."

Inaaya grasps my hand and gives an almost inaudible squeal of excitement.

"Roomies," she whispers, and I grin. And I say a silent prayer of thanks that I'm not paired with Dani. It would be great for the ratings, but *not* good in all other ways possible.

"For the boys," the PA continues. "Malik and Adam, and Hakulani and Paulie." She pulls a set of four bamboo stir sticks from her pocket. "Each pair will draw a straw and the first one to draw the short straw will get the master. Who feels lucky?"

Hakulani nudges Paulie, who stumbles forward and picks a straw.

The PA smiles at him. "Sorry, no short straw for you."

Inaaya is still holding on to my hand. "You draw," I say, giving her hand a squeeze.

As she steps forward, Lola swoops in and snaps the next pick.

It's shorter than Paulie's.

"Does that mean we get the master?" Dani asks.

The PA shakes her head. "They're all different sizes. You'll have to wait."

Inaaya steps up again and draws ours. It's longer than Paulie's. Inaaya gives me an apologetic look.

"It's no big deal," I say, shrugging my shoulders. "It's not like we're going to be here that much anyway." Adam and Malik play rock-paper-scissors to see who's going to draw for them. With Adam losing two out of three, he steps forward to take the last straw. Holding it against Lola's, it's obvious that he and Malik aren't going to be enjoying the master suite, either.

The PA directs us to take the room at the end of the hall, and Lola and Dani head off to explore their room. "Boys are in the middle. Sorry, guys. You have to share a bathroom. Peyton and Inaaya, you can use the bathroom across from your room."

"Is our luggage here?" I ask as Inaaya tugs me toward our room.

"It'll be delivered shortly," the PA assures me over her shoulder as she walks away.

We pause at the door to our room. "Welcome home," I say before opening it.

The room is like something out of one of those high-end store catalogs. Every piece of furniture is in the perfect place, and there are bistro lights running from the light fixture in the center of the ceiling to various points around the room, creating a canopy effect. The closet doors have two full-length mirrors hanging on them and promise a space twice as big than what I have back home. In one corner there's a cozy, expertly designed seating area with two plush chairs and a side table between them where I can only assume my roommate and I are going to have many heart-to-hearts for the camera. But the pièce de résistance is the pair of twin beds that are adorned with the fluffiest comforters I have ever seen in my life.

"This is so pretty," Inaaya says, running her hand along the soft comforter on her bed.

I nod and take a seat on the bed. I practically sink into it. "Yeah," is all I can think to say.

"Let's go check out the rest of the house," Inaaya says, pulling me off my bed and down the hall just as Lola swings open the door to her room and pops out her head.

"Isn't this great?" she says, opening the door wider.

I try not to be jealous as I take a quick glance into her room. It's bigger than ours, but there aren't any fairy lights. In fact, their room is nice, but neutral. Maybe that's because it was the one room up for grabs for either the guys or the girls. Well, they can have their space because I like our room better.

"Can you believe this place?" Lola asks, motioning to the floor-to-ceiling windowpanes. From their room you can see the skyline. "It's like living in a hot-air balloon." She pauses and rolls her eyes. "Obviously, it's a very big hot-air balloon. But we're high enough that the people almost look like ants."

I smile at her excitement. "We're going to check out the rest of the apartment. Wanna come with us?"

"Sure," she says, before turning back toward her room. "Come on, Dani."

I resist the urge to sigh. I still haven't figured Dani out yet. Everyone else, so far, has been open and friendly, but she has been nothing but guarded the whole time. Plus, finding out that she is the daughter of a famous chef makes me pretty suspicious of her motivation. As we head down the hall to the living room, I wonder if there is something that she could be hiding. But that thought is pushed away when I see the view.

The open floor plan kitchen, dining room, and living room make it easy to enjoy the spectacular view no matter which direction you look. The skyline of New York sprawls before us, and the sun is just now beginning to set, reflecting off the tops of the buildings and making them glitter like jewels.

"Unbelievable," someone says from behind us, and we all

spin around to see the guys have snuck up behind us. Hakulani's eyes scan the horizon, before turning to me and continuing, "Don't you think so?"

"I do," I say with a nod and step forward into the room. "Wait, there's a balcony?" I ask, clapping my hands. As I approach the door, I am aware of gears whirring as the cameras mounted high on the wall spin to follow me. I don't think there's a dead spot anywhere in the apartment.

I step out on the balcony and see two more cameras pointing at us. I expect Hakulani to join me, but instead, Malik squeezes in next to me.

"Big Brother really is watching, isn't he?" he says with a laugh.

"Yeah, but it's worth it," I say as I take in the city. "I feel like I should pinch myself."

Lola sticks her head out. "This is far enough for me," she says. "I don't mind looking at the view, but I prefer to not have my life hanging by just a couple bolts and brackets. Besides, the balcony in our room is bigger."

"You have a balcony? In your room?" Malik says.

Lola grins. "Regret losing the luck of the draw?" she asks him.

"Maybe," he admits, "but I think I'll manage."

We follow her back inside and walk through the kitchen. "Isn't this kind of small?"

"For New York?" Dani asks in amusement. "No, it's actually pretty big."

"Oh," I say. "I wonder how much a place like this goes for."

Dani crosses her arms over her chest and leans back against the counter. "In this part of the city, somewhere in the ballpark of twenty mil."

"No way," I say.

"She's right," Paulie says as he begins to rack the pool balls on the table located in the space between the dining room table and the sitting area of the living room. "Maybe more."

"I don't think my entire town is worth twenty million dollars."

"Well, it *is* the penthouse," Dani reminds me.

I survey the room, not sure that's enough of an explanation. I mean, a million dollars could do a lot for my town. I can't imagine what twenty million would do.

The more I think about it, the more it actually makes me a little sick to my stomach. Someone who can afford to live here probably doesn't know what it's like to make payment arrangements just to keep your power on. They probably don't even pay their own bills. Some guy named William Barnswallow III probably does it for them.

I open another door, expecting to find a closet but instead find something that takes me by surprise. "Hey, check this out. Stairs."

I hear the pool cues clatter on the table behind me as everyone rushes over.

Hakulani peers over my head. "Where do you think they go?"

"My guess is up," I say.

"Yeah, I got that, but what's up there?"

I grin. "Only one way to find out."

I step into the stairwell and jog up the stairs. At the top is a steel door. I push on it, surprised to find it unlocked, and step out into the muggy evening air. "Holy crap," I say, clapping my hands together. "It's a rooftop patio."

And not just any rooftop patio—it's an apartment-sized outdoor living and entertainment area. Everyone files out, exploring the bonus space and chatting excitedly. Around the roof are several seating areas. I move to the one at the farthest corner and sit down on a large, curved couch, putting my feet up on the edge of the gas firepit. Tilting my face to the sky, I take a second to pinch myself—I'm not dreaming.

Then the little voice deep inside me cautions that, just like any dream, it's one that I know I'll have to wake up from someday. But, thankfully, that day is not today.

CHAPTER NINE

WE HAVEN'T BEEN ON THE ROOF LONG WHEN WE hear the door open.

"Who could that be?" I ask, shifting to mentally count us. "Aren't we all out here?"

Leaning forward to get a better look at the door, I see Caitlin Merriweather, the show's producer, sauntering toward us, her high heels clicking on the stone floor.

"Hey, Caitlin," Dani says, jumping up and running over to hug the new arrival.

The rest of us aren't as quick to move, but it doesn't take long for us to circle up around her.

"How are you all settling in?" she asks. Without waiting for us to answer, she looks around and adds, "I see you found the rooftop. Isn't it amazing?"

"It's pretty awesome," Adam agrees.

"Well, we wanted you guys to have a place to relax when you aren't filming. I assume we did a good job?"

"It's great," Lola gushes. "I did have a question, though. When are we getting keys so we can get back into the apartment if we decide to go out?"

Caitlin looks perplexed. "Did the PA not tell you?"

"Tell us what?" Adam asks.

"When you aren't filming, you need to stay in the apartment."

"What?" I say as a chorus of groans and shouts erupts around me.

"You're locking us in when we aren't filming?" Adam asks again after looking around at everyone.

"We can't have you being exposed to the public before the show airs," Caitlin explains. "Besides, you'll be busy filming during the week, and we've got some special surprises planned for the weekends. It won't be that bad."

"I was hoping to see the city," Inaaya says quietly.

Caitlin smiles at her. "And you will. Jessica is going to tell you more about this tomorrow. Really, it's more for the audience than anyone else, but you'll be doing what we're calling Landmark Challenges. These outings will give you a chance to see the city and also, if you're the winner, earn an advantage for the elimination round."

"What are we supposed to do for food?" Malik asks.

I realize I'm so tired that I can't remember the last time I ate something.

"During the week you can have dinner delivered here. There are dozens of menus in the kitchen, and we have accounts set up with all of them. Of course, during filming you'll have full access to craft services. And you'll find the kitchen is well stocked.

"If you have special requests, make sure you get those to the PAs after the last elimination challenge of the week. And of course you can always order in." Caitlin must have realized she was losing us because she quickly changes the subject. "I'll make sure the PAs talk to you about this tomorrow. What I want to do is show each of you something very special." She scans the group until her eyes land on me. "Peyton, let's start with you."

Malik leans forward as I stand up. "Um, Caitlin. We haven't eaten."

She looks surprised, as though she hadn't thought that we would be hungry after cooking all afternoon, but she recovers quickly. "What was I thinking? Take a look at the menus. Pick a place, get an order together. At this time of night, it would be faster if I had a PA pick it up for you." She turns to me. "Peyton, we can chat after you order your food."

I nod, not sure what the producer of the show wants to talk to me about. But if there's one thing I've learned from eavesdropping on the PAs, it's that when Caitlin says jump, you don't ask how high. You jump and hope it's enough.

"Sure, Caitlin," I say, giving her my brightest smile.

It takes about ten minutes for us to all agree to order from a Thai place a few blocks away. After placing my order for pad priew wann and spring rolls, I head out of the kitchen to find Caitlin. It doesn't take long. She's standing outside a door near the master bedroom scrolling through her phone. As I approach, she looks up. "Peyton. Let's talk in here." She pushes the door open to reveal a small office. Or at least it used to be an office, but now the space has been converted into a small studio with a barrel chair facing a camera. Behind the camera is another chair and a small table.

"What?" I ask. "Wait, is this the confessional room?"

"Something like that," Caitlin answers. "From time to time, you will all come in here and have one-on-one chats with the PAs. You know, so the audience can get to know you a little better."

"Right."

"I want you to look at something," she continues. "This is the package we're going to show when we introduce you on the show. I thought you might like to get a peek."

Without another word, she pulls a tablet from her purse and sets it down on the little table. I sit down in the chair closest as she starts the video. As the technical credits role, she flips off the light. The first shot is of me sitting on the rail of a horse ring, looking off into the distance. It was shot at a horse ranch near my house. In all the preparation to get here, I'd totally forgotten about it. My red hair is blowing in the wind, and my eyes look even greener than they do in real life. Then the voice-over starts, and a stranger begins to sum up my life story.

I watch as the images blur from the tears that I refuse to let fall. The package is emphasizing the very things and moments in my life that I came here to escape. For three minutes, I watch as this edited version of all the hardships and pain in my life plays out in full color. They talk about everything from my dad going to jail for embezzlement to my mom losing the house and her ballet studio when she couldn't keep up with the bills. There's even an interview with my boss at the diner. He talks about how I always pick up double shifts and how the customers love my pies. This part makes me smile, but only a little.

The part that sends me over the edge is when the voice starts talking about how we were forced to move in with my aunt. They even got a nice big shot of my aunt's double-wide trailer, complete with the lattice fencing that hides the frame it sits on. As the final image of me sitting in the community garden looking thoughtfully toward the horizon transitions to a promo shot of me in my turquoise jacket (which they must have taken during today's filming), I'm clenching my fists so hard I know I'm going to have fingernail cuts on my palms.

"What do you think?" Caitlin asks as she flips the lights back on.

"Is that what y'all think of me?" I ask, unable to bite back my accent. I don't know if it's ever been this thick before, but then again, I don't think I've ever been this angry. "That I'm some sort of trailer trash pauper looking to be magically lifted from squalor by this show?" I can feel the heat even in the tips of my ears.

"No," Caitlin assures me. "Of course not."

"Because it really seems like that from the package."

"Peyton," Caitlin says, her eyes wide with astonishment. "No one meant—"

"I don't care what you meant; I look pathetic. I came here to give myself a shot at getting away from all of that. Now the whole world is going to see me as the poor girl trying to claw her way out of the trailer park one cupcake at a time."

She tries again. "I—"

"You even interviewed my dad. In prison."

The next thing I know Caitlin is sitting in the interview chair. The woman moves with the grace of a cheetah, and there is a glint in her eyes that reminds me of one. She meets my glare, unapologetically. "I'm sorry you didn't like the package. I'll see what we can do and maybe we can change a few things, tone it down here and there."

"That's a start."

"But it's not going to change much," she says, shaking her head. "Everyone on the show was selected based on two criteria: Could they cook better than the other applicants, and did they have a compelling backstory or quirky personality? Something to keep the viewers wanting to know more or see what they do next."

My eyes narrow as I process what she means. "I take it I wasn't picked for my quirky sense of humor."

Caitlin rolls her eyes. "No, but your story is compelling. In spite of what your family has gone through, you've taught yourself to cook. And not just to cook, but you've proven yourself to be one of the best in the country."

"Wait, so you're saying that without my sob story, I wouldn't be here?"

"Does it matter? You earned your spot because I said so. The way I see it, you didn't do anything to deserve the consequences of your parents' actions, so why not use them to your advantage? Show the world that you are resilient. It's a great angle."

"What if I don't want to do that?" All this time I had been under the delusion that I was someone special. That maybe I had enough talent to achieve my dreams. But in one fell swoop, Caitlin smashes all my confidence and hope.

"Oh my God. Peyton, you are *the* rags-to-riches story. We brought you here with the hope that you will be the one who reinvents herself. And from what I'm hearing, that's what you want, too."

"Yeah, but I don't want to be a national laughingstock."

"I don't want that, either," she says, slapping her hands on her thighs as she stands. "We want you to show everyone that they can transcend the life they are born into and become the star they are meant to be."

I resist the urge to roll my eyes. She's the producer, after all. "It just feels wrong."

"What?"

"Exploiting my parents. Using my past to get sympathy."

Caitlin shrugs. "You gotta give the audience someone to root for." She reaches into her bag and pulls out a folder, tossing it next to the tablet.

"What's this?" I ask.

"Your profile."

"My what?"

"Your profile. It's why we chose you. This is who we want you to be for the show."

"But this is a cooking competition. I came here to bake, not act."

Caitlin pauses for a moment, and I swear I can almost hear her counting down from ten before continuing. "This is reality television in the form of a cooking competition."

"Right. The key word being *real*."

"And it is reality." Caitlin slides her arm around the back of my chair and leans over me. "A very carefully and meticulously planned reality."

Her words deliver the warning she intended. I flip the folder open and begin reading. According to my profile, I'm a small-town North Florida girl from a low-class family. Okay, that's not great, but it's the truth.

"So, what, you just want me to open up about my—" I lift up some of the papers and begin reading "—'bittersweet relationship' with my locked-up father. Oh, and how embarrassed I am to accept charity from my aunt just so we have a place to live since my mom 'can't hold down a job.' Is that all?"

"Did we miss anything?"

I look up at her. "Can't I just focus on cooking? You don't know what it's like to be the family the whole town talks about when you walk down the street. If I talk about this on camera, it's going to make it worse for my parents."

"So?" Her face is unreadable. "That was their life. This is yours." She straightens up. "Do you want to win?"

"Yes. I wouldn't be here if I didn't."

"Then do what it takes to win."

"But my parents—"

"Are grown-ups who can deal with it."

Okay. That was harsh. But Caitlin isn't finished. "Do you think your dad was thinking about you when the FBI showed up at your house to arrest him? Was your mom worried about you when she spent who knows how long crying in her bathrobe instead of getting up off her ass and taking care of her daughter? I'm willing to bet they weren't."

I have seriously misjudged Caitlin. At the live auditions for the show, she struck me as a sweet, earnest person who wanted to help me achieve my dreams of going to culinary school, but I was wrong. She is stone-cold when it comes to doing her job. "So?" I ask back.

"So this is the moment when you need to think about Peyton. You need to put Peyton first." She takes the file out of my hand. "As far as I can see, if you don't, nobody else is going to care about you."

Stone. Cold.

I slouch back against the chair, shaking my head.

Caitlin lets out an exasperated sigh. "I'm not saying you should say anything bad about your parents. In fact, I would prefer that you keep the story focused on you. But the audience needs to know where you come from. They need to know you're a survivor. So let us show the world that you are more than just a small-town girl who got dealt a bad hand in life."

"And if I don't?"

She slips my file into her purse. "Then you can kiss any chance of winning the scholarship goodbye."

"What?"

"The network wants ratings, and I want to keep my job."

"Are you threatening me?"

Caitlin sighs. "No, I'm trying to help you. Believe it or not, I want you to do well in this competition. I was the one who fought to get you on this show."

"Why?"

"Because I know it can change your life. And quite honestly, you deserve a shot. Let this show be your shot."

I'm quiet for a moment as her words sink in.

"Here is a question for you. When this competition is over, what are you going to do next?"

"I plan to win and go to culinary school."

Caitlin laughs, but the sound is hollow to my ears. "You all think that, but only one person can win. What if it's not you?"

Her frankness stops me in my tracks. What would I do? Would I go back home and work at the diner? Marry the least loser guy I can find and hope he doesn't run off with the divorcée three trailers down? No thank you.

"You don't have a plan, do you?" Caitlin asks. "Well, let me give you something to think about. Let's say you stick around on the show long enough, you're going to get fans."

I can't help but laugh. "Are you serious? Me? With fans?"

She nods. "Even the person who leaves day one will have some fans. But it's the ones who make it through the early eliminations that will start to get the real followers. People who are invested in what happens to you and are rooting for you to win."

"Yeah, but there's no live vote on the show. They can't save me from elimination."

"True, they don't have that kind of power. But they can make a big difference after the show is over with their feet and their 'cha-ching.'" She rubs her thumb and middle finger together to indicate cash.

She watches me to make sure I'm following before continuing. "When this is all over, there will be restaurants lining up to hire you. You might even be a reality celebrity. At least for a while."

"Whatever," I scoff.

"I'm serious. Restaurant owners are going to be willing to pay top dollar for you to work in their kitchens. You'll bring in customers who'll spend money to eat your food. They'll take pictures of it and post it on social media and rave about how amazing and sweet you are when they meet you in person."

"Seriously?"

"Of course. It's free publicity. But how many of those fans do you think are going to come to see you in that pit of a diner we found you in?"

She doesn't wait for me to answer. "None. But play your cards right, and you could end up touring the country, hosting pop-up kitchens acround the globe."

"And all I have to do is . . ."

"Try not to burn your signature dish again."

I groan.

"There is one more thing," she adds.

"What?" The more Caitlin talks, the less I trust her.

She just smiles. "It's nothing, really. I mean, there might be a storyline or two that you're involved with, but we have to see how things shake out during this first week."

"I'm not very good at acting."

Caitlin rolls her eyes. "And no one expects you to. Just be yourself. We'll give you the nudge when you need it. Just do what I tell you, and I promise everything will work out. Do you think you can do that?"

I turn and look out the window, my eyes scanning the skyline. Things like this show don't happen to girls like me. And they sure don't come around a second time. This could be my only chance.

I nod my head.

"Great," she says, pushing herself away from the wall. "Now, I need to talk to the rest of the cast members. I trust everything we've talked about will stay between us."

I look at the camera. "I suppose you'll know if it doesn't."

"True. But Peyton—" she pauses "—this competition can really change your life if you let me do my job."

With that, she walks over to the door and leaves without another word.

I follow Caitlin back to the living room, where Lola and Paulie are playing pool with Hakulani and Malik. Caitlin motions for Hakulani to follow her.

He hands me his pool stick as he walks past me. "Fill in for me?"

"How do you know I'm not bad at pool?" I ask.

Malik snorts. "Trust me, you can't be any worse."

The others laugh as they turn their attention back to the table.

Leaning over the rail to line up the cue ball, I think about what Caitlin said about putting myself first. She has a point. And as much as I don't like the idea of making my life into one big sob story, this experience, win or lose (though hopefully it's going to be a win), could change my life. I mean, I can't throw this chance away, right?

CHAPTER
TEN

BY THE TIME THE PA ARRIVES WITH OUR FOOD, I'M starving.

"Do you think they'll care if we take our food to our rooms?" Inaaya asks.

"You know what they say: it's easier to ask forgiveness than it is to get permission," I answer, picking up my containers and a set of chopsticks.

She grins, picking up her own meal and following me down the hall.

"Where are you going?" Hakulani asks as we pass him. It's the first time I've seen him since he left to talk to Caitlin.

"Roommate bonding time," Inaaya says. "See you tomorrow."

When we get to our room, our luggage is sitting in a pile.

"Oh good. It came," Inaaya says.

"Yeah, but *when* did it come? I didn't hear the door open and we were in the living room."

"Maybe there's a secret entrance we don't know about."

"It's like they're watching every move we make," I say, putting my food down on the nightstand.

"They are," Inaaya reminds me.

"Right. Well, they can watch me unpack later. I'm starving."

I reach for my dinner and she does the same. "So, what did you really think of the competition today?" she asks, peeling back the aluminum lip that was keeping the lid in place.

I breathe in a deep whiff. "Holy cow. What is that?"

"Spicy basil fried rice. It's my favorite. Want some?"

I shake my head. "It smells amazing, but I'm good."

"So, about the competition," Inaaya presses.

I pick up a spring roll and dip it in the sweet-and-sour sauce before taking a bite. I chew thoughtfully before answering. "It was chaos."

She pauses, chopsticks halfway to her mouth. "Of all the words you have to describe the day, you go with chaotic?"

"Well, those of us who aren't in the front of the class might have had a different experience," I say.

"I didn't ask to be put up front. Besides, it sounded like you guys were having more fun than we were. I heard you laughing all day."

"It was especially hilarious when I sliced my hand and the medic took his time getting it wrapped up." I hold my hand up for her to see.

"Is that when your pie burned?"

I groan. "Yes. It was so embarrassing."

"But you had everything ready to make another one," she says.

"I got lucky. If I hadn't, the judges would have raked me over the coals."

She nods. "Yeah. I get the feeling Angelica is that judge that rarely has anything nice to say about anything."

"Totally agree. But do you think she's like that because deep down she's got a heart of gold under that tough exterior?" I can't stop from laughing.

"It must be really deep down," she says, kicking off her shoes as she slides across the bed until she's leaning against the wall. "I haven't been on my feet this long since my summer waitressing job."

"I waitress, too," I say, surprised that we have anything in common, much less that we wait tables. "It's your typical small-town diner where the only strange faces belong to people whose cars break down on the highway."

Inaaya smiles, but it quickly turns into a yawn. "It was brutal, but I wanted to get some restaurant experience. My parents are members at this yacht club, and they talked the maître d' into hiring me. Personally, I think they were hoping I would change my mind about culinary school and decide to go to med school."

"Is that what they want you to do?" I ask.

"That or be an engineer like my dad. But even as a little kid, I would rather make mud pies than build things with Legos. And I hate the sight of blood. My dad even offered to pay for everything if I went to college instead of culinary school."

And just like that, the common ground of us both being waitresses slips away. I work at the diner to help keep the lights on and food on the table. Inaaya was a waitress to prove a point to her parents. "So you turned him down?"

She shrugs. "What can I say. Cooking is my passion. Mud pies and all."

I force a laugh. "I was more of a Play-Doh girl myself. Even had the cake and pie shop sets."

"Did you have the pizza oven? It was my favorite."

"No."

"You know," she says, pulling one of the decorative pillows close to her stomach, "now that I think about it, it's my parents' fault that I want to be a chef in the first place."

"How so?"

"They came here from India. Dad was on a scholarship, and Mom followed for love. Ticked my grandparents off like you wouldn't believe. And living in Chicago wasn't cheap. When Mom started law school at Northwestern, they both got jobs at this Indian restaurant near campus to make ends meet."

"Is that where you learned to cook?"

Inaaya nods. "The owners had come over from India years

before, and the wife knew my grandparents. They took a liking to my parents, and when I was born they let us move into a little apartment they owned above the kitchen. They'd watch me so my mom could study. Dad was working all kinds of crazy hours."

"That was lucky that they had help."

She nods. "So, what got you into cooking? I mean, aside from the Play-Doh?"

I pretend to yawn and stretch my arms over my head. "My story's pretty boring, and I'm exhausted."

She looks at the clock. "I can't believe it's only nine back home. I'm normally a night owl, but I don't know if I can stay up much longer. But tomorrow, you have to tell me your boring story."

I smile and stand up to get my pajamas. "Sure." And by that I mean not a chance.

We take turns using the bathroom to get ready for bed. I let Inaaya go first and finish putting away my clothes. When I slip into the shower to finally wash the kitchen residue off my body, my mind starts racing. The conversation with Caitlin still has me on edge. Her expectation that I play the poor girl from the wrong side of the tracks might help me in the competition, but is that really what I want people to think about when the show is over? That I was some sort of pity contestant?

And how will the people back home look at me? Like Gerri at the diner, who gave me a job busing tables when I was fourteen because he felt bad that I was walking around town with holes in my shoes. Or my mom, who, yeah, hasn't always been able to take care of us but has done the best she can. I don't want them to feel like I don't appreciate what they did. And Aunt Jenny didn't blink when Mom asked if we could move in with her. She opened her doors and made room for us in her life. To slam on the trailer on national television would be a betrayal in her eyes. I lean my head against the cool tile, and the water slides down my back. I wish it could wash away the uneasy feeling in the pit of my stomach.

I turn off the water and dry myself with a fluffy towel before pulling on my pajamas. When I quietly open the door, I hear soft snoring coming from Inaaya's side of the room. The walls in the trailer are pretty thin, and I'm used to Aunt Jenny sawing logs, but even so, I toss and turn for almost an hour. I just can't fall asleep. Finally, tired of trying, I flip the covers off and slip out of the room.

When I turn into the kitchen, I see Paulie peering into the fridge. Leaning against the door frame, I say, "Still hungry?"

He startles and looks at me, his eyes wide. "Geez, Peyton. You scared me."

"Whatcha doing?" I ask, slipping farther into the room and peeking over his shoulder.

"Couldn't sleep," he says. "I saw some sandwich stuff in here earlier."

"So, what did I miss this evening?"

"Not much," he says, pulling out vegetables and packages and dropping them on the island. "Caitlin kept pulling in people to watch their packages. I was last."

"She's gone, then?"

He nods.

"How was your package?" I ask, avoiding his eyes, focusing instead on selecting an orange from the fruit bowl.

"It was good. I mean, they interviewed a couple of my sisters. That was embarrassing. But overall, it wasn't as bad as I thought it might be. What can I say? I am the loud Italian guy who loves his mama's sauce, but not as much as he loves his mama."

I raise an eyebrow. "Did you come up with that?"

"Nope. That's the tagline they want me to record tomorrow. I just wanted to hear it out loud."

"I didn't get a tagline."

"Maybe Caitlin forgot to tell you yours. I'm sure it will be equally cheesy." He begins to pile meat, cheese, and veggies onto a slice of whole-grain bread.

"I don't know if that bread is ready for all those toppings," I say, beginning to peel my orange.

He squirts spicy mustard in a practiced zigzag motion, twists his wrist, and goes back the other way. "Ye of little faith." He plops the second piece of bread on the top and slices it in triangles before picking one up and taking a big bite.

"Nice," I say, giving him a slow clap before going back to peeling. A piece of tomato slips from between the bread. Paulie looks up at me and grins.

Between bites, he asks, "How was your package?"

I shrug, crossing my arms over my chest. A beat passes before I say, "I don't know. It wasn't what I expected."

He pauses, his sandwich halfway to his mouth before putting it down. "You didn't like it?"

Paulie seems like a nice guy, but after what Caitlin said, I don't know who I can trust. My first reaction is to tell him, but I hold back.

"I don't know. It was weird seeing my past pasted together like that. Seeing my life put up for the world to see."

He nods. "I get that. And far be it for a cradle Catholic like me to quote Buddha, but he once said, 'Do not dwell in the past, do not dream of the future, concentrate the mind on the present moment.'"

"What does that mean?"

"No idea," he says. "But it sounds profound, right?"

"Why do I get the feeling you know exactly what it means?" I ask, pulling the orange apart and popping a wedge in my mouth. "Holy cow," I say, quickly taking another bite. "This is a good orange."

"You sound surprised."

"I'm from Florida, remember? Most of our oranges are so sweet and juicy that they make the best juice. My standards are pretty high."

"Right."

I bite into another wedge, a drop of juice landing on the counter. I grab a paper towel and wipe it up. "What do you think the Landmark Challenge is going to be like?"

"Not sure, but I hope we go somewhere cool like Madame Tussauds."

I laugh. "I wouldn't count on it. It's not like that place is only in New York. Besides, what kind of cooking challenge could they come up with in a place like that?"

"Fondue?"

I laugh. "Melted stuff; well played."

"Thank you," he says, giving a small bow before turning his attention back to his sandwich. He looks thoughtful while he chews. "I don't know what it is about your past that you don't like, but we all have things about our lives we wish we could change. That's life. Just remember: the past can't hurt you anymore, not unless you let it."

"Another quote from Buddha?"

He shakes his head. "Alan Moore. *V for Vendetta*."

"Of course," I say. "I should have known."

Paulie pops the last bite of his sandwich into his mouth and wipes down the counter. "All right, I am ready for bed. You want me to wait for you?"

I shake my head. "I think I could use a little reflection time, but thanks."

"No problem," he says and turns to leave the room.

I gather up my peels into a neat pile before dumping them in the trash. It's easy to say that your past can't hurt you, but it's quite another thing to be brave enough to put that to the test. And there's too much at risk if I fail.

CHAPTER ELEVEN

THE MORNING DAWNS BRIGHT AND HOT. WHEN I enter the kitchen, everyone is grabbing something from an array of bagels, muffins, and breakfast sandwiches. I grab one with sausage and sit down to eat.

"We're supposed to meet the PA at the bus downstairs," Malik says, spreading cream cheese on his bagel.

"When did they tell us this?" I ask, sinking my teeth into the soft English muffin.

He points his knife toward a dry-erase board on the refrigerator.

"The PA elves must have come in early this morning."

He nods. "I was up when they snuck in." He rinses off his knife before putting it in the dishwasher. "Almost scared me to death."

"Hey," Lola says as she sits down in the seat next to me to fix the strap on her bejeweled sandals. She stands and says, "How do I look?"

"Perfect," Malik says as she tops off her outfit with a black fedora and a pair of aviator sunglasses.

"Looks like we get to wear street clothes for the Landmark Challenges," she says.

"So it would seem," I say, looking down at my own outfit. "This was in my closet with today's date on it."

"It looks cute," Lola says.

"Yes," Dani adds, sneaking in behind Lola to grab an apple. "Very wholesome and innocent."

I smooth the fabric of my white short coveralls. From most people that would sound like a compliment, but from Dani it's definitely not. Pulling up the sleeves on what's supposed to be an off-the-shoulder crop top with eyelet ruffles, I turn my attention back to Lola, who seems to be trying to make up for Dani's snide comment.

"I like your necklace," she says, pointing to the long knotted gold chain that hangs down to my belly button.

"Thanks," I say. "It matches my sunglasses." I have never been so coordinated in my entire life, and when Dani snickers I realize that my comment just fed into her impression of me. "Of course, I'll have to take it off when I cook. Otherwise, I'll probably shut it in the oven."

The other drawback of my look today is the stylists had left strict instructions for me to wear my hair down and full of curls. Which would be okay, except the humidity today is like

90 percent, and I'm going to have to pull it back when I cook anyway. They might as well have told me to stick a fork in a light socket, because the result is going to be the same. Thankfully, I found a white scrunchie in one of the front pockets.

"Do you have any idea what the Landmark Challenges are?" Lola asks, and I shake my head.

"We were talking about that yesterday," I tell her. "Does Dani know?"

"Nope. Not a clue."

"We better go," Malik says, tucking an apple juice under his arm and grabbing a bunch of grapes.

Everyone springs into action and we head to the front door. Adam, Hakulani, and Paulie are coming from the bedroom hall-way when we see them.

Paulie rubs his hands together. "Let's do this," he says, giving me a wink.

"Why don't you save some of that for the cameras," Hakulani says.

"Someone's not a morning person," Paulie says with a grin.

"It's two in the morning back home," Hakulani groans. "Jet lag is no joke, man. I'd like to see you be all bright-eyed and bushy-tailed."

Adam turns and heads to the kitchen, reappearing a moment later with two bottles of iced coffee. "Will this help?" he asks, handing them to Hakulani.

"It can't hurt. Thanks."

With everyone ready to go, we file onto the elevator and down to the lobby, where two slightly annoyed PAs are waiting for us. "You're late," one of them says.

I glance at my watch. "By three minutes."

"We were supposed to leave at eight. Not meet at eight," the other one grumbles. "Let's load up."

Inaaya slips into line next to me. "And Paulie thought Hakulani wasn't a morning person."

"He looks like a chirping robin compared to them," I agree.

We climb aboard the small bus. Each of us has an assigned seat with our name on it, and we sit down. From across the aisle, Hakulani offers me one of his coffees.

"Thanks, but no. I'm nervous enough as it is. Add caffeine to my system and I'll be bouncing around like a jackrabbit."

He smiles. "Good. I was just being polite. I'm going to need both to get started."

"I hadn't thought about those of you from out west and how the time zone difference might impact you. Do you think it will make it harder for today's challenge?"

He shrugs. "I don't think so. By the time we actually start cooking, I'll be ready." He turns slightly. "Why? Thinking of going easy on me?"

I laugh. "Not a chance."

"Good. Because I hope we both stick around for a long time."

I shake my head slightly, tossing my hair off my shoulder, and turn to look at the city.

From behind us, Adam calls out, "When are you going to tell us where we're going?"

Without turning around, one of the PAs says, "When we get there."

Hakulani leans closer to me and whispers, "Have you noticed that there are some really cool PAs, and then some of them act like we're inconveniencing them?"

"Maybe they aren't morning people either," I say.

"You like to find the good in people, don't you?"

I look down at my hands. "I don't know about that, but sometimes we make assumptions about people and never really get the chance to know the real them."

He nods, looking at me thoughtfully. "There's a story behind that answer, isn't there?"

"I don't know what you mean," I say, starting to wish I had never said anything. Thank goodness Inaaya stands up and moves next to us.

"Wardrobe malfunction," she says. "I need my roommate to help me out."

Hakulani places his hand on the seat in front of him and pulls himself up. "Wouldn't want to get in the way of fashion." He moves to the back of the bus, where Paulie and Malik are in an intense debate about college football conferences.

"Thanks," I say as Inaaya sits down.

She gives me a quizzical look before glancing over her shoulder at Hakulani, then back to me. "For what?"

"Nothing. Just thanks."

She doesn't press me. "I really do have an issue," she says, holding out a bracelet. "This snagged on my pants and I can't get it back on."

I take the bracelet as she holds out her arm. "You look amazing, by the way," I tell her, pulling back the clip and reattaching the clasp.

"Thanks," she says, smoothing out her red and black harem pants. "Thank goodness they paired it with a T-shirt or I would look like a character out of a Disney cartoon."

"Well, it looks amazing on you."

"Back home I normally just wear jeans and T-shirts," she says wistfully before shrugging. "Oh well, at least we get to keep the clothes."

"We do?" I ask, surprised by her statement. "Who told you?"

"Caitlin, last night. When I met with her in the confessional room."

"You get to keep the outfit you wore yesterday, too?" I ask, thinking about the pants and shirt I wore. They weren't anything special, but I wasn't going to complain. "That's awesome."

She laughs. "I would hope so because I brought that one from home." She quickly adds, "At Caitlin's request."

"But any clothes we wear on the show?"

"Are ours to keep."

It would seem Inaaya's conversation with Caitlin was very different from mine.

"Well that's nice to know."

"I did a sneak peek at my clothes for this week, and I'm more than happy." She looks down at my outfit. "Is this how you dress back home?"

I almost laugh. There is no way I'm going to find something like this at the thrift store back home. "Uh, not really. I'm like you. Jeans and tees mostly."

The bus slows down and we all turn to see where our first Landmark Challenge is going to take place. At first, all we see are a bunch of white tents, like the ones you see at family reunions and weddings. Everyone is so busy trying to figure out where we are that no one notices Jessica join us on the bus.

"Today is your first Landmark Challenge," she says, and we all turn around. "Are you guys ready?"

"For what?" Dani asks, stepping into the aisle.

"Well, come down off the bus and see."

In a single line, we file off the bus, everyone talking excitedly about what comes next. But Jessica doesn't take us far, as the PAs order us to line up in front of the bus where a camera crew is waiting to capture everything.

Once we're all settled, Jessica looks straight at us and

launches into her introduction. "Welcome to your first Landmark Challenge. Today, you are going to get a chance to explore one of New York City's most famous attractions. You'll have two hours to explore, learning everything you can. Once your time is up, it'll be time for you to create a special dish, on-site. The winner of each Landmark Challenge will be determined by some very special judges. But you'll meet them later."

She turns to us. "Chefs, are you ready to find out where you are?"

We don't have to feign excitement as we all answer, "Yes."

She looks back at the camera. "Follow me."

We traipse around the bus and are instructed to look surprised and excited. Which would be a lot easier if we knew what we were so excited about. We must do a good job because it doesn't take long for the director to call cut.

Jessica turns and smiles at us. "I know it's weird, but we couldn't get you coming around the bus to see the location in real time because of Production City."

"Production City?" I ask.

She waves her arm toward the tents. "Welcome to Production City. Here we have our entire team ready to deal with any emergency that could arise. The big tent is craft services. It's packed with snacks, drinks, and especially coffee for as long as we're here. That's where you'll get your lunch once you've finished your exploration."

"Which brings us back to: Where are we?" Malik asks.

"And I will tell you as soon as you're on your mark and we start filming."

Taking the hint, we all hustle to the color-coded marks on the ground. The crew must have been here hours ago to get everything set up.

The cameraman counts us down before throwing the finger toward Jessica.

"Welcome to your first Landmark Challenge. Today, we're at the largest metropolitan zoo in the country. The Bronx Zoo."

Excitement ripples down the line as we clap and cheer.

Jessica waits for us to settle down before she continues talking. "You could spend all day walking through its two hundred and sixty-five acres. But you have just two hours to see as much as you can." She pauses, looking at us. "This field trip isn't about sightseeing," Jessica continues. "It's about finding inspiration for your next challenge."

Everyone begins talking at once.

"What kind of challenge do you think we'll have to do?" Adam asks.

"It has to do with animals, right?" Lola asks.

"Maybe we have to make a meal for one of the animals?" Inaaya suggests.

"No," Hakulani says. "Those animals are on a really strict diet. They wouldn't let us monkey around with it."

Paulie grins. "'Monkey around'? Nice pun."

Hakulani dips his head. "Thank you."

"Would you two be serious?" Inaaya says, rolling her eyes.

Jessica waits for us to settle down before continuing. "I can't tell you about your competition yet, but I will tell you that you need to report to Dancing Crane Plaza in two hours. If you're late, you will not be allowed to compete in this round, and trust me, you want a chance to win the advantage." She pauses as we nod. "So, are you ready to know what your challenge is?"

"Yeah!" we cry in unison.

She throws her head back and laughs. "And you will."

We wait for her to say something.

"In two hours, at Dancing Crane Plaza. Go explore the zoo," she says, but no one moves.

Jessica looks surprised. "Your time has already started. You might want to go."

She doesn't have to tell us twice. We sprint through the entrance and race down the pathways that lead to the different exhibits. I have no idea where I'm going or what I'm looking for, but I really need to find some inspiration and find it fast.

CHAPTER TWELVE

THE CAMERA CREW ASSIGNED TO FOLLOW ME does a pretty good job of keeping up. Not that I'm a fast runner. I generally lean into the idea that one should only run if your life is in danger and all other options have been exhausted. I glance to my left and see Adam, who looks more like he is participating in a 5K than a cooking challenge.

I wander the path, stopping to watch the sea lions as they bask in the morning sun. They lift their heads, giving a little bark as if to let me know that I am intruding on their quiet time. Then they lie back down and proceed to ignore me. So far, I'm not feeling very inspired.

Not too much farther down the path I see the Madagascar exhibit. The grand column and intricate carvings of lions are a stark contrast to the aluminum sculpture entry sign with its seafoam tree branches, bright red lettering, and pale-yellow silhouettes of lemurs and snakes.

"Lions and lemurs, oh my," I say aloud and make myself smile.

With the sun inching across the sky, the air is getting hotter. I can feel sweat dripping down the back of my neck, and I slip the scrunchie out of my pocket and wind my hair into a messy bun. With my hair firmly in place, I pull open the door to Madagascar and am transported to a different world.

The enclosure for the Coquerel's sifaka exhibit doesn't look or feel like any building I've been in before. The ceiling is painted to look like a bright blue sky with white puffy clouds. It doesn't look painted. It looks real. And the depth of the space is so deep the creatures hopping from branch to branch disappear into the distance. I stand close to the glass, resisting the urge to press my face against it just to get a little closer, as I watch three babies wrestle, trip over each other, pause to look around, and then repeat. Their antics make me laugh out loud.

A door on the darkened wall opens, a stream of light pouring in, and it momentarily destroys the illusion that I'm on a tiny island in the Indian Ocean.

"Oh," says the woman in a khaki jumpsuit and a name tag that reads Dr. Brenda. Her eyes widen before glancing at her watch. "What are you doing here?" she asks quickly. "The zoo doesn't open for another two hours today."

"I'm part of the show that's filming here today."

She doesn't look impressed. "Right," she says. "That teen cooking show."

"Uh, yeah. *Top Teen Chef*," I stammer. Out of the corner of my eye, I notice her arm shake. Looking closer, I see the pet carrier in her hand and a little paw reaching out through one of the air holes. "What's that?" I ask, bending down to look inside. Instinctively, she turns, the crate angled so I can't see.

"An infant lemur," she says abruptly. "Look, you might be here to have fun, but I have a job to do, so if you don't mind—"

"Can I help?"

"What?"

"With the lemur. Can I help you?"

"I'm just taking it back to its enclosure," she says, dismissing me. "Besides, I have no interest in being a prop in your show." She glances at the camera crew that followed me in.

If she only knew just how much I understand what she means. "I can help. And I signed a waiver so the show can't hold you liable for anything that happens to me."

She shakes her head.

"Please," I beg. "I've never seen a lemur up close." And by up close, I mean ever.

She spins toward me, fire blazing in her eyes. I'm impressed at how steady she holds the carrier. "Look, I'm short-staffed because every employee around here is out playing tour guide for you and your friends. But I'm not going to entertain an entitled reality star just so you can brag about how you got to pet a lemur. Now if you don't mind, I have animals to feed."

I like this woman. She's brutal, but at least you know where you stand with her. "I can help you," I say, stepping forward and hoping she doesn't kick me out of the exhibit. "You said you're short-staffed because of the show, so let me help. Please."

She glares over my shoulder, pointing to the camera guy with her chin. "There's no room for your crew," she says. I bet she thinks that's a deal-breaker.

"Even better," I say quickly. "Now you're helping me get rid of them." The camera crew doesn't look pleased, which makes me even more determined to help Dr. Brenda.

After several long seconds, she says, "Come on, then." I follow her through an unmarked door and watch as she swipes her badge over the card reader.

It flashes green and then the doors begin to open by themselves. I follow her down a long, narrow hallway to another door. Again, she flashes her badge and the door unlocks. "You need to wash your hands," she says, flipping on the lights.

I hurry over to the sink, glancing briefly inside the dark cage. I can't really see anything, but I can hear what sounds like a barking dog that's swallowed a squeaky toy. "Doesn't like being in a cage, does it?" I ask, turning on the water and pumping soap into the palm of my hand.

"Would you?" Dr. Brenda asks, shaking her hands before drying them with a clean towel. I do the same.

"Guess not."

As I dry my hands, Dr. Brenda puts the cage on a table and begins pulling things out of the refrigerator. The screeches get louder.

"Shh. It's okay, Zara. You're okay," Dr. Brenda says over her shoulder, her voice very different from the hostility I'd just encountered.

She reaches into the refrigerator and pulls out a silver bowl. "Here," she says, handing it to me. In the bowl are slices of bananas, strawberries, and mangos, and chunks of passion fruit. "Hold this."

"Sure," I say as she picks up the carrier. "What are we doing?"

Walking toward a door at the far end of the room, she looks back at me. "Time to reintroduce Zara to her family."

Dr. Brenda leads the way into the lemur exhibit, and I can't help but think how amazing this is. I've never in my life dreamed that I would be walking into a zoo exhibit for lemurs, of all things.

The leaves begin to shake as creatures move, still hidden from view. As Dr. Brenda puts the carrier down, I can see curious faces looking at us from behind tree trunks.

"Wow," I say. "They're adorable."

Dr. Brenda unlocks the latch of the carrier and places her hand in the opening. A split second later, a small lemur scurries up her arm and balances on her shoulder, its head rotating around, taking everything in.

I notice a bald spot on Zara's haunches. I peer a little closer to see a slight scar. "What happened to her?"

Dr. Brenda holds a grape in her hand and holds her arm out straight. Zara makes her way to the grape, reaching out for it before rushing back to perch on her shoulder.

She coaxes the lemur down again, holding out another grape. "Here," she says, pulling Zara from her arm and holding her out for me to take.

I hold my hands up and step back. "What?"

"You said you would help. Give her a strawberry."

I pick out a large strawberry and put the bucket down. From beneath the leaves I hear sounds of excitement. Dr. Brenda leans down and snatches the bucket up.

To my surprise, she's smiling. "You almost got attacked by some very adorable but hungry lemurs."

"Sorry," I say, holding the strawberry out for Zara. "Will she bite?"

"Probably not."

That's not reassuring at all. But I hold the strawberry out a little farther.

Without warning, Zara leaps from Dr. Brenda's arms and catapults herself toward me. "Oh," I say in surprise. I have no choice but to catch her. Zara's eyes never leave the strawberry as she grabs it and begins munching on it. "What if I drop her?" I ask.

"You won't. She's used to scampering up trees. She knows how to hang on." She points to a bucket next to the door. Dr. Brenda pulls a small bowl out of her pocket and fills it with fruit. Holding it out for me, she says, "Don't let her eat it all at once."

"How did she get the injury on her leg?" I ask.

She shakes her head. "Probably got it during a fight for dominance. Her mother is the leader of the troop, but little Zara has to earn her place just like any other newbie."

Zara pauses her eating as Dr. Brenda kneels down. From the cover of leaves and brush, several lemurs make their way to Dr. Brenda. Each is rewarded with a piece of fruit when they get close enough and each scampers away, a little closer to us than before.

"Are the females always in charge of the group?" I ask as Zara picks up a piece of banana to gnaw on.

"Troop," Dr. Brenda corrects me. "And yes. In the wild, eventually, the male lemurs would be pushed out to go join another troop." Zara grabs the bowl with one hand and rummages around until she pulls out a chunk of pineapple. When the bowl is empty, she jumps down and joins the crowd that's surrounding Dr. Brenda.

"They really like fruit," I say as Dr. Brenda stands, taking the bucket with her. The lemurs voice their opposition.

"Wow," I say, resisting the urge to cover my ears as the sound echoes off the enclosure. "They're loud, too."

Dr. Brenda smiles and tosses the remaining fruit toward the tree line. "You can hear the call of some lemurs from over a mile away."

As the lemurs scamper away, Dr. Brenda turns and heads toward the door. I give one last look at Zara and her adorable friends before following. A moment later, we're back in the small room, and I help Dr. Brenda tidy up.

I glance up at the clock on the wall and gasp. "Oh no," I say, turning to hand Dr. Brenda the bucket. "I lost track of time and I have no idea how to get back to the entrance."

"Head out the front doors and take a left," Dr. Brenda says, swiping her key card so I can get out. "You won't need a card for the next door," she assures me.

"Thank you so much for letting me help. Lemurs are pretty cool."

She smiles. "They really are. And hey . . ."

"Yeah?"

"Good luck on your show. I hope you do well," Dr. Brenda says. "If this cooking thing doesn't work out, you might want to think about working with animals. You might be a natural. Zara doesn't like too many people."

"Thank you," I say, starting toward the door. "And thank you for letting me help. It was a lot of fun." What I don't tell her is that if I can't afford culinary school, no way is a four-year degree in my future. I burst out the doors and into the hot summer sun. I race past the groundskeepers and college students opening the souvenir kiosks. By the time I reach the fountain, I'm out of breath and have less than ten seconds to spare.

"That was close," Paulie whispers as I fall in line.

I bend over and try to catch my breath. "Who knew cardio would be so important for this show?" I gasp.

"Heads up," Hakulani says, walking behind me to his spot. "Camera guy is coming this way."

I snap up, brush the wisps of hairs from my face, and plaster on a smile.

Jessica takes her place in front of us and smiles. "All right, guys. It's time for your first Landmark Challenge. I hope your exploration of the Bronx Zoo inspired you, because you have some very hungry judges."

My smile falters as I realize I spent all my time in one place. Talking with Dr. Brenda and feeding Zara was fun, and informative, but what if that's not enough to complete the challenge? What if I have to complete a map of the park using food or something off-the-wall like that? I'm in big trouble, that's what.

"Don't forget, Peyton," Jessica says sweetly. "You have a five-minute penalty."

CHAPTER THIRTEEN

THE DIRECTOR YELLS "CUT!" AND THEN THE CREW moves into action to set up for the competition. A couple PAs come up and usher us to the craft services tent, where we are treated to a wide array of choices.

"What did you see?" Hakulani asks, coming up behind me.

I jump slightly before looking up at him. "Lemurs. You?"

"I was going so fast I don't even remember," he says with a laugh.

The line moves quickly, and before I know it, I'm sitting at a long table with the rest of the cast. Jessica waves at us before heading our way.

"I hope you guys had a good time at the zoo," she says. "So, while you're eating, I'm going to tell you what your challenge is, and then you'll have about thirty minutes to decide on your dish for today."

"We get a heads-up?" Paulie says.

Jessica nods. "I mean the audience won't know, but do you

really think we're going to expect you to come up with something with no prep time?"

"After yesterday," I say, "that's exactly what I thought. Will it be like this for every challenge?"

Jessica shakes her head. "For the Landmark Challenges, yes; but for the elimination challenges, no."

"At least we get something," Malik says, dropping a stuffed olive into his mouth.

"What's our challenge?" Dani asks.

Jessica leans forward as she explains the details of the challenge. "You will have two hours to make a treat that could be sold at any zoo snack bar. The snack should be inspired by your time here at the zoo."

Jessica nods at something behind us, and a pair of PAs drops notebooks and pens down in front of us. "Start planning. You can check out the pantry to see what we have for you when you're done eating."

Everyone practically starts inhaling their food. Except Dani. She doesn't take another bite. Instead she picks up her tray, goes to the closest trash can, and dumps it.

Everyone watches her before looking back at each other.

"Anything to win," Malik says, and he follows after her.

A minute later, only Paulie and I are left.

"Aren't you going to go?" I ask.

"In a minute," he says, spooning another bite of pudding

out of a cup. "Why aren't you out there elbowing to see the goods?"

"What's the point?" I ask. "It doesn't matter what I want to make. With my five-minute delay, I'm going to be lucky if I can find enough stuff to make something edible."

"That penalty is turning out to be a lot worse than I thought it would be," he says. "You want me to snag something for you and then sneak it over to you when the eyes aren't looking?"

I laugh. "What? Are you going to bake it in a cake and slide it across the floor when you pretend to drop your pencil?"

He shakes his head. "It's that thinking that got you the penalty. You gotta be smooth." He glides his hand across the air in front of him.

"Okay, that was mean," I say, but I'm not mad. It's hard to be mad at Paulie.

He glances at his now empty tray and then back at the tent where the crowd of contestants has thinned out a little. "I better go."

"Good luck."

"You too," he says, picking up his tray. "You sure you don't want me to pass you something on the DL?"

"Tempting," I say, "but I think I'm going to play it straight."

"Your call, but don't say I didn't try."

I shake my head and use my fork to pick up the last bite of my salad.

I watch as the PAs begin to direct everyone to where Jessica is standing outside the competition tent and decide I better head over there before someone is sent to track me down. She turns to look at us, and I see Paulie stand up a little straighter, so I do the same.

"Chefs, are you ready for your first Landmark Challenge?"

"Yes," I call out, my voice blending with everyone else's. My stomach tenses up in anticipation.

Jessica clasps her hands together in front of her and laughs. "Today, you will have two hours to create a menu item worthy of the Bronx Zoo. And you'll need to make one hundred samples."

"In two hours?" I say under my breath.

But Jessica's not done. "But there's a catch." She pauses, scanning our faces. "The only appliance at each of your stations is a single cooktop."

This challenge keeps getting worse.

This news doesn't go over well, and there are a few audible gasps from the other end of the lineup.

"Don't worry. We've still got the blast chillers, the ice cream maker, and two ovens." She pauses. "For you to share."

She's not making this any better.

"Unlike the elimination challenges, each Landmark Challenge will have a special guest judge, or in this case, judges." Another pause. "Are you ready to meet your judges?"

I clap, and everyone follows, but I'm nervous about who we're making these one hundred treats for.

Jessica smiles and motions down the path where a parade of children are marching toward us. "The Boys and Girls Club Day Camp from PS 89."

Her words are drowned out as the kids begin cheering.

I turn to Hakulani. "They're so cute."

He nods. "And there are a lot of them."

"Hey, kids," Jessica says, waving. They all wave and yell hello back.

Several of the cast smile widely, but a couple of them look as nervous as I feel.

Jessica continues. "When I count to three, everyone but Peyton will be allowed to go to the pantry to get everything needed for your treat."

She looks directly at me. "Peyton, since you came in last in the initial challenge, you have a five-minute penalty. This means not only will you be the last to get your supplies, but you will also have less time to plan and finish your dish."

I nod my head and look nervously at the big countdown clock perched over the tent opening. This is the worst-case scenario.

"Three," Jessica says, beginning the countdown.

"Two."

Everyone except me crouches down in a half-racing stance, preparing to bolt into the tent and get the best ingredients before they're gone. Meanwhile, I still don't have an idea about what I'm going to make. I take a slight step back so I don't get caught up in the rush forward of the others.

"One," Jessica says, and I can feel the whooshing as everyone sprints toward the tent.

A moment later, she is standing next to me, facing the clock.

"Good luck, Peyton," Dani calls from the tent. "You're going to need it."

I know she's taunting me on purpose. I just can't understand why she suddenly cares so much when she barely gave me the time of day before.

Jessica either doesn't hear Dani or pretends not to. I glance over and see her smile in place, just in case the cameras turn on us, but each crew member is currently busy chasing after the rest of the cast and getting set up in the tent. "In a couple of minutes, we'll do a little chitchat, and then I'll send you into the tent," she says, smoothing her hair down. This only serves to remind me of my wild mane that is threatening to break loose from the scrunchie at any minute.

I nod and try to come up with ideas for things that are quick and easy, but also appealing to kids. Inside, I can see everyone racing back to their prep stations, their arms loaded with all kinds of ingredients. Sitting here, on the sidelines, sucks. As I watch Malik and Lola come back from the second trip into the pantry, I stop trying to figure out what I'm going to make.

There's no way, even without my five-minute penalty, I could bake something, but the thought of being in that tent, working with icing or chocolate while the heat just keeps building, sounds like torture. Besides, even if I had an idea, the chances of the ingredients still being available are going to be pretty slim. I take a deep breath to slow my racing heart and try to stay focused. It's not like I haven't made dinner from a bare cabinet before, I remind myself. I'll just have to get creative. Like the time I made homemade peanut butter and chocolate cups for my elementary school bake sale in fifth grade. They were the hit of the sale, and no one knew that everything came from the local food pantry.

Jessica clears her throat, and I look up to find the camera moving in front of us. "You ready?" she asks.

I nod.

"So, Peyton, tough luck about the five-minute delay, huh?"

"To be honest, I don't even know what's going to be left. But I'm pretty good at thinking on my feet. Hopefully being at the beautiful Bronx Zoo will give me some inspiration."

Where did those words come from?

Jessica seems pleased. "Let's hope." She glances at the clock. "You can go in three. Two. One."

The word still lingers in the air as I run so fast I almost knock over the camera guy as he swings around to follow Malik.

I was right about one thing. By the time I get to the pantry, almost everything in the refrigerator is gone. And the bread pile is obliterated. I grab a few packages of marshmallows and milk chocolate chips, which are the only sweets left on the shelf, and head to the fruits and vegetables that, while pretty worked over, still have a decent selection. I pick up a couple of pineapples, the last four packages of strawberries, and every banana I can find.

Turns out Zara is going to be my inspiration after all. I quickly set up a double boiler on the cooktop and drop the chocolate chips in so they start melting. Grabbing a sharp knife, I slice the prickly skin off the pineapple and chop it into chunks. I check the chocolate, giving it a quick stir before turning down the heat. As an afterthought I quickly run back into the pantry for some cinnamon that I can sprinkle in to jazz it up a bit. Grabbing a fork, I dip it into the chocolate to make sure I haven't overdone it. The chocolate is rich and full of flavor. No generic ingredients in this treat.

Dumping the strawberries on my prep station, I sort through them, picking out the best ones before cutting off the green leafy tops. When I check the chocolate once more, I'm happy to see it's almost ready.

Finally, I peel the bananas and chop them into pieces. The smell of the chocolate attracts Paulie's attention.

"What are you making?"

"Wouldn't you like to know?"

"What I know is that chocolate smells like I need to put it in a glass and drink it."

"Don't you dare."

I turn off the heat on the cooktop and set up cooling racks before sliding parchment paper underneath.

"What are you doing?" Paulie asks again.

"Chocolate-covered everything."

"When this is over, you have to tell me what you saw in the zoo that made you think chocolate piles would be enticing. Because I was over by Happy the Elephant's enclosure, and—"

"Just stop right there," I say, holding up the chocolate-covered spoon. "Or I will splatter you. I mean it."

"All right," he says with a laugh, holding up his hands. "Calm down."

Once I'm done, I line up one hundred pieces of each fruit on separate racks. I take a deep breath before spooning the chocolate over each piece.

"Twenty minutes," Jessica says over the din of the chopping and stirring.

I glance up in disbelief, but the countdown clock that matches the one outside confirms it. Somehow a hundred minutes have flown by.

"You gonna make it?" Hakulani asks on his way back from grabbing his mini cookie bowls out of the oven.

I gape at him. "You baked? How?"

"I'm not giving away my secrets," he says with a laugh.

Paulie snorts. "You mean your pre-made cookie dough secret?"

"Hey," Hakulani says, pointing at Paulie. "I didn't see you making the krispie treat from scratch."

"You guys keep talking," I say, picking up two racks and rushing over to the blast chiller. The other two shelves already have sheets on them. "Crap."

"You need one?" Inaaya asks. "My stuff should be out in a minute or two."

I look at her. "Seriously? I thought we were friends outside the kitchen but cutthroat in it?"

"Oh, no, we're still cutthroat . . . you just owe me now."

I smile. "Fair enough." I return with my third rack just as Inaaya is pulling her trays out.

While the chocolate coating is hardening, I pull out one hundred long lollipop sticks, count out two hundred marshmallows, and lay out more parchment paper. I'm down to fifteen minutes. I have to focus. Of course, that is made even more difficult with Hakulani and Paulie trying to one-up each other on either side of me as the camera hovers back and forth over my station to catch every second of the banter.

Racing back to the blast chiller, I retrieve all three pans before frantically sticking one piece of strawberry, pineapple, and banana onto the stick with a marshmallow in between.

I finish the last one with one second to spare. But my dish is done, and all things considered, I'm pretty happy with the way it turned out.

One by one, we present our treats to the kids while staff members pass around the samples. When it's my turn, I step up to the microphone and tell them what I learned about lemurs in the Madagascar exhibit. "While little Zara probably hasn't had chocolate before, I know for a fact that she loves strawberries and pineapple and bananas. In fact, watching her eat her treat is what inspired me to make these banana split kabobs."

I hear a couple of giggles and even some squeals of delight as the kids bite into the kabobs. Unfortunately, it isn't enough to win. In fact, when the voting is over, there's a tie for first between Dani and Paulie.

Jessica calls up both of them. "Since you each got the same number of votes, you will both have an advantage in the elimination challenge that you can use—or *not* use if you decide. And you'll find out about that . . ."

Trademark pause.

". . . when we get back to the kitchen."

There is a collective groan, but Jessica just laughs.

"It's only a day away. Until then, happy cooking, everyone!"

A few beats pass and the camera operator says, "And we're out."

"You won," I say to Paulie, giving him a hug. "That's amazing."

"It's a tie," he says, wiping down his station.

Why is he not feeling the same excitement about his win the way I am? "Do you see Dani pouting over the tie?"

He glances over at Dani, who is high-fiving Malik. "You're right. I am happy."

"Yeah, you are. And you know how these advantages work. There's a good chance you'll be able to inflict culinary pain on any of us. I would kill to have a tie with anyone right now and not be at the bottom."

I'm joking, of course. I haven't watched enough unsolved crime shows to get away with murder.

CHAPTER FOURTEEN

AS THE PAs BEGIN TO PACK UP PRODUCTION CITY, we're led back to the bus. I feel like I've been up since yesterday. While the rest of us are on the bus, Jessica and the camera crew ask Dani and Paulie how they feel about winning the first advantage. I try not to feel envy, but I thought I would come here and be a big deal. Turning away from the interview, I look out the window as the city rushes by and remind myself that just getting on the show is an opportunity of a lifetime.

No one talks during the elevator ride to the apartment. As the first person to step in the hallway, I head straight to the bedroom with the intention of grabbing my things and getting a hot shower.

"It's my feet that are killing me," I groan, dropping into the plush chair in my room.

"No kidding," Inaaya says, sitting next to me. "I must have run all over that zoo. What was your favorite part?"

"That would be the lemurs."

She tilts her head. "I didn't see any lemurs."

"They were in a building with lions in front of it?"

She looks at me like I might be joking. "Yeah, that might have thrown me. What else did you see?"

"That's it."

Her eyes widen. "That's it? You went to one exhibit. A whole zoo to explore and you went to one exhibit, and you were still able to come up with something to make?"

I shrug. "What can I say? Inspiration can come from anywhere."

"Well, all I can say is that if this is any indication what the elimination is going to be like, I should probably get sleep. Tomorrow is a big day."

"You're not going to get something to eat?" I ask.

"Mmm. I don't think so. Since I got to present first, I went back to craft services and ate. I think, just this one time, I pick sleep over food."

I had been so nervous presenting my snack bar creation that I hadn't even thought about going back for food. It's something to keep in mind for next time. Assuming there is a next time. "I'm going to see what's in the kitchen. Are you sure you don't want me to bring you something back for later?" But Inaaya is already asleep, her body curled up into a ball.

I leave the room, careful to shut the door behind me as quietly as possible. The door to the other girls' room is shut, and

I can hear hushed voices coming from inside. In the kitchen, I find Malik and Adam standing in front of the refrigerator, staring inside.

"Anything sound good?" I ask, standing on my tiptoes to look over their shoulders.

"Someone went grocery shopping, but I don't know what they were thinking about when they bought this stuff," Malik says.

"Well I'm making grilled portobello mushroom burgers," Adam says, reaching around Malik to pull out a couple packages.

"You can't call something a burger if it doesn't have meat," Malik says with a scoff.

"I just did, so obviously you can," Adam countered.

Malik shakes his head. "Leave half the grill for me to make my world-famous burgers," he says, pulling out a package of ground sirloin. "Peyton can be the judge."

"Oh no," I say, stepping back and holding my hands up in surrender. "Hasn't there been enough judging for one day?"

"Oh come on, Peyton," Adam says. "There aren't any high stakes."

Malik grins. "Bragging rights are the highest *steaks* of them all. Get it?" he asks, holding up his package. "Steaks?"

"Ha, ha," Adam says, nudging him in the ribs with his elbow as he moves past Malik. "Oh, we could do steak fries in the air fryer. I saw some russet potatoes in the pantry."

Malik nods. "Okay. I can get behind that."

Adam ushers me out of the kitchen. "You can't see the magic. You're only judging the final process."

"I didn't say I was judging at all."

"You are," Malik says, waving me out of the room.

I'm trying to pin down the moment when I agreed to this but realize I'm getting a free meal and decide to go with it. "Fine, I'll be on the roof. But if you try to serve those steak fries with regular ketchup, I'm docking points."

"Oh, I wouldn't dream of it," Adam says in complete seriousness.

Malik grins. "Girl, you know I'm going to bring it. Now get out so I can show this fool who's the king of the grill."

"You talk too much," Adam says, but his grin softens the words.

I pull open the door that leads to the roof and climb the steps. When I emerge, I see Hakulani reclining on one of the chaise lounges, soaking in the late afternoon sun.

"Hey," I say as I approach. "Mind if I join you?"

He swings his legs around. "Actually, I was just getting ready to move. If I lie here another minute, I'm probably going to fall asleep."

"Inaaya's crashed out in our room right now."

"So is Paulie."

I laugh. "This competition might turn us into a bunch of old people."

"Are Malik and Adam still staring into the fridge?"

"Oh no. They are now in a burger cook-off."

Hakulani's eyes widen. "Seriously?"

"Oh yeah, and I get to be the judge."

"Can I get in on this action?"

I nod toward the door. "Better let them know I recruited you."

Hakulani jumps up, then heads down the stairs. While he's gone, I stand and walk to the railing, leaning over to look at the street below. It's the first time I've been alone since I entered the set two days ago. A slight breeze picks up, blowing my hair off my neck. In the absence of people, the surrealness of the situation drops on me like a ton of bricks—and with it comes the gravity of tomorrow. This entire experience could be over in just twenty-four hours and tomorrow night I could be on my way back to Florida with nothing but a couple of memories and a wistfulness of what might have been.

Thankfully, my downward spiral is interrupted by Hakulani's pushing open the metal door.

"Good news," he says, pausing to turn on the grill before coming to stand next to me. "I was able to convince them that you were in need of an additional judge. They agreed and now I don't have to figure out how to feed myself."

I smile at him as his arm brushes mine. "I know the show probably thinks they're being nice to us by letting us make our own food, but after working all day in the kitchen to make food for other people, sometimes all I can do is crack open a blue box of mac and cheese for dinner," I say.

"Really?"

"Oh yeah. It's good Adam and Malik are cooking because I've even been known to make it in the microwave from time to time."

"Wow," he says, leaning away from me, taking the warmth of his arm with him. "Microwave mac and cheese is so bad compared with stove top."

"I know, but desperate times being what they are . . ." I say, letting my words fade away.

"You work in a restaurant back home?" he asks.

Had I told him that? "Um, what?"

"You said you work in a kitchen to make food for other people, so I guess you must work back home."

"Oh yeah. I mean it's just part-time, after school and sometimes on the weekends. I mostly make the pies." I leave out the part about waitressing so I can help Mom with the bills. I know Caitlin wants me to play up my life back home, but in this moment I feel awkward. Like playing to an audience is one thing, but doing it to Hakulani feels so forced.

"Yeah, I have a part-time job back home, too."

"Doing what?" I ask.

"Working in a kitchen." He grins. "What else? It's not one

of the three-star Michelin places, but it's still a good place to work. Plus, the chef has been giving me tips. But after this show, I hope I'll catch the attention of some of the top chefs on the islands."

"But when will you surf?" I ask, grinning.

He looks down at me, his brow furrowed. "There's always time for surfing." He smiles again. "You should come visit. I could teach you how."

"Surf or cook?"

"You pick. I could also teach you how to hula."

The blush that spreads over my entire body is a full-out sprint. Hakulani, perhaps one of the most attractive people I have ever met, is definitely flirting with me.

With him so near, I struggle to find words. "I can barely work a Hula-Hoop, so I'm pretty sure hula dancing is out of the question."

"You never know. A good teacher might be able to change your mind."

Did he just use such a cheesy line? Out in the open? Where every word and gesture is being picked up by the camera? Oh no, the cameras. The mere thought of this conversation being captured right now breaks the moment and I shift uncomfortably.

Hakulani, to his credit, notices my discomfort and asks, "You okay? I didn't mean to be that guy."

"That guy?" I ask, pushing away from the railing and taking a seat on one of the patio chairs nearby. A seat for one. "I don't know what you mean."

"Yeah, you do. You know, the guy who takes an innocent situation and says just enough to turn everything creepy?" He sits down on the seat across from me, the firepit separating us.

"That's not what you did."

"It's a little bit what I did," he says.

We are both quiet for a moment, the sounds of the city below drifting between us.

"I have to be honest," he says.

"About what?"

He motions to the camera perched by the stairs, pointing straight at us. "These things make me nervous. And when I get nervous, I tend to say stupid things."

"It's fine," I say.

"No," he insists. "I'm not the kind of guy who goes around and offers hula lessons to girls I've just met."

"So the camera made you do it?" I ask, trying to make it come out playful, but utterly failing.

"Yes." He pauses. "And maybe no."

We look at each other, and I give him a small smile, hoping it's enough to let him know that it's okay. After a second, he smiles back, albeit a little apologetically. "So, was I wrong?"

"About what?" I ask, not sure what he's talking about.

He nods back to the railing. "Before. We were having a moment, right?"

I mean, in my head, we went from talking about judging burgers to suddenly having him offer to teach me how to hula dance, and it completely caught me off guard. I haven't really dated, like ever, because when would I have had the time or the extra money, so I'm not exactly the best judge when it comes to romance. Was that a *moment*? Then, in the back of my mind, another question creeps in. And even if it was, was it a real one or was it all for the show?

By the grace of whatever deity is looking out for me, I don't get a chance to answer him because Adam and Malik burst through the door with their food ready to put on the grill.

"Keep your cow carcass on your half of the grill," Adam says, but his face is lit up with a good-natured smile.

"Hey," Malik says, lifting the grill lid to start our dinner. "I'm letting them be free range." He waits a beat before adding, "Just kidding. I know vegetarians are sensitive to sharing cooking space with us carnivores." He pulls out a roll of aluminum foil and proceeds to make a temporary shield that will keep the juices from splashing over to Adam's side.

"Thanks," Adam says, nodding his head and looking at Malik. "I really appreciate that."

Malik shrugs. "It's no big deal."

With the addition of two more people, the energy shifts

quickly, and the rooftop becomes a boisterous place to be. By the time Adam and Malik have pulled their burgers off the grill, Lola and Dani have joined the party. Lola immediately takes the spot next to Hakulani and begins peppering him with questions about Hawaii.

With the four of us acting as judges, the winner of the burger cook-off is decidedly a tie. Which is exactly how it should be.

"I bet Inaaya and Paulie are going to be sorry they missed this," Dani says. She's been surprisingly quiet tonight and, while it's unnerving, it's also been nice not to have to endure her subtle, and not so subtle, digs.

Over dinner, Hakulani catches my gaze and gives me a quick, relaxed smile along with an eye roll as Lola continues her never-ending chatter. I have to hand it to her; she can make a full-blown conversation out of small talk like no one I have ever seen before. I sit back, taking in this moment. For one of us, this is going to be the final night, so I want to enjoy every bit of it while I'm here.

CHAPTER FIFTEEN

WHEN MY ALARM GOES OFF THE NEXT MORNING, I refuse to open my eyes as I try to hit the snooze button. Five minutes later, I do the same thing. By the third time, Inaaya has obviously had enough because she launches one of her pillows across the room and it hits me in the head.

"Hey," I say, more out of surprise than anything else.

"Get up or turn it off. Either way, make it stop."

"Well you're in a good mood," I say, slowly pulling myself up into a sitting position, gathering my blanket around me.

Inaaya groans and buries her head in her one remaining pillow. "I was up all night," she says, her words muffled.

"Couldn't sleep?"

Her head nods into the plush pillow.

I pick up her other one and gently toss it back on her bed. "Me neither. I kept having this dream that Angelica was chasing me with a stalk of celery."

Inaaya's shoulders shake in the dim light of our room, and

I'm pretty sure she's laughing at me. After a moment, she lifts up her head and turns toward me. "One of us is going home today," she says quietly.

"No," I answer. "One of *them* is going home. You and me, we're still going to be here tomorrow."

"You sound so sure, but you don't know."

"I have a good feeling," I say, sounding way more confident than I feel. "Besides, if either of us should be worried, it's me. I've already lost one competition."

"You're trying to inspire me by saying that you'll go home and leave me here with Dani? Is that supposed to inspire me?"

"My Grams used to say that if you don't have the power of positive thinking, you've already lost," I say, scooting back against the wall.

"So we're not packing, because we are not going home?" she says.

"Right, because of the power of positive thinking."

"You know there's no scientific proof that you can make something happen because of positive thinking."

"Trying to disprove PPT does not make it any less powerful," I say, shaking my head, then turning to face her, my tone more serious. "Look, do you want to be here?"

"Yes."

"Then make it happen." I am so good at giving advice that I know I won't take myself.

She doesn't look convinced, but instead of arguing with me, she says, "Well, if for no other reason, I want to stick around long enough to find out what's happening between you and Hakulani." She pauses, tapping her chin with her finger and looking at the ceiling. "Or is it with you and Paulie?"

"I don't—"

"Oh, please. It's so obvious that they're both interested in you. So do you want to see what happens? Yes or no."

"What? No," I say, but I'm not sure she believes me. "Both guys are nice, but I can't let myself get distracted. This show is the only way I can go to culinary school."

"Good," she says, crawling back under her covers. "Because I am not wasting valuable time handing you tissues when it all blows up in your face."

"Wow, that's supportive," I say with a laugh. I glance at the clock and spring out of bed. "We're going to be late."

Inaaya races out of her bed and to the bathroom. "I'll make it quick."

"You better hurry or you'll miss our ride to the studio."

Hoping that I have time to grab some breakfast before she finishes, I step into the hallway, checking to see if anyone is coming. When I reach the kitchen, I find Adam leaning over a bowl.

"Hey," I say. Out of everyone here, Adam is the only person I can't seem to read. Not even a little.

He motions to a basket of bagels and pastries. "The PA elves dropped these off this morning."

"Are you ready for today?"

He shrugs. "What's going to happen is going to happen, right?"

How can he be so nonchalant about this? By the end of the day, one of us will have our hopes crushed while the others drink sparkling grape juice on their proverbial grave.

"Yeah, but it's the first elimination," I say. "I wonder what kind of challenges they're going to throw at us. You know they love to throw in a twist—it makes for good ratings."

"Yeah, ratings," he scoffs. "It's all about the ratings."

There is a knock at the front door and I jump.

"Relax," Adam says, spooning his last bite of cereal and slurping down the almond milk. "Time to go."

I assumed everyone was going to be a bundle of nerves and anxiety like me as we got closer to the studio and that the bus ride would be a hotbed of silent fidgeting. Instead, everyone else is laughing and joking around.

"Well," Dani says, giving Paulie a rueful smile, "just be glad the judges aren't judging on biceps or Hakulani would be wiping the floor with you."

Everyone laughs, including Paulie, but it feels like I've landed in an alternate universe. Yesterday, he would have growled at Dani for saying something like that, but today he is just nodding and smiling. And Dani sure as hell wouldn't be missing a chance to slam me, but instead she seems to be completely ignoring me now. When we arrive at the studio, Paulie slides out of the bus, turning around to help me out. "Are you ready for this?"

"You bet," I say, trying to not think of the million things that could go wrong today. I could poison the judges or set the building on fire. *Or,* a very tiny voice in my head says, *you could wow the judges and secure a spot in the next round.* I roll my neck, trying to release the tension. Inaaya turns from the front of the group and gives me a sly thumbs-up as we head into the studio.

After a quick trip to my dressing room to get dressed in my turquoise chef's jacket and black pants, I head to hair and makeup, before finally walking to the set. Adam is already there rearranging everything at his station when I enter. "Hey," I say.

"What's up, Peyton?" he asks, looking up at me. "You ready for this challenge?"

I shake my head. "No, but then again, I don't think I'll ever be ready. Are you?"

"No, but it doesn't matter." There is a quiet beat before he adds, "Like you said, I don't think I'll ever be ready. I just have to have faith and know that I've done everything I can to win while still being true to myself."

I give him the best smile I can manage, but his words and his overall attitude aren't like the Adam I've gotten to know the last couple days. When I met him, he always had a calm, collected personality, and last night he was fun to be with because it felt like he wasn't here to prove anything—he was just comfortable being himself. Now his energy seems different, and I wish I could think of something deep or thoughtful to say to cheer him up or encourage him a little. But of course I'm way too nervous, so I spout off the first thing that comes into my head. "Well, I've spent most of my time here in last place and trying to not burn down the building when I bake a pie. Not sure that means anything, but hopefully it will save lives." I hold up my crossed fingers.

He gives me a polite laugh as some of the others start to come onto the set and take their places. "We just have to remember that we're here to cook," he says. "If my cooking isn't good enough, then they'll send me home. If it is, then I'll stay."

A PA begins to make the rounds, telling us it's time to take our marks, and we all hustle to the front of the set. Once we're all in place, Jessica stands in front of the camera and starts beaming at us in her usual upbeat way. But my mind is replaying Adam's words.

"Today's challenge is all about having fun with food," she says. "With that in mind, the judges would like you to create a full day's worth of meals for kids in just three hours. That means breakfast, lunch, and dinner.

"Your dishes will be judged on creative plating, concept, and, of course, taste. And—" she picks up a picnic basket and sets it on the table next to her "—every item in this basket must be used in at least one of your dishes."

I stifle a groan. Any time a mystery ingredient is involved, you can bet it's not going to be something easy like strawberries or eggs. Instead you're getting stuck with cow tongue or falafel chips.

"But before we begin, there's one more thing we need to take care of. Would Dani and Paulie please step forward?"

She waits as they come up and stand beside her, both looking excited about winning the Landmark Challenge and the advantage that comes with it. Then a PA wheels in a large fishbowl and sets it off to the side near Jessica, who is now looking back and forth between the camera and Paulie and Dani.

"Inside this bowl are a variety of sabotages you can dish out to any one of the remaining six chefs. However, you can't use it on each other," she says, giving them a quick glance. "Step up and choose your sabotage."

Dani reaches into the bowl and pulls out a folded piece of white paper. Jessica nods for her to open it. As she reads it, a slow, evil grin spreads across her face.

"Take away one electric appliance from any opponent and replace it with the hand version."

Dani looks up and her eyes roam up and down the line of chefs as if she is trying to decide who she is going to unload her punishment on, but I'm not fooled. She is just buying airtime. I watch her eyes pass over me twice before she finally makes eye contact. "Peyton."

Big surprise. She was just toying with the other chefs. But me? She plans to eliminate me.

"And what appliance?" Jessica asks before giving me and the others a helpless sort of look like, if she could, she would totally rescue me; but since she can't, oh well.

"I think Peyton should lose her mixer," Dani says, and immediately a PA dressed all in black comes on set and takes not only my stand mixer, but my electric hand mixer too. She returns with a hand-crank beater and places it at my station.

I accept the change with a forced smile. "Thanks, Dani," I say. I try to tell myself it's just part of the game and not personal, but it really feels personal. I sense a fire starting inside me, and know I have to win a Landmark Challenge, even if it's only so I can give Dani a taste of her own medicine. Besides, a little revenge is good for the soul, right?

Paulie steps up to pick his sabotage. He gets along with everyone, so I have no idea who he is going to pick. As he reads his card, he begins to laugh. After taking a breath to compose himself, he looks right at Hakulani and says, "Sorry, man." Then he reads, "The chef who receives this sabotage must do all their prep and cooking in a miniature kitchen using only miniature utensils." He walks over to Hakulani and hands him the card.

As with my sabotage, the PAs quickly descend, unplugging

Hakulani's entire kitchen unit and wheeling it away while another team brings in what has got to be the smallest working kitchen ever created. No one can stop themselves from laughing as Hakulani tilts his head to one side and then the other as he tries to envision how he is going to fit. I try not to laugh too loud, but once he sits down on the tiny stool provided and puts on a tiny chef's hat that has a string to go under his chin so it stays on, I can't help it.

He looks up at Paulie. "You know this is war, right?" he asks in a good-natured way. At least, it seems good-natured, but his gaze is fiery.

"Worth it," Paulie says with a wide grin.

Hakulani doesn't look convinced as he starts testing things. However, he does look impressed when water comes out of the mini faucet.

"Oh yes," Jessica says, clasping her hands in front of her mouth, probably to keep from laughing. "It's fully functional."

She allows for one more round of giggles before getting us back on track. "All right, chefs, with three hours on the clock, please head to your stations, where your baskets are waiting for you."

As I jog back to my station, I watch Hakulani struggle to figure out how to cook three different meals on what is essentially a play kitchen for toddlers, and I decide that losing my mixer isn't really all that bad.

CHAPTER SIXTEEN

"ALL RIGHT, CHEFS," JESSICA SAYS ONCE WE'RE behind our stations, with our hands on the lids of our baskets. "It's time to find out what four ingredients you'll be working with today." She smiles brightly, letting the tension build. "Remember, you must use at least one of the items in each of your dishes." I glance nervously at Paulie, who gives me a quick head nod and a wink. "Open your baskets," Jessica says.

Pulling the lid back, I unpack each of the mystery ingredients and place them on the table.

Salami. I can work with that. It's spiced meat, so the possibilities are limitless.

Popcorn. This one could be interesting, but I've seen it on other shows before. The trick is going to be using it in a unique and unexpected way.

The next two items stump me. The first is a spice that looks like it should be on an old-fashioned Christmas tree. And the second looks like a sea urchin. As I study it, I feverishly hope that it's not a sea urchin.

Once everyone has put their baskets away, Jessica clears her throat to get our attention. "In your basket, you have four ingredients to use in your dishes. The first is salami."

At least I got that right.

"Second, there's star anise."

I pick up the star-shaped spice and sniff it. It reminds me of fall. I take an even deeper sniff, and it definitely has a cinnamon-like scent.

"Next, you have one of my favorite nighttime snacks," Jessica says, rubbing her hands together like she's about to steal some of our kernels. "Popcorn."

I pick up a piece and pop it in my mouth. The slightest hint of salt comes through and I feel a small bubble of relief. Too salty and it might have overpowered the sweetness I have planned for it.

"Finally, you have rambutan."

I pick up the sea urchin–looking ingredient. I'm still stumped, and I have absolutely no idea what dishes this is traditionally used in or how one would cook it.

"Get ready to create a day of meals that will blow the mind of even the pickiest young eater." She pauses, giving time for the camera to pan over our faces. "Three. Two. One." Another long pause. I think that this is the part I hate the most: the long, awkward pauses.

"Go."

Just like that, we're all sprinting across the set and into the pantry, grabbing everything we might need. Over the din of packages being opened, all of us racing back and forth, and warnings that someone is claiming the convection oven, I suddenly hear Jessica reminding us that the pantry will be closing in five minutes.

By the time I get back to my station, my arms are laboring under the weight of the ingredients. I quickly spread everything out on my counter and sort them by dishes before quickly taking inventory.

"Thirty seconds," Jessica calls out as the timer over the pantry flashes red.

I glance at my supplies.

Something is missing, but I can't figure out what. My mind races through each of the recipes, mentally ticking off each ingredient on my fingers. "Crap," I say, pivoting on my heel and making a mad dash back to the pantry for rice. I barely slip between the doors as they shut, closing the pantry off for the rest of the day. I wonder what would have happened if I'd still been in the pantry when the time was up: Would they have just shut me in and left me there?

As I start getting to work, I notice that an eeriness settles over the set. It's not silence—far from it. With the whirl of the fans keeping the equipment cool, knives against cutting boards, and the clink of pots and pans being slammed around, it's actually pretty loud, but there is no talking. The jovial mood of the bus ride here is gone.

I guess that's what happens when you know you have one chance to keep your dream alive or watch it collapse like a undercooked soufflé. I glance over my counter to watch Haku-lani measure flour with the tiniest measuring cup set I've ever seen—it's more like a thimble for a giant—and I smile.

"Do you have an Easy-Bake Oven, too?" I ask as I walk by him on my way to get a mixing bowl.

If looks could kill, I would be knocking on the pearly gates right now. "Hope your arms don't fall off using that hand mixer," he fires back.

After a split second, we both laugh and something about the sound breaks the tension on the set. Okay, sure. One of us is going to be leaving tonight, but that doesn't mean we have to act like we're at a funeral. Plus, it doesn't make for good television.

"You know he's going to get you back for the kitchen," I tell Paulie as we stand next to each other at the fryers.

"Still worth it," he says, pulling the fried dough from the hot oil.

I give him and his dish a glance. "Are you making funnel cakes?"

Paulie smiles and waggles his eyebrows at me. "Wait and see." Then he turns on his heel and heads back to his station, and I head back to mine.

If Angelica wasn't a fan of my fritters, I can't imagine she would ever be happy eating a funnel cake. At least my fritter had protein; Paulie is basically serving fried carbs.

"Hey, Peyton," Jessica says, coming over to check on me. "How are you handling the mixer situation?"

"It's definitely a challenge," I admit, forcing myself to smile and laugh a little. "But I have a few tricks up my sleeves."

Jessica beams. "I can't wait to see what you come up with. Can you give us any hints about the meal that you are creating?"

"Maybe a small one. You know how, as kids grow, they become more mature?"

Jessica laughs. "Oh yes. I've got three kids at home, all different ages. Trust me, I know."

"Right," I say, laughing with her. "As they grow, their taste in food changes too, right? So rather than focusing on one age group, I decided I want to try to elevate the taste palate for each meal. Starting with breakfast."

Jessica nods. "I think that's a great idea."

"Let's hope the judges agree with you," I say, and we both laugh.

Thankfully, Jessica doesn't come back to my station for the rest of the prep time. It's just the camera crew getting close-ups of my simmering pots and getting in my way as I try to pull a tray out of the oven. If they don't watch out, they're going to get burned. Unlike the first challenge, the time seems to go by much faster. Luckily I manage not to cut off another fingertip. Amid cooking, worrying, and plating, all of a sudden Jessica gives us the one-minute warning, and then, in what seems like ten seconds, the buzzer goes off. I throw my hands in the air just as I pop the last silicone straw into my rambutan, mango, and dragon fruit smoothie.

Hakulani leans over my station and gives me two high fives before clapping Malik on the shoulder, and I accept a hug from Paulie.

"Did you get everything done?" he asks.

I nod. "Barely. I needed every second."

"Same," he says, and we smile as the camera approaches.

Jessica redirects our attention as she claps for us from her host spot. "Well done, all of you. It's always amazing how, even when using the same ingredients, chefs can come up with such different dishes! I know the judges are eager to try them, so let's get started."

We line up and wait as, one by one, each of us presents our dishes to Billy, Angelica, and A. J. When Jessica calls my name, I take a few seconds to collect my thoughts before walking over to her and standing in front of the judges. I played it safe and to my strengths, so I'm not presenting any questionable dishes. Overall, I feel like I created a visually appealing meal, and I used all the ingredients, so the only thing that can sink me now is bad presentation.

Jessica talks for a few more seconds before handing the floor over to me.

"Thank you, Jessica," I say. "For today's challenge, I wanted to explore the evolution of the childhood palate, starting with the most important time of the day and the most discerning eater of the lot."

I don't even know where these words are coming from, but I'm not going to complain. "Breakfast and toddlers. For this energetic bunch and their little fingers, I created mini waffles with bacon bits, and brown sugar syrup for dipping. This dish also introduces these burgeoning foodies to the combination of sweet and savory. I've also paired this morning treat with a fruit smoothie."

Not bad, I think. I managed to work in my theme and explain each dish without tripping over my tongue.

A. J. is the first to speak. "The smoothie is an inspired taste," he says. "There's enough of the rambutan in each sip that it's obviously the star of the drink, while still being well balanced with the mango and dragon fruit. However, the sweetness of the smoothie and the syrup are a bit overwhelming. Each dish by itself would be delightful, but together I think they battle for dominance."

The other judges nod in agreement. "I think that's a great way to put it," Billy says.

Angelica is silent, which is more unnerving than when she has something to say.

"Okay, thank you, judges," Jessica says, clapping her hands together. "Let's bring out your lunch."

The cameras keep rolling, focusing on the judges as they take notes and then on my face as some PAs bring out the next set of plates. Once everything is in place, Jessica turns toward me again. "Tell us about your lunch dish."

I nod. "This lunch is inspired by the bento boxes of Japan. The sushi is made with carrots, cucumbers, yellow and orange peppers, cream cheese, and rice rolled in nori sheets. Next, there are breaded chicken chunks with a yum-yum sauce and a salad of fresh greens. And, of course, no lunch is complete without a sweet treat, which is where the star anise shortbread cookies come in. I've served the meal with a set of chopsticks, in keeping with the theme."

"Very creative," Billy says, picking up the chopsticks and dunking a piece of chicken in the sauce.

Angelica takes a small bite of the sushi roll. "This lacks any flavor." She reaches for a glass of water before barely dipping her chicken in the yum-yum sauce. "And you were too heavy-handed with the garlic powder in the chicken."

A. J. looks up at me, pity flitting across his face. "Presentation-wise, this is great, but I agree with Angelica. Your pitch at the beginning of your presentation was that each course would be elevated above the last. So far, this isn't quite cutting it."

"Thank you, chefs," I say. I was prepared for Angelica to criticize me—I kind of expected it after the first judging—but A. J.'s feedback feels like a blow. Maybe I was wrong, and playing it safe wasn't the way to go, but how do you please everyone all the time? They're all looking for something different, and it seems what they want is never what I'm offering.

The PAs set a record time for clearing and serving. It's like even they don't want to be on set with me.

"For your third meal," Jessica says once the lunch boxes have been replaced with dinner, "what have you brought for us?"

I take a deep breath. "This meal is for the hungry teenager who never seems to get full. I've made a salami and mozzarella calzone with marinara sauce, and fried asparagus wrapped in bacon and sprinkled with parmesan. For dessert, caramel popcorn cupcakes with salted caramel buttercream frosting."

Each judge digs into this meal. Behind my back, I cross my fingers. They have to like this one. Everything, including the dough for the calzone, was made from scratch. Without a mixer.

A. J. looks up, his mouth full of calzone. "This is good," he says. "I think you could have done something with the crust to up the elegance of the dish, but we didn't ask you to cater a black-tie event. We asked you to prepare a meal kids would eat." He bites into the asparagus, chews, and once he swallows, he adds, "And that's exactly what you have done. This is the best meal you've presented to us."

Billy unwraps the cupcake. "After your key lime pie, I have high expectations for this cupcake."

I smile. "I hope you like it."

He takes a bite and moans. "This is what I was hoping for. The caramel corn gives an unexpected crunch, which is awesome. My only critique is that the frosting could be a little fluffier."

Stupid Dani and her stupid sabotage.

Angelica clears her throat and I snap to attention. "Overall, it's fine, but I have to wonder if you're cut out for this competition."

Suddenly, I feel like a spotlight is shining down on me and the walls are closing in. The blinking red light on the camera seems to move closer and closer until it's a beacon. I glance at Jessica, and her eyes are as wide as mine feel.

"What do you mean by that, Angelica?" Jessica asks.

Please, let the floor open up and swallow me. Is that too much to ask?

"Nothing you've presented us shows me that you have what it takes to cut it in the culinary world." That's bad enough, but Angelica is only just getting started.

"So far, it's been twists on simple dishes—diner food and daycare treats. The winner of this competition is going to be someone who is going to take chances, be innovative, and be passionate about their creations. With the exception of your desserts, Peyton, I'm just not sure that you have found your drive or your passion yet. You are just *okay*."

The entire set goes silent and, in that moment, it's like Angelica and I are the only ones here. Then, after what seems like a lifetime, Billy coughs gently. A. J. shifts in his seat but keeps his eyes on the plate in front of him.

"While I don't completely agree with my wife's assessment," Billy says, giving Angelica a loaded glance, "I do agree that the one thing your food doesn't seem to capture is your love of cooking. That said, I see potential in what you've presented, and if you can find a way to bring that out in your food, I think you'll do just fine."

Somehow, I manage a quiet "Thank you, chef," before stumbling back to my place in line.

Of course, Dani is next to present, and her first dish is met with glowing compliments.

"You okay?" Hakulani whispers as the PAs start to bring out her next set of dishes.

"Great," I whisper back, my throat growing hot. "I mean, I'm obviously going home tonight, but otherwise I'm doing great."

He doesт't say anything else, because what can he say? That I'm not leaving? I listen as the judges go on and on about Dani's food and her clever use of color. Every word I hear is like a knife stabbing into my very essence.

When we finally cut so the crew can reset for the elimination, my legs feel like they're cement. It isn't until Paulie grabs my arm and practically drags me back to the waiting room that I remember how to put one foot in front of the other. He doesn't talk to me, though a couple of the other cast members try to. But all I can think is that they're glad it's me and not them on the chopping block this time. They can all breathe a little easier now because there is no way Angelica is going to let me through to next week.

Silently, Paulie guides me to one of the stools in the waiting room, and I drop my head to the table hoping to avoid any further looks of pity. Angelica's words ring through my brain. "Okay," I mutter to myself, "she said I'm just *okay*."

Except for your desserts, I remind myself. My throat gets even tighter, and I think: *Screw the power of positive thinking.*

After a few minutes, a PA comes to collect us, and the disembodied voice tells us to line up, so I start to prepare for my imminent departure as I force myself back to my spot. As Jessica announces that Lola is the winner of this week's elimination challenge, the disembodied voice tells me to look more excited. Easy for him to say.

Jessica goes on to tick off the rest of the top six, and it's no surprise to hear that I'm in the bottom two. What is surprising is that Adam is standing next to me. However, unlike me, who probably looks like someone stole my dog and set fire to my house, Adam is staring straight ahead at the judges' table with defiance—like he is daring them to send him home. I glance at him and he is holding his head high and meets each judge's gaze, and right now, I would give anything to be more like him.

I'm so sure that it's my name Jessica is going to call, so consumed by the inevitable demise of my dreams, that it doesn't register when Jessica announces who is going home. It isn't until Adam puts his hand on my shoulder and pulls me into a hug that I realize it's not me. It's *him*. Instinctively, I hug him back, and despite the relief rushing through my body, I wonder: How is this possible?

"Don't trust any of them," Adam whispers in my ear before giving me a final squeeze. Before I can ask him what he means, the rest of the cast descends on us. Everyone looks as stunned and confused as I feel. Adam could have been a fan favorite, and he can certainly cook better than me. Heck, I was even thinking about trying to incorporate a few vegetarian recipes into my arsenal after tasting his portobello burger last night. But somehow he is going home, and I'm staying.

Adam has only a couple of minutes to say goodbye before he turns and walks through a set of doors on the far side of the set. We are asked to return to our marks as Jessica wraps up with the show's tagline, and then the cameras cut off. Out of the corner of my eye, I see Angelica and Billy in a quiet, heated conversation. Then Billy quickly stands up from the judges' table and storms away toward his dressing room. A. J. follows him, his cell phone pressed against his ear.

Inaaya comes up to me, blocking the rest of the scene as she links her arm with mine. Inside, I'm a fireworks display of emotions. Obviously, I'm glad and relieved that I managed to survive the elimination round, but Adam's warning rings in my ears. *Don't trust any of them.* Who is *them*?

Inaaya is saying something to me, but I can't seem to follow any of it. Malik glances my way and gives me a weak smile before leaving the set without a word to anyone. In the back of my mind, I acknowledge his behavior is kind of odd, but I'm still trying to figure out how I was spared and Adam was sent packing. The one thing I know for sure is that unless I do something drastic, there might not be another miracle in my future. Fun and games are over—now it's all about survival.

CHAPTER SEVENTEEN

THERE ISN'T MUCH TIME TO PROCESS ADAM'S departure before we head back to the apartment. Once we load up, the ride there seems to take forever. Members of the camera crew encourage us to sit in our assigned seats, so they can have continuity when they start editing the footage, but Inaaya ignores them and sits next to me, leaning her head on my shoulder.

"That was brutal," she says with a little sniff.

I don't say anything. Instead, I nod and close my eyes. I wish I could say that I'm sad Adam is gone, but I can't. In that moment, it was him or me—and I *want* to be here. But as determined as I am to stay, watching him walk out the door was harder than I expected it to be.

The rest of the cast is pretty quiet, too. Lola and Dani talk in soft voices in the middle of bus, while the guys are spread out in the back. The camera crew, to its credit, stops trying to get our reactions and leaves us alone.

Inaaya sniffs again, rubbing her hand under her eyes. "But you're here, and that's what matters, right?"

I nod. "I am here, but I'm still not sure how."

"Because you were better." She lifts her head off my shoulder and looks at me.

I look down at my hands for a moment before I look up. "We both know that's not true."

She seems to want to argue but instead says, "We don't know what went into their decision. Maybe they see something in you that makes you special."

"Yeah, but the competition isn't a 'you can do it' kind of gig."

"Well, then, do you want to go back to the judges and demand they send you home and bring Adam back?"

I hesitate, not because I need to think it over, but because even though I feel guilty, I also know that I'm being selfish and silly for complaining about having this opportunity to prove to the judges—well, mainly Angelica—that I belong here. "No, I do not want to do that."

"Then this is a good thing, and I'll hear no more pity from you."

She lays her head back on my shoulder, and I turn to look out the window. Could Inaaya be right? Could the judges have seen something in my cooking that they didn't see in Adam's? Something that made them want to give me a second chance? If that's the case, then I really need to find a way to up my game.

From now on, it's all about the food. If I have time to hang out on the roof or chat with someone, then I have time to work on my skills.

Back at the apartment, no one seems to know what to say—even Dani, who I figured would be the first to point out that I don't belong, is keeping her thoughts to herself.

As we all step out into the hall, Malik turns to us and says, "Roof. Fifteen minutes. *Everybody*," before turning toward the kitchen. Paulie follows him, and the rest of us head to our rooms to change and clean up.

"You going to shower now?" Inaaya asks, reaching for her caddy.

I drop into one of our armchairs and shake my head. "You go first; there isn't enough time for both of us. I'll shower after whatever mysterious activity Malik has planned."

"If you're sure."

"I am. Besides, you take forever in there." I give her a quick smile. "I think I need a quick nap."

She smiles, closing the door as she leaves the room. I sit in the chair for a beat, summoning the energy to get up, then I stand and go to my closet. After pulling on a pair of jeans and a loose T-shirt, I turn off the overhead lights, flip on the twinkle lights, and flop onto my bed. Staring up at the shimmering lights, I let the events of the day wash over me. The whole thing was a mixture of exhilaration and terror. Just thinking about it makes my heart start to race. I loved every second that I was at my station cooking—it was so different from anything I'd ever experienced that I don't know if I could ever go back to just working in the kitchen at the diner or even cooking at home. I hate that the judges' critiques affected me so much. I thought I could handle anything they would say, but Angelica should have basically taken my chef's knife and stabbed me with it. That would have been less brutal. But worst of all, I hated the look in Adam's eyes when he told me congratulations.

Then there was his cryptic message. *Don't trust any of them.* But who was he talking about? I close my eyes and take a breath. The cast? No, we're all in the same boat, so why would he tell only me that? Well, maybe I should watch out for Dani, because she is definitely trouble and not exactly in the same boat as the rest of us. Was he talking about the judges? Maybe. Could he have meant the judges and Jessica? But then why wouldn't he just come out and say that? Ugh, I am not the mystery kind of girl. I'm more of a fantasy-with-a-heavy-dose-of-romance kind of girl.

Just then, Inaaya returns, drying her long black hair with a towel. "You ready?"

I open my eyes before rolling over to look at her. "More than you are." I laugh.

With a quick flick of her wrist, all her hair is pulled into a loose bun. "Not anymore," she says with a smirk.

"Then let's go," I say, pushing off the bed. I'd rather stay in bed and not have to face everyone, but Malik was clear: he wants all of us on the roof.

The hot summer air has given way to a rare cool front, and the sounds of the city drift on the wind as Inaaya and I walk up to the roof. We're the last to arrive, and everyone else is standing and chatting in a loose circle around Malik, who has a pitcher of iced tea in his hands.

As we find a place with the others, he nods to three champagne flutes sitting on the table near him. "Grab one," he says. Inaaya and I look at each other, then at the rest of the cast, before walking over and picking up our glasses.

Normally, when I'm on the roof, I don't hear the cameras whirring to follow our every move; but right now, I am acutely aware of the sound. Inaaya and I step back into the circle, glasses in hand. I'm between Malik and Lola, and Inaaya is between Hakulani and Dani, who are directly across from me. When I look up and meet Hakulani's gaze, he looks disappointed, but it's probably just my imagination. I glance at Malik and give him a small smile. He and Adam seem to have really connected and maybe even become friends in the few days we've been here. Back on day one, whether he really meant it or not, Malik and I made a pact to have each other's back, and even if he is upset that Adam left and I'm still here, I want to try to let him know that I am still here for him.

He gives me a slight smile before handing me the pitcher. "Pour your glass and pass it around."

"Is it sweet?" I ask, teasing just a tiny bit.

He scoffs, but there is a softness in his gaze. "What do you think?"

"Sweet it is," I say, filling my glass halfway before passing it to Lola.

Malik strides over to the table and returns with the remaining glass. One by one, each of us fills our glass until the pitcher is back on our side of the circle. Malik accepts it from Paulie and fills his own before setting down the almost empty pitcher on the arm of a seat behind him.

He raises his glass and we all follow suit.

"It occurred to me on the ride back that when one of us is eliminated, that's it. There's no goodbye, no time to reminisce. Just a quick round of hugs and a one-way ticket home."

Everyone looks around the circle as condensation begins to form on the glasses.

"But I think that's a punk way to go out. So I propose a tradition. Now, in the South, traditions are a part of our everyday life."

I smile because he's not wrong.

He looks at each of us in turn. "I'm serious. I swear, my auntie has a tradition for every day of the year—but there's not enough time to get into all that. What I'm saying is, when one of us is whisked through that door, we should take a moment to remember them."

"With sweet tea?" Dani says skeptically.

Instantly, I'm with Malik. "Hell yeah, with sweet tea," I bite back. "My Grams used to say, 'It's the house wine of the South,' and since I doubt the network is going to let us toast with anything stronger, sweet tea is as good as anything."

Dani raises her eyebrow like I did something she didn't expect, then shrugs her shoulders. "If you say so."

Malik clears his throat and all eyes return to him. "As I was saying, I would like to propose that we each take a minute to recall and share something about Adam."

Everyone nods.

"Peyton," Malik says, turning to me. "Why don't you start?"

"Me? Uh, okay." I rack my brain, but the only thing that comes to mind, other than his cryptic warning, is the portobello burger he made for us just the other night. "Adam had a way of making the ordinary extraordinary," I start, turning toward Malik. "Case in point: the burger cook-off between you two. It wasn't just that he could turn a fungus into a mouthwatering burger; it was that he was full of passion, and even during an intense moment, he could still have fun and be silly."

"Agreed," Hakulani says. "And the man knew how to grill a mushroom."

"He still *does*," Lola says, rolling her eyes. "It's not like he's dead. He's just going back to his normal life.

"But in keeping with this sentiment"—she looks at Malik—"which is really a cool idea, by the way, I will say this about Adam. It felt like you could never stay mad at him. Adam was a genuinely good guy. I mean, he wanted to win this competition, but he still took time to get to know you as a person. And he showed me how to turn carrot peels into yummy fritters, which is something I never would have thought of."

Paulie nods. "He is super innovative. I think he told me about fifteen different ways to make meatless meatballs."

Dani is quiet for a minute before she adds, "Adam didn't try to be anyone but himself."

We all wait, but that's all she says. There is another pause before Hakulani clears his throat.

"As much as he was willing to teach other people," he says, "Adam also loved to ask questions of other people—to really get to know them."

"He is noble," Malik says, before raising his glass. "To Adam."

"To Adam," we all repeat.

The sweet tea coats my throat on the way down, and, for a moment, I feel a twinge of homesickness. There is nothing that says home more than a tall glass of ice-cold sweet tea as you sit and watch the sun set over the horizon. Or, in our case, the New York City skyline.

After downing her tea, Dani clears her throat. "That was nice, Malik, but now that the 'Kumbaya' moment of the evening is over, can we cut to the heart of the matter?"

And just like that, everything is shattered, and we all just stare at her.

Finally, Paulie asks, "What are you talking about, Dani?"

"How did *Adam,* who we have all just acknowledged is one *hell* of a chef, end up going home, while Little Miss Trailer Park, who can barely manage to prepare something edible, is still here?"

"Dani!" Inaaya says, shocked.

Hakulani turns toward her, blocking me from her sight. "Whoa, out of line."

Malik pours the remaining tea from the pitcher into his glass, muttering, "Here we go."

I'm so angry and fed up with Dani that I can't hear anything anymore, but I see Paulie's face as he says something to her. Lola is trying to keep the peace and diffuse the situation, but it doesn't seem to be working. I just stand there thinking that it's one thing for me to question why I didn't get sent home, and it's an entirely different thing for Dani to call me out in front of everyone and suggest . . . what exactly?

Finding my voice, I squeeze between Hakulani and Inaaya, meeting Dani's defiant gaze. "Say it," I tell her. "To my face. Go ahead, just say it."

"*You* shouldn't be here," she says calmly.

Every word from her mouth just ticks me off more, but even as she is insulting me, I'm in awe of the fact that, with five people standing up to her, she's not backing down. In fact, she seems unfazed by the resistance.

"I just have this nagging question," she continues, looking me dead in the eyes. "Why are you here in the first place? And why are you *still* here? It's one thing if they brought you on the show to be a charity case, but then why keep you when you clearly don't meet anyone's standards?"

"Dani," Lola says quickly, trying to pull her away by her elbow. "Maybe we should go back to the room before you say something you don't mean."

Dani yanks away her arm. "I don't think so," she says. "Doesn't it seem weird to any of you? I mean, you've been at the bottom since day one, and it's clear that the judges don't think you are good enough to be here, so what else do you bring to the show? It's not like you could afford to pay off any of the judges or anything." Her face is completely straight as she delivers the final blow, but I can see the smile in her eyes.

Hakulani takes my hand and starts to pull me away. "Enough. If you won't leave, then we will."

I try to pull back my hand at first, but then I let myself be guided away because I don't really know what else to do. She's only saying what I've been thinking.

"Dani, I thought you had a little more class than this,"

Hakulani says over his shoulder as he marches me to the far side of the roof.

Lola finally pulls Dani from the rest of the group and shoves her through the stairwell door. After a minute or two of awkward shuffling, it's clear the mood is ruined, and the rest of the cast retreats to their rooms.

"Ignore her," Hakulani says as he leads me toward the firepit. "She's just being—"

"A pain in my ass?" I provide.

"I was going to say 'herself,'" he says, "but your word works, too."

"The problem is, she's not wrong. I mean I didn't do anything to make them keep me here, but I would never . . ." I wipe a tear that's threatening to slide down my face. "But I shouldn't be here. She is *right*; Adam's a better chef than me."

"Yeah, but Adam's choice to only use vegetable-based ingredients could get old after a while. And what if there is a beef or chicken challenge in the future? They can't bend the rules for him. Plus, he may not want to do the challenge if they don't."

"You've really thought this through," I say, sitting on the sofa.

Hakulani flips a switch to turn on the firepit, and suddenly we are accompanied by the soft crackle of flames. "Well, when it was just the two of you, I realized I didn't want you to go." He sits next to me. "I mean, I like Adam, and he is a nice guy, but you, you're my *friend*."

I sniff again as I feel the all-too-familiar rush of heat on my skin, and I know it's not from the fire. "Thanks, but I don't want to be someone's pity project."

"You're not," he says, putting his hand gently on top of mine. "You're here for a reason, and I, for all selfish purposes, don't care why. What I do know is that I'm glad to have another round of competitions to get to know you better."

My hand might as well be on fire. "I'd like that," I say.

Then he reaches up, his fingers barely brushing my cheek, so I look up at him, and suddenly, it's like I'm in one of those rom-com movies where everything about the moment is perfect. Hakulani is gazing into my eyes, practically seeing into my soul, and the moon is just starting to make its march across the sky. I swallow once and resist the urge to lick my lips in anticipation for what will most likely be the best kiss of my life.

"Hey, Peyton?" Paulie's voice drifts from the stairwell. "You still up here?"

Just like that, the magic evaporates, and the moment is gone. I pull my hand from under Hakulani's and try to keep my voice steady as I call back, "Yeah, I'll be down in a minute. Thanks."

"Yeah, *thanks*, Paulie," Hakulani says under his breath. "Where else did he think you'd be?"

"For what it's worth, I'm kinda glad he came looking for me."

The instant the words leave my mouth, I want to kick myself, and I see the hurt look on his face. I feel a stab of guilt. "Not because I didn't want to," I say, trying to backpedal as fast as I can, "but because one of these days it could be you and me in the bottom two . . ."

"I get it," he says, straightening up. "And you don't want to deal with a broken heart when you go home."

Suddenly the romantic mood shifts into a playful one, and I breathe a sigh of relief—I really don't want any awkwardness between us.

"I was going to say I didn't want to have to pretend I was sad to see you go when I win the entire competition, but, you know, your scenario could happen too, I guess."

He laughs and stands, offering a hand to help me up. "It's these little moments that I will mention at the toast when you head back to Florida."

I take his hand but give it a little tug as I stand so that he is pulled off balance. "Oh, you'll be saying aloha before me, buddy."

"That is the fighting spirit," he says, before adding quietly, "Forget Dani. She just needs to be the center of attention."

Without another word, Hakulani walks me down the stairs and into the living room, where Malik and Paulie have just started a game of pool.

"I'll play winner," Hakulani says, taking a seat and kicking his feet up on the table.

"And I'm going to bed," I say, giving a slight wave. "Goodnight."

A chorus of goodnights follow me down the hall as I head for my room. Inaaya is still up, though she is tucked into bed with a book when I walk in.

"You okay?" she asks.

"Yeah, but I'm pretty sure I'm going to be on the show calling Dani a pain in the ass, so that should be fun."

"You didn't!" Inaaya gasps, looking up from her book with a small smile on her lips.

"It just slipped out," I say. "Loudly."

"You want to talk?"

Picking up my shower stuff, I shake my head. "I want to take a hot shower, slip into some clean pajamas, and forget tonight ever happened."

She nods and turns back to her book.

Well, mostly, I think as my mind drifts back to the almost kiss. Which is then immediately followed by Adam's warning. I hear it ringing in my head as I turn on the shower and realize that I don't think that's going away anytime soon.

CHAPTER EIGHTEEN

THE NEXT MORNING, WE REPORT TO THE FRONT of the building, where the bus is waiting to take us to the docks at Battery Park where there is a private ferry to take us across New York Harbor. Adam's departure still hangs over us, and the casual banter and joking around has been replaced by a stilted quiet. On the ferry, I listen to the tour guide explain the history of the Statue of Liberty and about the countless people who came through the port of entry while I lean against the rail and watch the seagulls as they glide and dive over the water, the backdrop of New York City glimmering behind them. The rest of the cast is scattered around the boat, half-listening to the lecture, half-staring out over the water.

"A gift from the people of France to the United States to symbolize the strong friendship between the two nations," the guide says into her microphone.

I sigh and wonder why the tour guide insists on using

the loudspeaker even though we're the only people on the entire boat.

Hakulani stands and slips away from the group to stand next to me. He takes a deep breath before saying, "I miss the water."

I glance over at him, but he is looking into the distance beyond the looming seafoam green statue that rises ahead of us.

"How often did you get to the beach back home?" I ask.

"Every day," he replies. "Morning surf, hanging with my friends. It wasn't 'going to the beach' for us. It was just living life."

"And school was just what you did to fill in the time?"

"That," he says with a grin, "and cooking."

"It must suck being so close to the water and not actually able to get in."

"The water back home is a little cleaner, so it's not that hard right now," he laughs, his hands gripping the rail as he leans back. "But I guess there are many worse places I could be." He nudges me. "Plus, I've met some pretty cool people."

I try to hide the blush that starts creeping across my face. Of all the things that go with being a redhead, this is the one I hate the most.

"I know what you mean," I say.

"About the cool people?"

I grin and look down at the water as it's pushed aside by

the boat. "About being by the ocean, or in my case, the Gulf. It's not quite the same as you. It takes over an hour to get to my favorite beach, and most of the time I'm too busy working to go there, but when I can it's like the crappy parts of my life disappear."

"Yeah." His voice is low and smooth. The back of his fingers brush against my elbow, and even in the sunlight I feel a small chill ripple down my spine. I catch myself and give myself a mental slap—I have *got* to get it together. I didn't come here to get in some showmance with a guy who lives beyond the other side of the country.

Pushing myself away from the rail, I say, "At least we get to do the Landmark Challenges. It's a chance to get out of the studio and see the city a little."

"I guess," he says with a nod. "But it comes with strings, doesn't it?"

I turn around so my back is against the rail, the warm metal against my arms. "Most things come with strings," I say quietly.

"You sound like you speak from experience," he says quietly, shifting his weight until he is standing close enough that I can feel the warmth from his body.

"My parents met each other when they were pretty young. Mom got pregnant with me, and they thought they could raise a child and live life on love and prayers."

"And?" he asks gently.

"Let's just say I'm not a big believer in the whole 'love con-quers all' stuff." Then, refusing to reveal any more of the drama from my life back home, I slap my hands on my thighs to break the mood.

I expect him to say something but am pleasantly surprised when he doesn't. We settle into a peaceful quiet and watch as the statue comes closer into view. Well, it would have been quiet, except the tour guide is going on and on about the reno-vation that took two years to complete back in the 1980s. As we approach the island, Production City comes into view.

"It looks like the circus has come to Liberty Island," Haku-lani says.

I nod. "I guess that makes us the animals?"

He chuckles. "Something like that."

When the boat finally docks on the island, we join the others at the gangplank and prepare to set foot on the island. The tour guide gives us a bright, practiced smile. "You have about thirty minutes to look around the pedestal before we head up."

"Head up where?" Dani asks from the opposite side of the gangplank.

"To the crown," she says.

"The crown?" Paulie, who is walking next to me, says excit-edly. "Are you kidding? I've always wanted to go all the way up, but the reservations fill up so fast." He turns to me. "This is going to be so cool."

His excitement is contagious and I can't help the smile that spreads across my face as I turn to Hakulani, ready to include him in our celebration, but he is ghost white.

"What's wrong?" I ask.

He just shakes his head and stammers, "Nothing. Who's ready for this?"

I touch his arm gently. "You're not afraid of heights, are you?"

"And tight spaces," he says, sucking in a slow, deep breath. He raises a hand to his puka shell choker, running his finger over the smooth surface as he looks up at Lady Liberty.

My eyes go wide as I follow his gaze up and then look back at him. "That could be a problem," I say quietly. "Does production know?"

He shrugs, chewing on his lip. "I don't know. I don't remember if I was ever asked about phobias during my interview."

I nudge Paulie in the side, pulling him from his excited conversation with Lola, and nod toward Hakulani. He takes one look at him and shoots me a questioning look at the same moment the tour guide opens the gate and we head down the gangplank.

Jessica is waiting for us just outside the pedestal. "Hey, guys," she says brightly. "Find your mark and we'll get started."

It only takes us a few moments to locate the silicone dots on the pavement. Once the cameras are in place, Jessica makes eye contact with all of us.

"Today we are visiting one of America's most iconic symbols of freedom and hope. For immigrants coming to the nation by sea, the Statue of Liberty was a welcome sight after so many weeks on a ship." She directs our attention to the monument. "Now it's a time capsule for those who helped build this country."

Malik scoffs so quietly that had I not been standing next to him, I wouldn't have heard it. I catch him rolling his eyes before turning his attention back to Jessica as everyone applauds. I quickly join in, though I'm not sure why we're clapping and cheering.

"Time for you to go exploring," Jessica continues. "Remember, this isn't just a sightseeing trip. Your experiences here will help shape your creations for the Landmark Challenge. Take it from me: this one is going to be *tres difficile.*"

"That was French, right?" Paulie asks as we head toward the first part of our tour. Hakulani trails behind us. I think about including him, but honestly, he looks like he probably needs some time alone.

"I think so," I say, then teasing, "I know it's not Spanish."

"Do you think it's a clue?"

I motion to everything around us. "We are standing in front

of the biggest gift ever given to us by the people of France. I don't think Jessica is winging it, do you?"

He shakes his head. "Maybe it's a classic Julia Child deal where we are supposed to find new ways to create French dishes?"

"Too obvious," I say. "They like to throw in twists to keep the show interesting."

He opens the door to the museum for me. "It's all about the twists, isn't it?"

"French fusion?" I suggest. He nods before putting a finger to his lips as if in careful thought.

Then Malik and Hakulani come up behind us—Malik walks over to a photographic display of the Statue of Liberty's arrival in New York, and Hakulani asks, "What are you guys talking about?"

"The challenge, of course," I say. "And how Lady Liberty fits into it."

"Check this out," Malik says, looking at the pictures on the wall. "Did you know that Lady Liberty came over on a ship and was packed in two hundred cases?"

I groan. "I swear, if we have to make two hundred of *any-thing*, I'll turn in my jacket on the spot."

"No, you won't," Malik says, calling my bluff.

Shaking my head, I say, "No. I won't."

Hakulani is still unusually quiet.

"You okay?" I ask.

"I'll be fine," he says, but I watch him wringing his hands, and I'm not so sure.

"Don't tell me you're scared," Paulie says, teasing him.

Hakulani shoots him a withering glare.

"Paulie!" I say, elbowing him.

"Ah, man, I'm sorry, I didn't know." Then he turns to me. "How was I supposed to know that was what you meant? I thought he was seasick or something."

I sigh and rub a hand over my face, while Hakulani is staring at the spiral stairs that lead up the center of the statue, and beads of perspiration start to form on his forehead.

"Talk to Jessica," I suggest. "Tell her you can't do it."

"No. I'll be okay." He smiles, now looking a little green under his tan skin. "What is it that they say about facing your fears?"

"I don't know what they say, but *I* say I'm going ahead of you on the climb up," Paulie says. "You know, that way if you puke, it won't hit me."

"Very funny," Hakulani says, looking less than amused.

"Just remember not to look down," I say, trying my best to encourage him.

"Thanks," he says as Jessica begins to wave everyone over to the base of the stairs.

True to his word, Paulie goes first, leading us up to the

lobby located in the pedestal. Displays of the statue's history are everywhere.

"Hey," I say to no one in particular as I look over some pictures of kids playing on the lawn outside of the pedestal. "Did you know that this place used to house military families back in the 1930s and even before then?"

"Seriously?" Lola says, coming over and reading over my shoulder. "That's so cool. Some kids actually got to wake up, go outside, and look up to see Lady Liberty watching over them."

We walk together for a few minutes, looking at the different bits of the display together, and I'm surprised Dani doesn't swoop in to break us up.

"Huh," Lola says, pointing to a close-up photograph of the statue's head. "I thought they were just part of her crown, but those point spikes represent the seven seas and continents."

"Really?" I say, moving in to read the marker. "I always thought they were rays from the sun."

Out of the corner of my eye, I see Jessica with a tour guide walking toward the stairs that will take us up to the crown. "Think we better go over?" I ask, nodding in their direction.

"Probably," she agrees.

We're actually the last ones to gather at the bottom of the steps. Lola splits off to stand next to Dani while I go to stand next to Inaaya and, looking over my shoulder, I see Hakulani hanging near the back of the group. I think about going over to say something, but then Paulie moves in next to him, and the two begin speaking quietly, occasionally glancing up at the staircase.

When we begin the climb to the crown, I'm pretty sure this is the quietest we've ever been. The metal rails are cool as we climb to the top, and I find myself wondering how many other people from all over the world have made this same trip. Paulie and Hakulani are bringing up the rear, and when the stairs turn in a direction that allows me a clear view behind and below me, I can see Hakulani taking slow, deep breaths, and Paulie is right behind him, encouraging him. When I look ahead, there is nothing but narrow spiral stairs.

Once we emerge into the crown, the view makes every step worth it. The sky is blue and clear as I stare through the window at Manhattan. From up here, away from the noise and the smells, the city looks a sprawling testament to human determination and spirit. When you think of everything the city has endured in its past, it's kind of inspiring. Even Hakulani, who still is a little shaky and pale, gazes out at the view with awe—while standing as far from the window and the stairs as he can.

There's not enough room in the crown for all of us at once, but somehow Jessica manages to crouch down and get a picture of everyone, even though Paulie and Hakulani are only able to poke their heads into the frame.

"Perfect," Jessica says. "Now, take some time to enjoy the

view, and then you all can head down when you're ready. We've still got a competition to do."

Right, I think as I soak up as much of the view and all the feelings it inspires in me as I can. I really need to win today. Then all the good will and inspiration that I felt during this walk through history only moments ago begin to crumble when I think about what could be at stake. I almost went home yesterday, and if I don't win an advantage today, things could get very, very bad for me.

CHAPTER NINETEEN

ONCE EVERYONE HAS CLIMBED DOWN FROM THE
crown, we gather in a circle near Production City.

"That was incredible," Lola says. "I could see forever."

Malik nods. "Couldn't have picked a better day."

Jessica arrives and motions for us to follow her to a clearing among the tents and equipment before turning to address us. Automatically, we begin to look for our marks and shuffle into our usual lineup.

"Don't worry about that," she says, laughing. "We're not filming this, at least, not officially. Right now, boxed lunches are being served in craft services, so grab what you want. Then you'll have about an hour and a half to explore the island, the museum, whatever you want. While you're doing that, you might want to come up with a plan for your meal."

A couple PAs appear and begin shoving two quarters into everyone's hands.

"And if you get curious about what's around the island,

these will give you access to the coin-operated binoculars located around the path."

"Are you going to give us a hint so we can plan?" Malik asks.

"French," she says. "And an extra hint: your judges know a fair bit about this island, so I would make sure you don't waste your chance to explore."

"Are you going to tell us who?" Lola asks.

"You'll find out soon enough."

I glance around, then mutter, "Hope they brought their appetites." As much as I love making food, I love eating it more, but that is kind of a requirement for being a chef or a baker. I couldn't imagine being a regular person trying to judge a contest where I could only take a couple bites before I had to decide if I like it or not—especially when my comments could mean the difference between someone doing well or possibly going home.

"I think they can handle it," Jessica says with a smile as she checks her watch. I blush, not realizing that I'd said that loud enough for her to hear. "All right, the clock is running, so you all should get moving."

As several of the cast head to craft services, I decide that I'd rather get a head start on exploring. Okay, and maybe give my stomach a moment to settle as well. Between the ferry ride, the adrenaline of being up in the crown, and the nervousness from the upcoming challenge, I'm feeling a little too jittery to eat. I glance back and see that even Hakulani, who looks a lot better now that his feet are on solid ground, is piling food on his plate. I just shrug to myself and start walking, enjoying the gentle breeze and the warm sunshine.

I wander around to the north side of the island and look across the river at Ellis Island. We'd passed by on our ride here, and I vaguely remember the guide mentioning that immigrants never actually went to the Statue of Liberty when they arrived but rather disembarked on Ellis Island.

I drop my two coins into a nearby stationary binoculars and press my eyes to the eyepieces. The black shades flip away and I swivel the viewfinder so it focuses on the island.

"You're with the group that's filming here, right?" a voice says behind me.

Startled, my head snaps over my shoulder. Standing behind me is a National Park Ranger. "You scared me."

"Sorry about that," he says. "Just wanted to know if you needed anything."

I start to say no, then stop. "Actually, I was looking at Ellis Island and was wondering—" I look back into the viewfinder. "—What are those run-down buildings?"

He steps forward. "May I?"

I step away as he takes a quick look.

"That's the hospital," he says, stepping away from the binoculars.

"I'm surprised it's so run-down. I thought Ellis Island was another tourist spot."

The ranger nods. "It is, but historical renovations are expensive. There's been a push to raise money, but so far, it hasn't been enough."

"I'm Peyton, by the way," I say, extending my hand.

"Ranger Jacob," he says, taking my hand and giving it a firm shake.

I expect him to ask questions about the competition or the contestants, but he doesn't. Instead, he slips into tour guide mode and gives me a brief history of Ellis Island, and the millions of people who came here looking for a better life—listing off the countries that they were most likely to come from at the time.

"Sounds like a lot of European countries."

"Yep. Most people who came here made it to the American shores—"

"Most?"

"Well, some were sent back to their countries, and those who were sick were sent there, to the hospital."

"Why were they sent back?"

"Most of the time, legal issues; but sometimes it was their health."

"And if they went to the hospital?"

"Fortunately, those who were sent there," he said, pointing

at the hospital, "had a good chance of survival. This hospital was actually ahead of its time, and the staff took great care to keep things clean and sterile. The tuberculosis patients had access to fresh air and sunlight, which, at the time, was thought to help them recover."

"Interesting," I say with a thoughtful nod. "Thank you so much."

"I can answer any other questions you might have, too," he says.

I laugh, waving my hands in front of me. "I'm good. I mean, it's interesting, but I really need to start thinking about my next challenge."

"That makes sense," he says, stepping back. "Good luck."

"Thank you. And thanks again for the history lesson."

"Hope it helps," he says, before turning to walk away.

When I get back to Production City, the only other contestant around is Lola, who is sitting at one of the tables, writing something. I grab a boxed lunch and head over to her.

"Hey," I say. "You're done exploring, too?"

Lola quickly rips the paper off the pad she's writing on and shoves it into her pocket. "Brainstorming."

"Same," I say, taking my lunch and moving to the other end of the table. "Is the food good?"

"As far as boxed lunches go, it's not bad." She leans back in her chair and watches me start to unpack mine. "How did you like the island? I saw you talking to a ranger over there. He was cute."

"Who? Ranger Jacob?" I focus on the sandwich in front of me. "I guess. He really knew his stuff."

Lola gives me a playful look. "I bet."

"One thing I forgot to ask him was: If Ellis Island was the main port for European immigrants, where were the other main hubs for immigration at the time?"

"Well, I don't know about 'main hubs,' but my family came from Cuba through Miami in the early 1960s," Lola says quietly. She runs her finger over a scratch in the table as she continues, not looking up at me. "But there wasn't a grand statue to greet them. And instead of fancy ships, they came on rafts. My best friend back home, her family came from Mexico through El Paso. They took trains until the tracks were blown up by the revolutionaries; then they walked."

"No big statues?"

"Not a one."

Around us we could hear the bustle of the crews getting everything set up for the challenge and the cry of seagulls overhead. I bite into my sandwich and think about what Lola said.

"Everyone makes such a big deal about the Statue of Liberty," I finally say.

"Yeah," Lola says before turning her attention back to her pad of paper. "It's a gigantic symbol, but it's only part of the story."

Her comment hangs in the air between us as the energy in the tent starts to rev up. Back from their exploration, everyone comes in talking and buzzing with anticipation for the upcoming challenge. I finish lunch just before the PAs arrive to hustle us to where we'll officially find out about our challenge so the crew can film Jessica's reveal and our reactions. As a few assistants touch up my makeup and there are calls for everyone to find their marks, I chastise myself because I *still* don't have any idea what I'm going to make. This is starting to become a habit. Angelica is right, I really need to manage my time better if I want to have any chance of staying on the show.

Jessica waits for us to give her our attention before she begins her introduction. "The Statue of Liberty was a gift from the people of France, celebrating the one hundredth anniversary of the American Revolution," Jessica says. "Without France's help, it's hard to say what the US would look like today. It's also important to remember the contributions of the countless immigrants who came to these shores looking for a better life. Take what you have learned during your sightseeing and let it be the inspiration for your dish today."

She pauses for the camera to pan over us. When it's clear they still aren't going to do more than a quick pan in our direction, she continues. "You'll have thirty minutes to plan and three hours to prepare a French fusion dish that will wow the judges."

"She should be giving out a lifetime achievement award

instead of hosting our show," I whisper to Hakulani, and I watch as he bites down on his lip as he chokes back a laugh.

I turn my attention back to Jessica as she lays out the details for the challenge. During the last Landmark Challenge, I was just winging it because of my penalty. With only thirty minutes to see what's available and then plan out a meal when everyone else is trying to do the same, the hardest part about this challenge isn't going to be cooking, it's going to be staying organized and making sure that I don't forget anything.

"Once your thirty minutes are up, you'll turn in your list of ingredients and your order will be filled and delivered to your station. Keep an eye on your time because as soon as those thirty minutes are done, your cooking time will automatically start. Make sure you ask for exactly what you want and no more, because not only will the judges be looking at whether or not your dish fits the French fusion theme, they will also decide how efficiently you used your ingredients. So wasted food is a big no-no."

I start to bounce on the balls of my feet but stop myself. I wish Jessica would hurry up and tell us who the judges are so we can get started.

I'd be lying if I said we didn't waste a lot of food during our challenges, so this is going to really test our planning ability on top of our creativity. If I'm going to have a shot at the advantage, I need to nail this challenge.

Jessica finally breaks the pause, motioning for people to

stand next to her. Before our eyes, ten members of the National Park Service take their places next to Jessica. Including Ranger Jacob. "Great," I say under my breath. I hope Dani didn't see me talking to him. I can only imagine the conspiracy theories she could come up with if she knew. I'm so caught up in my thoughts that I barely register Jessica telling us to begin, so I shake my head, reminding myself why I'm here. Taking a deep breath, I focus on the task at hand.

Fusion cuisine can be a lot of fun to play with, and I have tasted out-of-this-world combinations in the past. But mashing tastes and textures that you wouldn't normally think pair well together can also be a complete disaster. Luckily, I've checked out and read Julia Child's French cookbook from the local library multiple times. After looking over the list of available items, I settle on coq au vin enchiladas paired with chorizo fondue with crusty French bread. I really hope the judges are in a cheese mood. Thank goodness I don't have to bake the bread from scratch, but making red wine–braised chicken normally takes all day, and I have only three hours. I scan the special request appliance list and am relieved to see an electric pressure cooker on it. The ingredients are fairly simple. Thick-cut bacon, mushrooms, onions, and, instead of the traditional sauce, I decide to make mole.

I must not be the only one who realizes that this challenge is going to be harder than it seems, because Hakulani has his game face on and Paulie looks like he is trying to concentrate. Which is a blessing because it's much easier to think when they aren't joking around and trying to one-up each other all the time. Once my ingredients are delivered, I get to work prepping and sautéing everything on the stove with a bit of red cooking wine before piling it all in the cooker along with a few chicken thighs. Setting the timer for forty-five minutes should give me enough time to make the mole sauce, prep my other ingredients, cook the chorizo, and set up my fondue, before I have to start focusing on building the enchiladas.

"That smells amazing," Jessica says, peeking over my station as I put the lid on the chicken. "Is that coq au vin?" she asks in surprise. "In three hours?"

"More like one hour, actually," I say. "But yeah."

"I'm impressed," she says. "But that's a traditional French dish. Where's the fusion?"

"I'm pairing it with a mole sauce and making enchiladas. Then, as a side or appetizer, a little fondue with chorizo."

"My mouth is watering already," she says. "Good luck but watch your time."

I nod to her, and then rush to go grab my plates before all the good ones are taken.

In the end, smelling good wasn't enough to win. The top spot went to Lola again and her shrimp and chive tortellini with beurre blanc. But the good news is that I came in third and not last, because that, unfortunately, went to Paulie. As we all head off the set, I swipe the sweat from my forehead and remind myself that in *Top Teen Chef,* one day you can be on top, and the next, you're looking up from the bottom.

CHAPTER TWENTY

BECAUSE WE GOT STARTED SO EARLY FOR THE Landmark Challenge, we're back at the apartment by late afternoon.

"Great news," Jessica says as the bus pulls up to the apartment. "A. J. has invited all of you to come to his new restaurant this evening. It's not open to the public yet, so this is a really cool opportunity for all of you."

"That's awesome," Malik says. "Will he be there?"

"I think all the judges will be there," she says. "And Caitlin mentioned she might stop by, too."

The excitement in my gut twists and turns until it reshapes into raw anxiety. Having Caitlin on the set is to be expected. Having her just stop by? That didn't go so well last time, so I'm really not looking forward to this.

As we stand to leave the bus, Jessica calls after us. "Make sure to be ready at six o'clock. You don't want to be late for a sneak peek at one of New York's soon-to-be-hot dining spots."

"A night on the town," Dani says. "Finally. It's been real fun being stuck here with you guys, but I need a break."

"We *all* need a break," I say, meaning for my voice to be quieter than it is.

Dani laughs, and it's one of those laughs someone has when they really don't think something is funny, but they're gearing up to say something mean.

"I would suggest you order from the dessert menu so you could learn what real pastry arts are, but then again, the camera does add ten pounds."

"That's it," I say, standing up to show her just what I can do with my pounds, but Paulie steps in front of me and ushers me out of the room.

"You are going to have to calm down," he says, leading me away.

"Me?" I say, but it's more like a shout. "Did you hear what she said to me?"

"I heard, but if you haul off and deck her, you're gone. It's in the contract."

"Oh, but she can say whatever she wants, and I just have to sit there and take it?"

He shrugs. "I mean, you *could* say something back, but that doesn't seem to be your style."

I rub my hand over my eyes and let out an aggravated breath. "I just really hope I'm around on the day she gets sent home."

"That's right. Keep your eye on the prize," he says. "And don't forget that she is just trying to drag you into the mud and make you the troublemaker. Don't let her get to you, okay?" As he reaches to put his hand on my shoulder, I swear I feel his fingers brush my cheek. He gives my shoulder a gentle squeeze and says, "I'm going to get ready for dinner, and I'll make sure that Dani can't sit anywhere near you. Deal?"

"Okay," I say, taking a deep breath. "You're right."

I start to say thank you, but he's already down the hall.

"What was that about?" Inaaya asks, her eyes twinkling.

I shoot her a look but don't say anything as we walk into our room.

"Peyton, you have two guys trying to win your affection, and you don't even see it."

"That's because I'm trying to win a *scholarship*, not a boyfriend. Everything else is a distraction."

"Maybe," she says, twirling her hair around her finger. "But they're cute distractions."

I drop my head back and laugh. "They are—but cute distractions are the worst."

"On this we agree. Oh, I looked in the closet. Wardrobe sent over clothes for tonight."

"It's almost worth putting up with Dani's big mouth just for the clothes," I say. "Almost."

"What are you wearing?"

Inaaya walks over to her closet and pulls out a ruby red off-the-shoulder blouse with a pair of white pants and a jean jacket.

"It will look amazing on you, but I have to be honest. I'm going to have to resist the urge to salute you."

"I know, right?" she says, laughing as she puts the clothes down. "What about you?"

I tug on the zipper of the garment bag and find a white silky tank top with thin straps and a pair of ripped blue jeans. Digging a little deeper I find a lightweight, sheer, floral duster. I hold everything up for Inaaya to see.

"Cute," she says.

"It's not bad," I say, trying to sound nonchalant, but I can't help but grin. I'm going to a fancy restaurant in an outfit that is going to make me feel like a model. "I better get ready."

Less than two hours later, I join everyone else at the elevator to head downstairs to the waiting bus. Twenty minutes later, the bus rolls to a stop in front of a bustling diner in the heart of the Theater District. The worn letters on the window spell out MELLY'S DINER. As we walk through the door, we're instantly transported back to the 1950s. There's a jukebox that plays actual vinyl records, and the polished waiters and waitresses bop between tables.

"How do they stay so clean?" I wonder aloud. All of the waitresses are wearing white sweater sets, while the men have on long-sleeved, crisp white shirts. There's not a stain among them.

"More important, how have they not all dropped from heat exhaustion?" Inaaya asks, fanning her face with her hand.

There are so many people crammed in the restaurant, either sitting in a red leather booth or waiting for a seat, that we have to elbow our way to the host stand.

Paulie, who's ahead of me, pulls up short as a tall, blond woman with cat-eye glasses makes her way through the throng of tables. "I thought this place wasn't open to the public."

"Are we at the right place?" I ask, looking around for A. J. "I feel very overdressed."

The woman with the cat-eye glasses comes back, stopping for a second. "Are you all lost?" she asks.

"Um, maybe," I say. "We were supposed to have dinner here tonight, but I think we have the wrong address."

She looks over my shoulder and her eyes light with recognition. "Are you the kids from that show?" she asks.

I noticed several people around us craning their necks to look at us, and I realize the camera crew is behind us. I wonder what this pageantry must look like to everyone else. It's not like I'm completely used to it or anything, but here we are, a bunch of kids being followed by a full camera crew.

"Yeah," Hakulani says as he steps forward. "From Food TV."

"This way," she says, motioning us to follow her.

I look over my shoulder at Malik, who just shakes his head and motions for me to follow Hakulani and Paulie. The waitress leads us through the restaurant and up a narrow flight of stairs.

Though the upstairs space keeps with the fifties theme, instead of neon signs and over-the-top red, white, and black decor, we find ourselves standing in a swanky nightclub with crushed red velvet benches and round tables better for having intimate conversation than feeding a group of hungry teenagers. In the back is the most peculiar bar I have ever seen. Half of it is covered in metal, and instead of bottles of alcohol lining the mirrored shelves, there are tall jars of candy sprinkles in every color. In the center of the room, several benches have been pushed around a couple of tables covered in light-gray cloth.

"What's up with the bar?" Lola asks, leaning over the bar top to get a better look.

"That's not a bar," a voice booms from the back of the restaurant. "That's the world's most intense dessert experience. It's got a state-of-the-art dry-ice infusion tank, an anti-griddle to create delicate garnishes right before your eyes, and a temperature-controlled granite counter to temper chocolates and mix in anything you can think of into our ice cream concoctions."

"It's amazing," I say. If this dessert bar were human, I would marry it right here and now.

"Thanks, Peyton," A. J. says. "It's my pride and joy. And

tonight, this place is yours for the evening. You are the first guests at Prima il Dolce."

"Prima il Dolce?" Inaaya repeats. "I might be wrong, as my Italian is a little rusty, but doesn't that mean—" she pauses "—dessert first?"

A. J. smiles. "There's nothing rusty about your Italian."

"What did this place used to be?" Dani asks, running her hand over the gold tone railing on the bar.

"People say it used to be everything from a speakeasy to a front for the mob's money-laundering operations."

"And you're hoping to bring it back to its glory days?" Lola says. "I can respect that."

"Not the mob part, I hope," Paulie says, and A. J. looks at us like he forgot we were there.

His face lights up as he laughs. "No, not those days. I'm talking old-school Broadway."

"Broadway?" Lola asks, tilting her head.

"This is a Broadway institution," A. J. insists. "More than a few Hollywood types have signed NYC's finest thespians in this very room. And now it's a dessert bar."

I smile brightly. The mere fact that it exists means heaven can exist on Earth. "So, rather than appetizers, your patrons get dessert and then their entrée?"

"That's the idea," A. J. says brightly. "Assuming they would want an entrée."

"Why don't you advertise it out front?" Malik asks. "Someone walking by would never know this was here." He pauses. "Unless that's your gimmick."

I cringe slightly, hoping he hasn't offended A. J. by talking about his place like it's some sort of pop-up novelty show.

But A. J. takes the question in stride. "It kinda is the gimmick. Much like how it was during Prohibition, this place is going to be the place so secret everyone knows it's here. In this time of low-fat, no-carb diets, this is the new excess."

"You really think a place that specializes in desserts can be all that?" Inaaya asks, skeptical.

A. J. pauses for a moment before answering. "That's exactly what my investors asked me. I'll tell you what I told them. Anyone with a halfway decent menu can open a restaurant. What keeps people coming back for more is the experience. I'm not just selling extravagant ice cream delights and pastries, but creating a memory that they'll never forget. How many times have you heard someone say they really want dessert, but then they decide not to get one because they *shouldn't*. Here, it's expected that you're going to have dessert. So much, in fact, that we start with it."

"And I'm sure a bunch of teen foodie celebrities tagging you in their social media feeds when you open wouldn't hurt," a voice says behind us. I spin around to see Caitlin leaning against a half-wall, watching us.

A. J. laughs. "Only if they love the concept and the food." His gaze drifts to the stairs and then back to her. "I thought the others were coming."

Caitlin's smile falters. "Angelica had a headache."

A. J. raises an eyebrow, but he recovers quickly. "Another time, then."

An awkward silence falls over the group, so I blurt out, "What inspired you to build a menu all around desserts?"

"Because I like sweets," A. J. says with a grin. "So when I started looking for a building, I knew I wanted a location around the corner from a gym. This place just fell into my hands at the perfect time."

Everyone laughs.

"Now, take a seat so I can wow you."

We all move toward the table and, somehow, Dani ends up sitting between Caitlin and A. J., allowing her plenty of time to suck up to a judge and the producer. I, on the other hand, am sitting between Hakulani and Paulie, with Malik and Inaaya across from us. Three waitresses arrive to answer any questions as we pore over the menu. I can't believe how amazing everything sounds. I finally settle on a cheesecake milkshake topped with five different cookies, whipped cream, and a cronut.

"I thought cronuts were out?" Inaaya asks, teasing.

"Everything is new again when paired with cheesecake ice cream," I say with a laugh.

We don't have to wait long for the waitresses to return, and they aren't empty-handed.

"Compliments of the owner," a waitress says, putting a large platter on the table and giving A. J. a wink. "Baked Alaska with layers of chocolate cake and chocolate ice cream."

There are smatterings of excited exclamations as she passes plates family style around the table. Once everyone has a slice, we each get lost in the taste and texture of the delicate dessert. Several people dressed in black chef outfits take their place at the bar and begin putting together one sweet masterpiece after another until the air is so full of sugar you can taste it with each breath.

Unable to stop myself, I place my cloth napkin on the table and lean forward to catch A. J.'s attention. "Can I watch them?" I ask.

He nods enthusiastically. "That's the whole point. We want everyone who comes here to have their own experience. Go ahead and check it out."

I'm surprised that I'm the only person to stand, while everyone else is caught up in their own conversations and the bliss of our first dessert, but that's fine with me—more time for me to study what they're doing. Slipping away, I make my way to the dessert bar and peer over the edge as the man behind the counter pours a creamy mixture on a cold slab.

"Making ice cream?" I ask.

The chef looks up. "Something like that." As the mixture begins to crystalize, he takes two utensils and begins breaking up the sheet and smoothing it out again. He repeats the process over and over until he's satisfied. Once the cream has hardened, he picks up a spatula and begins to roll the ice cream, dropping each log into a dish. When the cup is full, he looks up at me. "What toppings do you think I should use?" he asks, sliding a laminated sheet toward me. "Go wild."

There are so many choices, it's hard to decide. "Okay, let's start with coated candy bits."

"Pretty common first choice, but all right," he says, a hint of a challenge in his voice.

I look closer at the name tag on his shirt. "Okay, Rex," I say, skipping over the more common add-ins. "How about donut sticks, cotton candy, a slice of red velvet cake, and, of course, if it's not too *plain* for you, sprinkles."

He calls over his shoulder, "Skye, fire up the cotton candy machine."

A young woman, about the same age as me, comes through the door that leads to the kitchen and flips a switch. A whirring sound comes from a large bowl set into the bar.

"Whipped cream and cherries?" Rex asks, beginning to pull my requested toppings from the cabinets below the bar.

"Of course."

It doesn't take him long to pull the entire thing together in a messy but eye-popping display of sugared bliss. I clap, shocked by how the ice cream, which was probably delicious enough to be the main attraction, has been perfectly crafted into the foundation of this decadent and calorie-laden creation. Rex hands the dish over to me with a flourish. "Enjoy."

I point over my shoulder at the table. "I ordered already, though."

He nods thoughtfully. "Then we'll put it in the blast chiller and you can take it with you. For later."

"Seriously? That could be a midnight snack for all of us."

"Even better. Now, is there anything else I can get for you?"

I bite my lip. "Is there any chance that I could go back there? Or maybe you could give me a few tips—show me some of your tricks?"

He smiles, his blue eyes twinkling. "Absolutely."

I spend the rest of the evening mixing exotic ice cream flavors. Rex, who is the head chef for Prima il Dolce, shows me how to make the cutest mini cotton candy flowers. He even lets me try out the flash freeze disk, but after a few failed attempts, he gently takes the scraper back, and I realize just how much I still have to learn—just because I'm in this competition and he makes it all look easy doesn't mean that it is. Skye shows me several different plating styles and designs before handing me a piping bag to practice.

It doesn't take long for the others to notice that I'm behind the bar, and they all wander over. When they begin to ask questions, Rex grabs a stack of plates, then has Skye prep some more bags, and the evening becomes a crash course in basic dessert plating. By the time I walk through the diner with my entire dinner—and my special creation—wrapped up for the trip back to the apartment, I have perfected several different smears and basic plating techniques, plus I can squeeze out a continuous spiral of jam with my eyes closed. (Okay, not really, but I'm working on it.) As I think about how I can use the things I've learned tonight in the competition, I smile because I actually had a good time, and I managed to avoid talking to Caitlin or Dani the whole time.

Honestly, the night turned out better than I could have ever predicted.

CHAPTER
TWENTY-ONE

THE NEXT DAY, I SOMEHOW MANAGE TO MISS MY alarm and oversleep. Even with Inaaya's help, I barely make it to the bus on time. The PAs give me dirty looks as I slouch in my seat and pick at the muffin I grabbed on my way out. I'm so frazzled about being late and trying to mentally prepare myself for today's challenge that it isn't until I'm through hair and makeup and heading over to the set that I notice the energy is different from the last elimination challenge. Unlike last time, now everyone knows what to expect, and it is like we've all made some kind of peace with knowing that if you don't put your best dish forward, you could be the one packing your bags at the end of the day.

I pause as I walk onto the set, trying to get my bearings, because the set looks different today—the walk-in has exploded to three times its original size, and it now looks like a small-town grocery store. I look at Malik and Lola, who are just as in the dark as I am, when the disembodied voice says, "We'll get started in about ten minutes. Feel free to familiarize yourself with your new stations."

As I take my place, I notice that it's much more compact than it had been last time. I pull open the top drawer, and where my sleek vegetable peeler once was is some vintage piece of metal that looks like it could cut off more than the tip of my finger. I glance at the kitchen gadget shelf on the other side of the set where they keep the food processor, electric pressure cookers, and air fryers, and everything is gone. Except the ice cream maker, but it has been replaced with a hand-operated version.

"What the actual hell," Lola says from the front row, standing up from behind her oven. "Check out how small it is."

"You're right," Dani says. "This is ridiculous."

"I've seen smaller," Hakulani says, and everyone laughs.

I tug open the drawer that normally has all of my mixer attachments, but it's empty. In fact, most of my drawers are bare. I look up at Paulie. "What is this? Some form of torture?"

He shrugs and then the disembodied voice is back, telling us to take our marks. We move, silently, waiting for Jessica to tell us what is in store for us, because I have a feeling, in this round, anyone could end up going home.

Jessica walks to her mark and beams at us as the crew gets ready to start filming. I can feel the anticipation building on set—especially when one of the PAs starts maneuvering a giant dartboard to the edge of the set, ready to be wheeled on at a moment's notice.

"Welcome to *Top Teen Chef*'s 'Flashback Grocery Challenge.'"

We all exchange looks of confusion.

"As you learned on your tour yesterday, Ellis Island closed to immigrants in 1954. So today we are going back in time—to that same year—to create your dinner for four." Jessica waits for the camera to catch our reactions. "Everything, from the size of your kitchen to the prices of the items on the shelf, is now retro."

"That explains the ovens," I hear Lola whisper to Malik.

He nods, his eyes never leaving Jessica.

"In today's elimination challenge, you will have just six dollars to plan a dinner for your family of four . . ."

She pulls out a poster, displaying it for all to see. "And that meets the nutritional guidelines of the US Department of Agriculture."

I look closely at the vintage print before I point out, "Wait, there are seven food groups."

"Yeah," Malik says with a grin. "And butter had its own wedge of the pie."

"I can get behind that," I say.

He laughs and reaches over to give me a fist bump.

Jessica waits for us to settle down. "Each of you has a copy of the guidelines at your station, along with a cookbook from the 1950s—for inspiration."

She motions to the dartboard. "The twist for today's challenge is a simple game of darts. You each will have one throw and whatever wedge your dart lands on will dictate the parameter of your purchases."

I look at the wedges. Some aren't too bad, like "No Fresh Produce" or "Ten Items or Less," but some are rough, like "No Fresh Meat" or "Lose Two Dollars." My mind is racing as I try to figure out the best way to handle this challenge, but I can't help but worry about how I'm supposed to make a meal for four with six dollars that also meets the guidelines. Making a family meal on a tight budget is one thing, but I have no idea how much food cost in the fifties.

"If you miss the dartboard altogether," Jessica continues, "you will lose thirty seconds of shopping time and two dollars from your budget. For this challenge you'll have two hours to complete your planning and preparation."

Another pause.

I wonder if she falls into this habit when she is at home. Like, she is talking to her husband, like, "Hey, dear." *(Pauses for a reaction.)* "Would you like steak for dinner? Or . . ." *(Long pause as she waits for the camera to pan.)* "Chicken?"

The thought almost makes me laugh, but then the sudden

movement of everyone rushing to line up at the dartboard snaps me out of it. Once we're lined up in front of the board, Jessica hands each of us our dart. Hakulani is the first to step up to the line and throw.

His dart lands on "No Fresh Meat." He tries to look a little disappointed (but I've seen what he can do with canned meat), but then he grins and says, "Spam is my jam."

I laugh with everyone else, glad to have his sense of humor to keep us from getting too serious and tense in front of the cameras.

I step up next, trying to aim for what I think will be the least devastating wedges. However, my dart has a mind of its own and lands squarely in "Frozen Food Only," and I groan. Not using fresh meat is one thing, but being forced to use frozen anything means I'll have to thaw it before I can start preparing it, which is going to cost me time. And time is one thing I *can't* afford to lose.

One by one, everyone steps forward to take their turn and almost everyone hits the target. Inaaẏa's dart hits the wedge labeled "Lose Two Dollars," but it bounces off, so her penalty is to lose the two dollars *and* thirty seconds of grocery shopping time, and suddenly my frozen food sentence doesn't seem too bad. I look up at Jessica, who is giving us the smile that I've come to recognize means there is another twist that is about to mess everything up.

"Lola," she says, and Lola snaps to attention. "Since you were victorious in the French fusion challenge, you've won a surprise advantage."

Lola gives a big smile as Jessica reveals another dart.

"You may use this dart for yourself, possibly gaining some additional ingredients beyond the middle aisle, or use it as a sabotage for one of your opponents to limit their options even more."

The middle aisle is basically all your packaged and canned goods. There's a lot of stuff there, but it lacks anything fresh. When I was younger, we shopped a lot from the middle aisles. If I were her, I'd take the chance to throw another dart since she doesn't have much to lose and she might even add to her ingredients. Then I catch Dani nudging Lola and giving her a pointed look before glancing in my direction. *This cannot be happening to me.*

For a second, Lola holds on to her dart, and I think I'm going to be safe, but then I can tell by the way her expression changes that I'm completely screwed. With a slight sigh, Lola looks at Jessica and says, "I'd like to give this to Peyton."

I clench my teeth and force myself to smile as the cameras pan to catch my reaction. I really hate Dani; but if I'm being honest, Lola is on my list right now, too. I take the dart with as much grace as I can muster and step up to the line. I aim for "Dairy Only," thinking that I could maybe make something work. However, my throw goes wildly off the mark and ends up on the "Bottom Two Shelves" wedge. The bottom shelves have a lot of generic foods and bigger, bulkier items that are going to take up some of my money, but it gets me out of the dilemma of only using frozen food. I look back at Jessica and I feel all my confidence drain from my body. Damn, there's that smile again.

"Combined with your earlier throw, Peyton," Jessica says, "you will only be able to use the bottom two shelves."

Pause.

Pause.

This is going to be *so* bad.

Pause.

"Of the freezer section."

I hear someone gasp behind me. I don't even know what's on the bottom of the frozen section, because in order to see that, I would have to crawl on the floor. This is a disaster, and Dani knows it. She smiles at me, her smug face begging for me to rearrange it. Paulie must know what I'm thinking because he puts his arm on my shoulder as if he is trying to cheer me up, but then leans in close, his mouth barely moving.

"Don't give the cameras anything to use against you," he warns me. "They can edit you like crazy, and the next thing you know, Dani's their new girl next door and you're the mean girl out to get her."

"He's right," Hakulani whispers. "Don't let her get to you like that."

It's easy for them to say, I think, as we all walk back to our stations. I pick up the orange cookbook that's sitting on my station. A young mother with a crisp white apron smiles up at me, a cherubic baby reaching up for her from its highchair. Through the window, two more children play catch under a bright sun. I'd like to throw the book in Lola and Dani's general direction. If it should happen to smack one or both of them in the face, well, maybe they should have been paying better attention. Instead, I flip the cover open and start looking for ideas. I raise my hand to get Jessica's attention.

"Can we use some of our prep time to look at the items that are available?" I ask when she comes over.

Jessica turns around to look at the spot where I assume the disembodied voice comes from.

"That's fine," the voice says.

A few of us take advantage of this option immediately, while the others continue to flip through the cookbook. In the pantry, I bend down to examine the bottom of the freezer section and am happy to see that I can use chicken. It's on the bone, but I can make it work. Farther down, I find fatty bacon and lots of vegetables. When I see the ice cream and frozen fruit, dessert becomes a no-brainer. I stand up and start ironing out my dessert recipe. I'm going to take store-bought ice cream and dress it up with rhubarb compote. I remember Grams used to say how much Grandpa loved rhubarb-strawberry pie, but I never quite got on board with that combination.

Back at my station, I begin to flip through the cookbook. I only have about five minutes left to figure out my main course when I see the recipe for duck à l'orange. I read through the ingredients and I realize that there are some spices I will need that apparently weren't in the frozen section back in the 1950s, but they are common ones and I might be able to work out some way to find substitutions. I know there is no duck in my section of the freezer, but I can use the chicken and some frozen orange concentrate, salt and pepper, and a packet of soy sauce from a frozen Chinese vegetable package and I think I can pull off chicken à l'orange. I flip to the sides section of the cookbook, the pages falling open to something called succotash. Lima beans? Seriously? Oh, but there's bacon and the rest of the ingredients are also available to me—in one form or another. I just hope I can stay within my six-dollar budget.

Jessica warns us that our prep time will end in one minute. I jot down everything I need to get, but as I am relegated to one aisle, the shopping part should be quick and easy. When the timer sounds, we stand in front of our stations, lists in hand. The cameras fire up, ready to follow us as we dash around the pantry. We each have a buggy, or, as Jessica says, a cart, to help us get all our items safely back to our stations.

"Remember," Jessica says, "you must check out during the ten-minute window. If you check out and have money left while there is time on the clock, you can return to the store. Anything in your cart at the end of the ten minutes must be checked out. If you go over your budget, you will have to give up some of your items."

I tap my foot, anticipation building. Can we get to the cooking, please? This challenge feels unique because it's far out of my comfort zone but also kind of familiar at the same time. I take a breath. It's bad enough we have to use limited ingredients, but we also have to get through checkout and spend no more than six dollars. I'm not sure I could buy a bag of frozen chicken for six bucks, let alone everything else.

I twist my hands on my cart, preparing to make a quick dash to the frozen food section. I doubt I'll have to fight too many people off, though. My biggest challenge is going to be thawing everything out, especially the chicken. I run through everything I need to do when I get back to my station and keep repeating to myself: *The sooner I get all my items, the sooner I can get things on the stove.*

As soon as Jessica tells us to go, it's a madhouse. Carts crash into each other and run over people's heels. Lola almost runs down a camera guy, and although she claims it was an accident, I'm not so sure. I have to do a few substitutions of items and buy other items I don't exactly need, like a mixed bag of frozen peppers because I need the red ones, but overall I am able to find everything I needed. By the time I'm through checkout, I have three minutes left to spare and forty-five cents in change. I'm stunned. Things really were cheaper in the good ole days.

I get several pots of water on the burners to boil. Working with frozen food can be tricky. I need to thaw out the chicken before cooking it, but I don't want to overcook it, either. Grabbing a plastic bag, I drop the chicken inside and gently lower it into one of the pots. I check the shopping clock and discover I still have about a minute left to buy things. I make one more trip through the tundra zone of the store, looking for something that might add another layer to the dessert. I lean down and far in the back I see a package of pie dough. I look for a price tag but don't see one.

I look at the shelves above and realize what happened. Somehow, probably during the stocking, a package of dough slipped behind the other shelves, landing on the bottom. I pull it out and look up and down the row, hoping I can get a clarification, but I don't see anyone. I walk to the end of the aisle and spot Jessica near the cashier's line and approach her. The timer buzzes just as I get to where she's standing.

"Everyone, stop what you're doing and report to the cashier's station. If you have already checked out and have started your dish, keep going. Hurry up. You're using your cooking time."

She looks at me and the pie dough in my hand. I think she's going to call me out for having it, but she doesn't. Instead, she ushers me into the line. "Check out, Peyton," she says, but I resist.

"I just need to know if I can use this," I say, holding up the package.

"Was it on the bottom two shelves of the freezer section?" she asks, looking past me to make sure the other chefs are leaving the pantry.

"Yes, but—" I begin, but she cuts me off.

"Then it's fine. Get through the line."

I feel a twinge of guilt, but I tried, right? I tried to get confirmation, she gave it to me, and now I have pie crust and can make a deconstructed strawberry-rhubarb pie à la mode for dessert.

Once I'm back in my station, I put the thought out of my mind. I did try to ask. And, as Jessica pointed out, the crust was on the bottom shelf. I need every advantage I can get here, and if Jessica says it is okay, then I'm going to take this inch and run with it.

CHAPTER TWENTY-TWO

"HOW DID YOU GET THE CRUST?" ANGELICA ASKS as she races up to my station. "I thought you were supposed to only use items from the bottom two shelves."

"It was on the bottom shelf," I say quickly.

"No, the only frozen pie crust was at eye level," Angelica says, eyeing me with suspicion. "I checked myself."

Of course, because you're a heinous pain. "I found it on the bottom shelf," I said. "Since it was the only one, I asked Jessica if I could use it, and she said if it was on the two bottom shelves it was fair game."

Angelica turns her gaze to the host. "Is this true?"

Poor Jessica looks like a deer caught in headlights, and it's a feeling I know all too well. I feel bad about throwing her under the bus, but I'm also not going to be reprimanded when I tried to make sure I could use the item.

"She did ask me," Jessica admits. "It was during the final seconds of shopping."

Billy tries to play the mediator. "Well, it sounds like it was an honest mistake."

"You can check the footage," I say quickly. "You had to have some camera on me. They're everywhere."

Angelica still doesn't look like she believes me. "Hugh, can you confirm what Peyton is telling us?"

And just like that, the disembodied voice has a name. "Give me a sec."

This is great. When they watch the tape and see I didn't do anything wrong, I'll be cleared. The only problem is there is a good chance Angelica is going to hold it against me for the rest of the competition. I glance over to see her, Billy, and A. J. in a hushed conversation at the judges' table.

The set is so silent that when the disembodied voice, I mean Hugh's voice, bounces around the set, several people are visibly startled.

"We've reviewed the tape," he says. "It looks like Peyton did get the pie crust from the bottom shelf and she did attempt to get clarification from Jessica."

"She should have checked the shelf," Angelica says, sitting back in her seat. "She would have known those ingredients were off-limits."

"Why don't we vote on it?" A. J. offers.

Angelica gives him a strained smile but doesn't object.

The outcome is two to one in favor of my dish being accepted for judging. Once the vote is taken, Billy turns to the other judges and says, for all to hear, "There's no reason to mention this issue once that camera starts rolling again, right?"

A. J. nods, but Angelica, her arms folded across her chest, says nothing.

"Angelica?" Billy asks, his voice making it clear that he's not really asking her.

"Fine," she snaps. "I just don't think it's fair to the other contestants, that's all."

Billy takes in a deep breath and turns to me, a forced smile on his face. "Do you need a minute, Peyton?"

I shake my head. "No, I'm ready."

And with that, the cameras get into their spots, and the PAs stream in with trays of my food. By now the ice cream is starting to melt and I can only imagine how soggy the crust will be. The crust that would have been fine ten minutes ago.

Maybe it's because Billy and A. J. felt bad about Angelica's attempt to get me disqualified, or because my dishes actually managed to impress them, but somehow I manage to land in the middle of the pack this time, which means that I am once again spared from elimination. However, my luck turns and my accomplishment is bittersweet because Inaaya is eliminated for her overcooked chicken croquettes. Everyone says their quick goodbyes, and I squeeze her in a hug for so long I thought a PA was going to come tell me to let go—then she is gone. Jessica wraps up the show as we stand quietly, and I try not to look devastated as the cameras pan over us.

Like after the last elimination, the bus ride back to the penthouse is silent, and back at the apartment I stand in front of the open door to our room, which I guess is just my room now.

"It's weird, right?" Malik says as he stops beside me. "Having the room all to yourself?"

"I feel guilty. Like it should have been me."

Malik chuckles, but there isn't any humor to it. "Trust me," he says. "I know exactly what you mean." He clasps a hand on my shoulder. "But you are here, so make it *count.*"

"You heading to the roof?" he asks.

"Wouldn't miss it," I say, following him to the kitchen to make the sweet tea.

Dani and Lola are the last to arrive for our toast to Inaaya. Much like last time, the mood is somber, but Malik does his best to keep it positive.

"To Inaaya," he says. "She always had a kind word for everyone."

"True," I say. "She could always make me laugh, even when I'd had a bad day in the kitchen. And she loved food as much as anyone I know."

This got some laughs. As we go around the group, everyone agrees that Inaaya was a kind, thoughtful person. If there had been a "Miss Congeniality" on this show, she would have won hands down. When the toast ends, I don't feel like sticking around, even though Hakulani and Paulie both try to convince me to hang out for a while. All I can think about is going to sleep so this day will finally end.

When I step into my room, the first thing I see is that Inaaya's side is completely bare. Not even a scrap of paper or hair-tie remains. I grab some things from my side of the room, swiping the tears from my cheeks, and head straight to the shower to rinse off the grime and sweat from the kitchen. Between the running around for the grocery game and the stress of Angelica accusing me of cheating, I reek. As the water peppers my back and I rinse the tears from my face, slowly the aches of the week are replaced by the anticipation of the one still to come. We only have two weeks left, and I have to survive the remaining elimination challenges.

Now just five people separate me from the scholarship that could change my entire life.

CHAPTER TWENTY-THREE

SATURDAY MORNING DAWNS BRIGHT AND CLEAR as I wake up to a half-empty room. With no filming planned for the weekend, Caitlin has scheduled time for each of us to meet her in the confessional over the next two days. Other than that, we can do what we want as long as we don't leave the apartment.

On the way to the kitchen, I stop to knock on Hakulani and Paulie's door to see if they want to play pool or watch TV. The door is slightly ajar, and I don't mean to eavesdrop, but something about the hushed urgency in Hakulani's voice sucks me in.

"Alaina, stop," he says.

I start to turn around, but his next words stop me.

"It's not like I *really* like her. It's just for the show. You are my girl. But . . ."

Then I realize that he must be on a phone. The PAs took our phones on day one—something about how it was in our contracts and it was supposed to prevent anything from getting leaked—so how does he have one? The second thing that pops into my head is that the "her" he is talking about is me. To someone who he *really* cares about. His girlfriend, maybe? As he continues to talk, I suddenly get this feeling of sudden clarity, and everything starts falling into place as my face gets warmer and warmer by the second.

In all the time we've been hanging out—in all the time he's been flirting with me—Hakulani has never mentioned anyone back home. Come to think of it, outside of his family and surfing, he doesn't talk much about his life back home. He always seemed to deflect or steer the conversation back to my life, which I was never going to talk about, so I'd change the subject, and—oh my God, I've been catfished in real life.

"It's not like that," Hakulani tells the other person on the phone, and I'm pulled back from my thoughts. "It's just for the show—it's like acting."

The other person says something. A lot of something, based on the long silence before Hakulani speaks again.

"You don't *understand*. They just want a story, and I have to give them a story or I'm *gone*."

Silence.

"Yes. They will, just like that. It's already happened to a guy here. First week. Out of nowhere, he was cut. No one knew why, but I saw him arguing with Caitlin, you know, the producer, the night before, and then *bam*. He was on the next flight back to the West Coast."

More silence.

"No, it's true. Caitlin told me that's why he was cut. They wanted him to do something, he refused, and then he was cut."

Adam. My heart slams in my chest, and a knot forms in my stomach. If Caitlin really did cut him because he refused to play by the show's rules, then me making it through that first elimination was all a lie. I feel all the heat leave my face as my heart drops, and I get a little light-headed—maybe the reason I wasn't eliminated during the last few challenges wasn't because of my cooking or because the judges saw something special in me, but because the show wants *ratings*. And if that's true, then doesn't that mean that it's not necessarily skill or cooking the best dish that keeps you safe from elimination? So, if the real rules are play the role you're meant to play or go home, then do I have more or less of a chance to win? Was Dani right this whole time?

I want to walk back to my room and pretend this never happened, to stop the questions from swirling in my head, but I'm stuck in this spot, unable to move.

"Alaina, please," Hakulani says, pleading. "I swear, I didn't mean to hurt you or for you to feel like you can't trust me. I've missed you so much, and I didn't want you to see the show later and think that I was keeping this from you or being unfaithful. I promise, you have no reason to doubt me."

More silence.

"I can't quit. I'm doing this for us, remember? For *our*

future. If I don't win, you know what's going to happen? Best case, I get a job working in some tourist trap kitchen. We'll be living the same life as our parents, barely scraping by while the haoles keep taking over more and more of the islands."

He pauses.

"But I want us to have more."

He pauses to listen.

"Then think of this as a part in a movie or play." He laughs ruefully. "The only thing that's really real about this show is the cooking, and even most of that isn't as real as it looks."

Then I jump about a mile high when I suddenly hear from behind me, "Hey, Peyton."

I turn and Paulie is standing in the hallway with a soda in hand. "Um, why are you hanging out in the hall by my room?"

Damn it. Leave it to Paulie, of all people, to bust me. Instead of answering, I walk past him, slip into my room, and shut the door. I'm resting my forehead against the wood and trying to keep my thoughts from racing, when a minute later there is a gentle knock on my door.

"Peyton?" Hakulani says softly. "Can we talk?"

I think about opening my door and facing him, but then all my anger and fire drains from me, and I'm left feeling confused and sad. "You know, I'm actually going to take a nap," I say, trying to force my voice to sound carefree and light. "Later?"

"Promise?"

"Sure," I lie. If his rooftop words don't mean anything, why should mine? I turn and lean my back against the door and wish Inaaya was still here. At least there would be someone to talk to. Instead, I lie down on my bed and stare at the ceiling until the twinkly lights grow fuzzy and then fade to black.

Later that afternoon I venture to the kitchen, my stomach insisting that I find something to eat. I grab some fruit before leafing through the take-out menus, settling on a local burger joint. After placing my order, I check the time and realize that my confession session with Caitlin is in five minutes. *Great.*

I turn the knob slowly and push to see if it's locked or anything, but it's not, so I open the door and step into the room.

"Hello, Peyton," Caitlin says from the chair behind the camera. "Please, come in."

"Hey, Caitlin," I say with a slight wave, letting the door shut behind me.

She motions to the other chair. "Sit down and we'll get started."

I do as she says, my stomach beginning to tighten. I'm glad I have to wait for my dinner until after this confessional. I'd hate to waste a good meal.

Caitlin presses a button on a remote, and the camera comes to life. "The way this works is I'm going to ask some questions, and then you'll answer them."

"What kind of questions?" I ask.

She smiles sweetly. I know that smile, and it's the opposite of sweet. "Oh, a little this, and a little that."

"So anything is fair game?" I ask.

She smiles. "Anything."

Great.

"Now, let's talk about how things are going so far this week. You seem to be getting along with everyone. Well, you and Dani seem to have some issues, but that's to be expected—not everyone can get along with everyone—but you seem to have developed a couple of good friendships. Especially with Hakulani and Paulie. Care to tell me more about getting to know everyone?"

"There's not much to tell. I've known them for a week. We get along all right."

Caitlin pauses the video. "Okay, Peyton. I need a little more dish from you. I need you to give me something I can work with."

"Okay," I say, not sure what I'm going to say.

Caitlin flips the camera back on. "Okay, so Paulie. You guys seem like you've been friends forever."

I smile at Caitlin, avoiding the camera. "Paulie's great. I mean, he's funny and loves to goof around. I'm really looking forward to getting to know him better."

I get a nod for my answer. "And Hakulani?" Caitlin asks. "He's cute, and I think he's interested in you. Any chance you feel the same way?"

I try to keep my face neutral. Caitlin is obviously working with some outdated information. Yesterday, I might have blushed while trying to answer this question. But after what happened earlier today, I feel like I somehow have the upper hand, so I answer, in all honesty, "Oh, Hakulani? We're just friends. He's not really my type."

Caitlin's right eyebrow rises. "Really? I was sure I picked up on some flirtation while watching you two on set together."

I shake my head. "Nope."

Her smile tightens just the tiniest bit, but she nods and moves on. "What about Dani?" she asks. "You two are positively combustible."

"Yeah, I would agree with that. Dani thinks she is the best in the kitchen, and it's annoying. Just because you come from a culinary family doesn't mean you're entitled to special treatment or that you're somehow better than the rest of us."

Caitlin smiles her approval. "And how do you feel you're doing in the competition?"

"I think I'm lucky to still be here," I say honestly. "But I'm still here, which means I still have a chance to impress the judges, so I'm going to do *everything* I can to win."

"So who do you think is going to win?" she asks.

I smile directly at the camera. "I am, of course."

"Of course," Caitlin says, before turning off the camera. "Well, I think that's enough."

"Really?" I say in surprise.

"Well, to be honest, Peyton, you're answers are pretty boring. I give you a shot to talk about Dani, who has been awful to you, and you *punt* the answer. I don't know how much extra footage we'll need for you."

"What are you saying?"

She gives me a serene look. "I'm saying there are more eliminations to come. If you want to make sure you stick around, it would be in your own best interest to give me something to work with." She holds my gaze for a moment, a chill traveling down my spine, before she looks down and starts writing something in her notebook. When she is finished, she looks up and seems surprised that I'm still here. "You can go," she says, waving me off with her perfectly manicured hand.

Stunned, I leave the room, barely aware of a PA calling my name and telling me that my food is here. Caitlin made it crystal clear where I stand in her book, and since I'm not playing the poor girl role or the drama that is being expertly crafted between me and my castmates, I'm no longer cut out for the show. So that means only one thing: I need to get my hands dirty or this week will be my last.

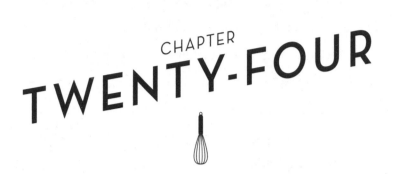

CHAPTER TWENTY-FOUR

AVOIDING SOMEONE WHEN YOU'RE TRAPPED IN an apartment with them takes a great amount of skill and determination, and it takes all that I have to manage to avoid Hakulani for the rest of the day. So what if I did it by spending most of my time in my room reading, planning, and only coming out when I absolutely had to?

When I wake up on Sunday, I have no idea what time it is or how long I've been asleep, but I can smell grilled meat and garlic, and it's too good to resist. I throw my hair into a sloppy ponytail, change my shirt, and clean off a bit of yesterday's makeup before peeking my head out the door of my room. I don't hear anything or see anyone, so I figure that I'm probably safe. I know that I'm not going to be able to avoid him forever, especially with Caitlin's not-so-subtle warning on repeat in my head, but I can try. I slip down the hall and turn the corner toward the kitchen, but I stop when I hear the dishwasher snap shut and someone moving around.

Panicking, I turn and twist the doorknob to the confessional room and almost gasp in relief when the knob turns. I slip through the door, closing it behind me with the slightest click. Leaning against it, I close my eyes. What am I even going to say when I see him? It's not like anything really happened between us, but still. I stand at the door waiting for whoever is in the kitchen to leave again, but judging on what I can make out, it might be a while.

In the end, my stomach wins out again, and I venture out in search of food. I slowly make my way into the kitchen, and I can hear the buzz of people talking on the roof and the occasional burst of laughter drifting in through the window along with the sounds of the city. I debate heading up to the roof—and the grill—and just letting the cards fall where they will, but after a few seconds, and the thought of Dani getting even an ounce more of dirt on me, I decide to retreat.

When I turn around to grab something out of the pantry, I find myself face-to-face with Hakulani. *Crap.* Seeing him for the first time since I overheard his conversation triggers a wave of emotions. I am so angry at myself for even getting caught up in all of this in the first place. How could I have been so stupid to believe Hakulani actually *liked* me like that? I spend a couple days with a guy who's my competition in this once-in-a-lifetime opportunity, and I wind up like your average rom-com character: smitten at first sight. What was I thinking?

"Hey, Peyton," Hakulani says quietly, fighting to hold my gaze. "Can we talk?"

I watch him with so much confusion, embarrassment, and anger gathering on my tongue. I want to snap at him and tell him that here is fine, but I also want to break this tension between us—to go back to how things were. In the end, all I can manage is, "Come to the confessional. I don't think there are hidden cameras in there."

He follows me back into the room, and I close the door. We sit down across from each other, neither willing to speak first. I cross my arms over my chest and sit back against the chair.

Finally, Hakulani lifts his head, and I'm surprised to see that he looks ashamed. "So, how much did you hear?"

"Enough to know you're a first-class jerk and to feel stupid enough to fall for the whole thing."

"Look, it's complicated."

I give him a sharp look. "Did Caitlin put you up to it?"

"Put me up to what?" He looks confused, but there is something else, too.

"To start something with me?"

He hesitates for a moment before nodding and dropping his head into his hands. "I'm sorry, Peyton," he says, looking up. "It wasn't supposed to be you—at least it wasn't at first, when we were starting to become friends."

"Then who was your victim supposed to be?"

"Caitlin told me that if I got something going with a cast member, I would have a better chance of staying on the show longer. She said Dani was pretty desperate to get some screen time, and I should try with her."

"So you decided you would just ignore the fact that you had a girlfriend, and start something with Dani to win a competition?"

"Oh, like you would have played it straight if you didn't have an angle?" he says. "But wait, you do. You're playing the poor girl from the unsophisticated country, like you're the only one here who has had problems or a rough life." His words are like blows, and there is a dark look that I've never seen on his face before.

None of that matters, though, as my temper flares and I skip past being embarrassed and head straight for being royally ticked off. "First of all," I snap, "it's not an act; and second, no, I would never try to sleep with someone just to score a chance at an extra challenge."

"Whoa," he says. "No one ever said anything about sex. I would never sink that low."

"Right," I say, letting the sarcasm coat every letter.

"Are you always this suspicious?"

"Well, I'm sitting in front of a guy who has been trying to hook up with me for the last week, and all the while he has a girlfriend back home. I wonder why I would have any reason to be suspicious."

"That's not what I . . . Look, Caitlin said I'm running out of *time*. If I don't create some sort of drama, they're going to cut me this week."

My brain immediately jumps to Caitlin's warning yesterday and why she might start threatening me *and* Hakulani, but another wave of emotion drowns it all out.

"So, I'm your insurance policy?" The anger has drained from my voice and I can hear the hurt in it now. "Why didn't you just ask me if I could help out? I thought we were *friends*."

"We are friends."

"Then we have very different ideas about what friendship is."

I watch the hurt look flicker on his face before he looks away. We both remain silent as the minutes tick by. I realize that, deep down, I want to trust him, and I want to believe that he was just doing what he had to in order to stay.

"Where'd you get the phone?" I ask, finally breaking the silence.

I expect him to avoid the question, but instead he sighs and looks me in the eye. "One of the camera guys. I traded him some of my clothes so he could give them to his kid. He smuggled in a prepaid phone for me."

"So, you are a *professional* hustler," I say.

"Peyton," he says.

I hold up my hands. "No, seriously. I mean, I'm the daughter of a guy who's done time for financial fraud, and I'm impressed."

"Come on. You don't know what it's like to tell Caitlin no."

"Oh, no, I do know." I sigh and rub my hands over my face before continuing. No turning back now. "I'm supposed to be this poor little trailer park, white trash girl with a prison dad and a mom so busy pining over everything she's lost that she can barely take care of her kid."

"So you know, then."

"Yeah. I know what she is capable of. But I haven't lied to people, and I haven't tried to make someone like me just so I can stay on the show.

"And I don't get to go home to a tropical paradise if I lose. I'm going back to a small nowhere town that doesn't have a working stoplight. If I lose this competition, I'm probably going to end up knocked up by some guy just passing through and then become a single mom trying to raise a kid on a waitress's salary and spend my twilight years with thirty cats."

"Is that a part of the act?" he asks with a small smile. "The kids and cats?"

I shake my head. "No, that's what happens to girls who stay in my town. I mean, some get married to decent guys, but every year it seems like there are fewer and fewer of them."

He stops smiling. "It won't be like that for you."

"How do you know?"

He hesitates, then continues. "Because you seem like the kind of person who isn't going to let the mistakes of her parents drag her down. You're a fighter. You have to be or you wouldn't be here."

Another round of silence. Maybe I am a fighter, but fighting can only get you so far. I need this opportunity. And I need to catch a lucky break.

"Have you ever heard of mutually assured destruction?" Hakulani asks, breaking the silence.

I shake my head.

"It's this military strategy where two or more groups or countries each have the ability to assure the complete annihilation of the other."

"Like how Russia and the United States have enough nukes that should one fire, the other would return fire, resulting in both being destroyed."

"Yeah, that's where I think we are now. You have something on me and I have something on you but, ultimately, neither of us wants to be sent packing." He pauses. "The only alternative is a truce."

"To have a truce, you need trust."

"You *can* trust me," Hakulani says, looking me in the eye and endearing me to believe him. "From now on, no secrets."

I study him, trying to see if this is some kind of trick, then decide: What do I have to lose? "Okay, I'm listening."

"I need a fake relationship to get Caitlin off my back, and you need to get out of the storyline that you hate so much."

"Yeah," I say, not really seeing how this truce is supposed to work.

"What if we pretend, until the final four Landmark Challenge, that we're into each other."

"'Into each other'?"

He nods. "We do the flirting stuff, spend time together, get caught trying to sneak off for some alone time. Stuff production would love."

"That helps you. What about me?"

"It helps us both," he says. "If you're in a showmance with me, then Caitlin isn't going to try to get you to dish about your life back home."

"Intriguing," I say.

But I must not convince him because then Hakulani asks, "Do you have a better idea?"

I'm quiet for a minute, but then I shake my head.

He nods. "All right, then."

"We need rules," I insist.

"Such as?"

"This relationship can't be a cliffhanger," I say. "When the time is right, we need a very clean, visible breakup. No questions asked. I don't want to end the show with people thinking we're still together."

He nods. "Can I make a public proclamation about Alaina?"

"Do you *want* the whole world to think you cheated on her?"

"You're right. Maybe I just say: 'As much as I like you, there's a girl back home I can't stop thinking about.'"

I nod thoughtfully. "You could get some sympathy from that."

"Okay, also no kissing," Hakulani says quickly. "Because kissing you would be like crossing the line of pretending and cheating—and I don't want to humiliate Alaina any more than I am already."

"Do you think she's going to see it that way?"

"I don't know."

"I don't kow if Caitlin will buy it, but okay. Anything else?"

"There's someone else who's going to get hurt in this," he says, looking at me like I should know what he's talking about.

"Who?" I ask. "Me?"

"Paulie."

I can't stop the small laugh from bursting from my lips. "Paulie? Yeah, right. Why would Paulie care that we were pretending to be into each other?"

Hakulani stares at me. "Are you serious?"

I look at him, waiting for him to crack and tell me he was joking, but Hakulani just sighs and leans back in his chair and stares at the ceiling.

"I have a feeling he is not going to like any of this." He looks back at me. "You know he is my roommate, right?"

"Oh, please, we're just friends."

"You might think you're all in the friend zone, but don't be surprised when something happens, because all I'm gonna say is I told you so."

"Okay, let's stick to the rules," I say. "I can't handle another distraction right now."

"We should start tonight," Hakulani says.

"Sounds good. The sooner we get this show on the road, the sooner we can break up."

"Good thing I'm the romantic in this relationship."

"I can be romantic."

"But can you?" he asks, skepticism dripping from his voice.

I stop for a moment and think about it. "I mean, I would be really bad at it."

"Yeah, you would."

"Shut up," I say, and Hakulani laughs.

We spend the next half hour planning how we're going to pull this off before finally emerging from the confessional room. Now that we've ironed out every detail, we head up to the roof, where everyone is hanging out and relaxing. Paulie presents me with a plate of steak, baked potato, and corn on the cob. Hakulani grabs his plate before leading me to a quiet corner and starts to point out the different constellations that have broken through the light haze of the city as we eat. As we spend the next hour or two together, I can feel the cameras—and the rest of the cast—following our every move. For once, I don't mind because it finally feels like I'm the one controlling the cameras and not the other way around.

Later, when we head downstairs and to our rooms, Hakulani stops at my door and says, "Goodnight, Pey."

I guess he is going to start using my nickname now that we are officially co-conspirators.

"Goodnight," I say, giving him a shy smile.

He leans down and gives me a quick kiss on the cheek. "See you tomorrow," he says with a wink, then whispers, "Let's give them a show."

CHAPTER TWENTY-FIVE

"I KNEW IT," LOLA SAYS AFTER SHE SEES ME WHISpering to Hakulani on the bus the next morning.

I can feel him laugh silently next to me, and I try not to laugh as well. We couldn't ask for anyone more perfect to "find out about us" than Lola.

"Inaaya is going to be so ticked when she learns that the two of you got together after she left."

"What are you talking about?" I ask innocently.

Paulie is the last to arrive and he doesn't even look at me when he slides in behind the driver's seat.

"Brrr," Hakulani says quietly to me. "How does that cold shoulder feel?"

"Maybe he's just grumpy because he didn't sleep."

"Yeah, right. That is exactly what it is, Peyton."

"Well, I can't do anything about it now," I whisper back.

He smiles like I've said something witty.

"Good grief," Dani says from the row behind us. "Get a room."

"So where are we going today?" Hakulani calls out to the driver, nudging me to ignore Dani's baiting.

"The Empire State Building," he says like a showman introducing the main event while closing the bus door with a flourish.

"Ooh," Lola says. "That is so romantic. Did you ever see that old movie where the guy was supposed to meet the girl at the top of the Empire State Building on Valentine's Day?"

"No," I say, shaking my head.

She looks aghast. "Seriously? When this show is over, I am going to have to send you a list of movies that you *must* watch."

The conversation on the bus continues to center on movies while Hakulani and I scrunch down in the seat, occasionally shouting out contributions and teasing the others about their picks. By the time we make it to the front of the Empire State Building, we have debated the best movies in several genres. Stepping off the bus, we find Jessica waiting patiently for us. Taking our spots, we wait, mentally preparing for the next Landmark Challenge. After the cameras are in place, Jessica launches into her introduction and begins a rapid-fire round of facts about the Empire State Building.

After a minute or two, Jessica is still talking and we all start to shift and shuffle, anxious to get inside and see what's in store for us. I try to catch Paulie's attention when I think he is looking my way and make a face as Jessica explains that if all 73 elevators magically broke down at the same time, we'll have to walk up 1,872 steps to the observation point on the 103rd floor, but he just ignores me. I try to brush off the dull ache I suddenly feel as he looks back at Jessica as she wraps up telling us that it took 410 days to build the structure, during which five people died, and how it was the tallest building in New York City from 1931 to 1972.

"Oh man, I thought it would never end," Hakulani says to me and Malik as we enter the lobby with Jessica and cut through the throng of people to the VIP line. Paulie walks next to Lola ahead of us and smiles as she says something to him. A few people in the waiting crowd start to complain until they see the camera crew and I hear them speculating about who we are and why we're there.

"Get used to it," Hakulani whispers in my ear. "Once the show starts, everyone's going to know who you are."

The very thought makes me want to hide in the potted plants.

In the elevator the tour guide informs us that the regular tour stops on the 86th floor observation deck, but that, for a fee, you can also visit the 102nd floor, which is where we're heading.

"For better or worse," Hakulani says, "you gotta admit, the show is letting us get some pretty cool experiences."

I grin up at him. "Well, those of us without a fear of heights. And how are you going to deal with this?" I motion to the ceiling of the elevator.

"Oh, were you under the impression that I was going anywhere near the ledge?" he chuckles. "You are sadly mistaken."

"Come on, lover boy," Paulie says, but there is an edge to his voice that I've never heard before. "I thought you conquered your fears back at Lady Liberty."

I glance over my shoulder. "Really?"

He stares at me. "What? I'm just messing with him."

I sigh and turn around. Maybe Hakulani was right about Paulie, but then again, maybe this jealous schoolboy act is just part of his role. Caitlin could have set it up so he's always supposed to make problems for Hakulani. I rub my forehead and wish that this competition really was only about cooking. My head is starting to hurt from trying to figure out what's real and what isn't.

When the doors open on floor 102, Jessica turns to us, backs out, and, sweeping her arms, says, "Welcome to the top of the Empire State Building."

"How did she get here before us?" I whisper to Malik, who shakes his head.

"The woman might have superpowers or something."

"It would make sense," I say with a giggle.

A strong breeze pulls at our clothes as we step out of the elevator and see that a small section of the floor has been roped off, and she ushers us to our spots before we can start to wander. We cram together in the roped-off area as the blinking red light of the camera reminds us to get along and smile for the audience at home.

"Today's Landmark Challenge is all about going big. Vertically, that is," Jessica says as the wind whips her hair around. "Take in the sights and wrap your head around ways you can add architectural features to send your culinary skills sky high. Don't forget, this next challenge is as much about presentation as it is taste. Because, in this challenge, should your creation be too short or fall, you'll be sorry."

I notice that there's not as much pausing today—probably because of the wind. And the initial shock of this challenge's twist wears off after the audio guy asks Jessica to repeat her instructions a couple times. Once they are satisfied, we are finally allowed to wander the deck.

Hakulani links his arm with mine and we walk the perimeter, with me on the outside, of course. Jessica hands each of us some change and motions for us to look out the binoculars stationed around the edge of the observation deck. At first Hakulani dismisses this outright, but after a little persuading, he steps forward and puts his face into the viewfinder goggles.

"Oh wow," he says. "You can see *everything*."

"Do you see Central Park?" I ask.

He nods and the binoculars jiggle a little and I laugh at the face he makes.

"Can you see our apartment?"

"This city really has a lot of buildings, Peyton."

"Yeah, I guess that is an important characteristic of a city."

He steps back. "Your turn."

I place my face against the rubber goggles, and just as my eyes start to focus, everything goes black. Hakulani feeds another quarter into the machine and, as if by magic, I am looking down at the city, a cloudless blue sky acting as a backdrop, and I'm in awe. From the ground, you can feel the heart of New York, but from up here you can see its soul.

Even though Hakulani says he's seen enough, I race to each side of the building, using the binoculars to see as much of the city as I can. I pull out a small notebook from the tiny backpack that was part of my outfit today and jot down some thoughts. All we know is that the challenge is going to require our dishes to be tall and taste amazing, but I have some ideas that I hope will blow the judges away if I'm allowed anywhere near an oven.

The ride back to the studio is better than the ride there. At least Paulie doesn't seem as mad as he did in the elevator. Lola is sitting with him, and she even gets him to crack a smile.

Once we are settled on the set, Jessica, now a little less windblown, tells us again that our next challenge is going to be a tall order. "You can make anything you want, but it has to be *big*."

"That sounds easy enough," Paulie says with a smirk.

"Wait for it," I mutter.

"There is a catch," Jessica says.

"Here it comes," Dani adds.

"You must successfully transfer your design to the measuring table to be eligible for the advantage. You can opt to accept the help of one of our PAs, but that's at your own risk. If you drop your submission before it's measured, you are out."

"That shouldn't be hard," Hakulani says, but Lola doesn't look as sure.

"Also," Jessica adds, "there will be a bonus for creativity. Think of it as a second opportunity for an advantage."

Finally, a challenge that feels like it was made just for me.

"There's one more thing," Jessica adds, looking proud of herself. "Your submission must be ninety-five percent edible."

"Is that it?" Lola asks.

Jessica nods, before pivoting for the cameras so they can get a shot of all of us together. "All right, time to get started. You have five hours to build your fantastically tall creations." On her mark, we all tense and then rush off to our stations when she gives the word.

I race to mine and start going over all the things I need to grab from the materials pile and the pantry. Paulie is already coming back with an armload of ingredients, but his usual smile and playful banter are gone.

"Ninety-five?" Hakulani says over his shoulder as we get started. "That's oddly specific."

"It's so you can use support tools," I explain. "Like dowel rods and the like."

"Oh," he says. "Don't you think it's weird that they gave us five hours? That seems like a really long time."

"You're adorable," I say, wrapping my arms around him quickly for a side hug before I shoo him away. "Now, I've got a lot of work to do if I'm going to win this thing."

He says something, but I don't hear him over the sounds of the competition and the hum of excitement in my veins. I pull out some paper that was provided in the materials pile and quickly start sketching all the sights I remember from my notes and what I saw from each side of the tower. Once I have enough ideas, I race to the pantry to gather as many bags of marshmallows as I can carry and powdered sugar, along with a tray of gel food coloring. My second trip to the pantry includes many boxes of rice cereal, along with some spices, cocoa powder, some dried fruit, and other sweet surprises. Back at my station, I begin to construct four pillars made of dowels that will support the main part of my building.

"So what do you have in mind, Peyton?" Jessica asks, looking over the supplies.

"I'm going to recreate the Empire State Building."

"Oh, so you're going for height?" she asks.

"No," I tell her. "I'm going for both height and creativity."

"The building is very iconic, so what is going to be your creative spin?"

"I've got a few ideas," I say mysteriously. I've watched enough food competitions to know not to set the expectations too high during the early stages of the challenge. Jessica gives me a mischievous look before moving on to talk to Malik.

Turning a pot on high, I begin melting my marshmallows, then when it's done, I blend in powdered sugar, adding water a bit at a time to get it to the right consistency. In another stock pot, I mix melted marshmallows with cocoa powder and a bit of cinnamon, which I'll fold into my rice cereal to make the first batch of my treats.

Hakulani steps beside me, a little closer than he would have a few days ago, as I drag my sleeve across my forehead. I'm still uncomfortable with his overt attention, but I think it's having the impact we wanted.

"Fondant?" he asks, making a face. "I hate how that stuff tastes."

I try to look offended, but I know what he means. In general, it's pretty awful. "I'll have you know I make the most simple and amazing fondant." I tear off a little piece and look up and over my shoulder at him. "Open up." He does and I pop the piece into his mouth.

He chews on it thoughtfully. "Okay, this fondant I like," he says with a smile before turning back to his work.

I can practically feel the silence and tension coming from Paulie's station, but I ignore it and focus on the fondant, cutting out all the decorations so they can harden a little before I paint them. When I'm happy with how they look, I turn my attention to assembling the tower and rolling the dyed gray fondant over them before smoothing down the sides. Once the edges are done, I grab my pot of rice treats and add bits of dried cherry to punch up the flavors, before spooning it out and molding it, then covering it in fondant.

To attach the decorations to my creations, I mix up some powdered sugar, vanilla extract, and water to make a thick royal icing, or what is essentially edible cement.

"That's pretty cool," Paulie says as he rushes by and glances up. "And tall. Are you going to be able to move it?"

I smile at him and hope that this break in his silence is an olive branch of some kind, before turning back to my work. Even though the structure is supported with thick dowel rods, I am a little concerned that it'll be too heavy to move by myself.

In the end, I opt to take advantage of the extra set of hands, and, carefully, a PA helps me move my creation from my prep table to the judging table.

Jessica joins me as we wait for the measurement. "So, Peyton, you have all these adorable decorations on the sides of your building, but what do they represent?"

"These edible decorations are the things you can see from

each side of the Empire State Building. There's the Rockefeller Center, which I represent with the ice rink, the Statue of Liberty, One World Trade Center, Times Square, and the Brooklyn Bridge."

Jessica looks impressed as she gets a closer look. "Wow, these details are really impressive." Straightening up, she adds, "Go ahead and stand back with the others while the judges prepare to announce the winners."

I smile and do as I'm told, taking time to survey the other submissions. Lola's tiered wedding cake is the second tallest, after mine, but it's plain. If I'm being brutally honest, there's not a submission that can top mine in either the height or creativity category. I try not to get my hopes up, but I can't help it—I feel like I nailed this challenge.

We all look forward as Jessica announces the winner. "With a structure measuring six feet, seven inches *and* decorations that are both creative and detailed, the winner of today's Landmark Challenge is . . ."

Another one of her legendary pauses.

I swear if Jessica doesn't say a name, I'm going to burst.

"Peyton."

I stand there in shock as the others congratulate me and applaud. I've just won my first challenge. And it feels *amazing.*

CHAPTER TWENTY-SIX

ON TOP OF WINNING MY FIRST CHALLENGE, IT seems like the arrangement with Hakulani is working out better than expected, and the production team is totally eating it up. In fact, a PA pulled us aside after the Landmark Challenge filming was done to remind us this is a family-friendly show and we should keep that in mind going forward. We tried to be serious and look embarrassed, but the whole time I could tell Hakulani was trying hard to not laugh. We barely hold hands or do anything more than stand close to each other and act cute, but people see what they want to see.

The next morning, we decide to have breakfast on the roof and catch the sunrise—perfect fodder for the cameras—except we lose track of time, and now Hakulani and I are running late. We hurry to catch our ride to the studio and barely make it. To try to make up some time, the driver takes a few extra risks, and the bus rocks and lurches as we speed through a yellow light, dodging a car that was trying to make a left turn. Looking around, everyone seems caught up in their own thoughts. Hakulani seems to notice, too, because he just stares out the window and is quiet for the whole ride.

"We're here," the driver says, opening the door so we can pile out onto the curb.

Hakulani holds out his hand to help me out of my seat and I giggle. Oh yeah, I've gone all in on this charade, and now I am a giggler. It's nauseating to do it because I don't like the girl-in-love stereotype any more than the next person.

"Oh my God, look," Dani says, stopping short. She points to a monitor where the promo for our show is playing. She grabs my arm in the excitement before realizing it's me, and not Lola. "Oh, it's *you*." Then she quickly lets go and turns on her heel, moving to the other side of the group. Lola catches my gaze and gives an apologetic shrug.

We watch, our eyes scanning each quick shot, waiting to see our picture or a clip that we're in.

"Did anyone see Adam?" Malik asks.

"I don't think I did," I say, "but it was so fast, I could hardly find myself."

"Yeah, and it's so hard to miss the red mass of tangles on your head," Dani mutters.

I turn my head slowly, giving her my meanest stare. "At least I'm not a bleached blonde."

"Okay, ladies," the PA says, ushering us through the door. "Save it for the studio. We don't need a scene out here."

We file in, Dani pushing in front of me when we reach the door at the same time. When she flips her hair and it catches me in the face, I can feel the rage building up. She's even worse than usual today.

Paulie comes up behind me. "You okay?" he asks. "It could be my imagination, but she seems to really have it in for you today."

I shrug, wondering if he is trying to cover up her earlier excitement. "Who cares. With any luck, she's going home today."

Hakulani comes over and stands close. "Are you going to use the awesome power of the advantage on her?"

"If given a chance, you bet."

He smiles. "That's my girl."

The way he says *my girl* send a chill down my spine. I know we're only playing at this whole dating thing, but the possessiveness of it all gets a little weird sometimes.

Paulie rolls his eyes and speeds up, putting some distance between us. Which is pointless because we're going to the same elevator. Still, when we enter the car, he pushes as far as he can into the opposite corner, and his eyes stay trained on the floor.

I keep smiling and chatting with Hakulani and Lola, but, in this moment, I miss the fun Paulie and I used to have—so much. Ever since Hakulani and I started hanging out more, he's been distant, and I know that if I said anything to Malik or Hakulani, they'd probably both tell me the same thing. I wish that there was something I could say to Paulie that would make everything go back to the way it was, but then I remember that despite what's going on with Hakulani, I'm here to win this competition and so is Paulie. We don't have time to be worrying about anything else, right? As the elevator doors open and we walk into the set, all my thoughts are pushed aside. Once again, the set looks completely different. Instead of the six separate kitchens we'd gotten used to, there are now three large stations forming a U shape in front of the judges' table.

"Hello, chefs," Jessica says. "Please step up so we can begin today's elimination round."

"Why does she always sound so cheerful when she talks about one of us going home?" I ask Paulie, who is standing on my right.

He doesn't say anything, but I see his chest move. I'm not sure if he is huffing at me or laughing but doesn't want me to know. Either way, I guess I should be happy I even got a response.

"Today our challenge is all about chance," Jessica says with a devilish smile. "Do you guys feel lucky?"

We respond with a round of "Yeahs" and "Bring it ons."

Jessica reveals a drawstring bag that she was hiding behind her back and gives it a little shake. "In this bag are six tiles. There are two tiles in three different colors."

"Oh no," Lola says, worry in her voice.

The rest of us stiffen because we all know what's coming next.

"That's right, chefs." Jessica pauses for effect. "It's a pairs challenge."

My stomach drops. A pairs challenge. During an elimination. This is a complete game changer from everything we've done so far. The best chef in the show could end up with a bad pairing and the next thing they know, it's time to hang up their jacket and ride into the sunset.

"When I call you up," Jessica continues, "step forward and select a tile." She looks up and down the line. "Dani."

Dani steps up and pulls out an orange tile.

"Please stand in front of the orange kitchen."

Next is Malik, who pulls out a red tile.

Jessica calls Hakulani up, and he pulls out a yellow tile.

Lola is next and pulls out an orange tile.

"Peyton," Jessica says. "You're up next."

I walk toward her, smiling as I do. When I glance over at Hakulani, he holds up his crossed fingers. Reaching my hand in, I feel the smooth surface of the two remaining tiles. I start to pick up one but at the last second change my mind. Closing my eyes, I pull out the tile and then peek. It's yellow.

I swear Hakulani is clapping louder than the rest. When I reach our shared kitchen space, I meet Hakulani's high five and I catch Paulie rolling his eyes, but at least he isn't shooting daggers with his eyes anymore. We watch Paulie go through the formality of picking his tile and he and Malik do a secret handshake I've never seen before.

Once we're settled, Jessica begins to explain the challenge. "In the last Landmark Challenge, you had to build high. In this elimination round, you're going to be tested like a real-life chef, and your creation will need to be not only high, but also stunning and tasty enough to serve as a dinner party centerpiece. Like the last challenge, you must move your structure from the prep station to the presentation stands, but be careful: if your structure topples or doesn't make it to judging, you will automatically be eliminated."

You can practically hear all of us start to sweat and panic a little. These structures aren't only going to be tall, but they're going to be probably much heavier than our last creations. Plus, taste wasn't as big of a component in the Landmark, but now we also have to contend with the palates of Angelica, Billy, and A. J. I glance at Hakulani's arm, and I swear he's flexing his muscles ever so slightly—either that or that's raw tension coursing through his arms.

A PA rolls out a cart with three baskets on it. "But the luck of the draw isn't over. In each of these three baskets is a mystery ingredient. This ingredient must be used in every creation you make." Jessica pauses while we exchange nervous glances.

"In the pantry we have a variety of food-safe support equipment you can use."

Another pause. "Are you ready to see what's in the baskets?"

We cheer, and Hakulani nudges my shoulder. "We got this," he says.

I want to ask Jessica what my advantage is for winning the Landmark Challenge, but I figure she hasn't said anything because it's not time to use it. Still, I was hoping I would get a hint or something.

"All right, chefs. Your time begins . . ."

I really hate the long pauses.

"Now."

Hakulani races to the cart in front of Jessica, grabs the basket in the middle, and hurries back.

"What do we have?" I ask as Hakulani begins to unpack.

Blood oranges, limes, and lemons.

"Citrus," I say, giving the counter an excited pat.

Hakulani reads the card on the inside. "Yep."

"So we need something made with citrus that can be stacked and will be light enough to transfer without breaking our backs."

"Are we baking?" he asks.

"Are you letting me make that call?"

"Why not?" He shrugs. "No one can touch you when it comes to baking."

"I have an idea, but I need to check something." I wave Jessica over and she pivots to come over, the camera crew following behind.

"What's up, Peyton?" she asks.

"Any chance someone in the building has aged eggs laying around?" I whisper.

"I can check, if you want," she says. "Are you making what I think you're making?"

"Maybe," I say slyly.

When she is out of earshot, Hakulani whispers, "Care to clue me in?"

"Macarons," I say. "They're light and quick to make. Since the cookie is pretty basic, all we have to do is color the mix and we have the bulk of the work done. Then the fillings can be one of a hundred citrus combinations."

He nods approvingly. "But we need aged eggs?"

"If at all possible. Now we need to find a way to make a stand that's at least ten tiers tall."

"Ten?" he says, looking a little panicky. "Why are we making ten different macarons?"

"Presentation, baby."

I race to the refrigerator and search through each shelf. "Nothing," I mutter to myself before race walking over to Jessica, shaking my head.

Without a word, she nods and walks over to a PA, who gets on the phone with I don't know who.

Jessica looks over at us and tries to look confident, but I can tell she isn't sure she'll be able to find what I need. How did they have conch on day one, but they don't have aged egg whites now?

The PA hands Jessica the phone and she begins to make our plea to other shows.

"How's this?" Hakulani says, holding up a set of stackable, clear trays. "Ten tiers exactly."

"It's perfect," I say, glancing back at Jessica who has her back to me. It looks like she's still on the phone. "But from the looks of it we better think of a backup plan in case the eggs fall through."

"Maybe we could do tartlets? Same flavor combinations, but we don't need day-old eggs."

I smile. "It's a good idea." And it *is* a good idea. But I feel like, compared with my vision of stacks of macarons, it doesn't feel like enough to really wow the judges. "What if we also think about adding—"

"Well, I have good news and bad news," Jessica interrupts.

"Good news first," Hakulani says quickly.

"We found three dozen egg whites—" she begins and then pauses.

"Just tell us," I say. "Please, I beg you."

"—that are two days old."

"Is that the bad news?" Hakulani asks, looking back and forth between me and Jessica like we are sharing some sort of baker's secret.

I break into a smile. "You are an evil woman," I tell her. "A lifesaver, but evil."

Hakulani still looks confused.

"There's no bad news. I just wanted to mess with you guys." Jessica throws her head back and laughs. "The eggs will be here in ten."

Hakulani looks at me as Jessica walks away. "Okay, we have the eggs. Now what?"

A smile spreads over my face. "Now, we win this challenge," I say as I turn to the oven and set it to preheat at 320 degrees.

It takes a little while for him to get the hang of piping out the dough onto the silicone mats, but eventually Hakulani is churning out the cookies like a pro, and I turn my attention back to the cream filling.

"What do you think?" I ask him, showing him the flavors I've chosen and written on a scrap of paper. "Do I need to add anything?"

"Blood orange," he says quickly. "That's strawberry and orange combined—it's so good."

I have my doubts, but add it to the list.

I continue to pipe out the cookies and put Hakulani on baking duty.

"You have to get them out as soon as the timer goes off," I tell him.

"What are you going to do?"

"Start the icing. You can help when the cookies are done."

In addition to blood orange, we also have lemon, orange cream, lemon-lime, and at least five other combinations that I hope will be enough to really wow the judges. I check the time and give Hakulani a heads-up that we need to wrap up this last batch so we can get to filling and assembling.

Sweat drips down my face as we begin to assemble and place all ten different flavors of macarons on the display. Hakulani is partial to the blood orange one, but I can't decide between the lemon raspberry and lime coconut. As I stack more and more of the macrons onto the display, I begin to worry about how hard it is going to be moving it from the prep area to the presentation stand. Hakulani asks me a question about where the other tray of blood orange macrons are, which pulls me away from my thoughts and helps me focus on the task at hand. I climb onto the counter and begin filling the top tier of the stand with the blueberry lime flavor as the seconds tick down.

"Hurry," Hakulani says, his eyes on the clock and not me.

"Less watching the clock, and more stacking," I mutter at him.

Then, just as I place the final cookie in its spot, the buzzer sounds, and the challenge is over.

"Can you help me down?" I ask, and a moment later his hands are around my waist, bringing me gently to the ground, and I can't help it—there's a warmth that spreads across my cheeks. "Thanks."

"It looks amazing."

It really does. "Do you know why I wanted to do these?" I ask as we move to stand in front of our stations.

"Because they are ridiculously light and fluffy?" he says with a grin.

"Well, yeah, but there's more. I made these for a wedding one time. It was a fairy-tale wedding complete with a horse and pumpkin-shaped carriage."

"Was it orange?"

"You're focusing on the wrong detail," I tell him. "But no, the carriage was white. Anyway, the couple was going to France for their honeymoon so the whole thing had a French theme. I just remember the first time I tasted this cookie, I thought that if people in France could make something this amazing with two-day-old eggs, then maybe there was hope for me."

Hakulani is quiet as the crew sets up for the judging portion.

"What?" I ask, self-conscious, but he doesn't answer right away.

We watch as the camera crew gets shots of the judges for a moment, before Hakulani says softly, "Why do you think the only thing that awaits you is nothing?"

"Well, when I win this show, that will change."

"Yeah, but why do you think that's all you deserve?"

I look at him, aware that at least one of the cameras is recording us. "What do you mean?"

"It's like, yeah, this competition could change anyone's life, but you seem to think it's the only thing that can save you from a miserable future." He pauses. "I don't know you that well, and what I know of you is influenced by the show, but you're a really good chef and an amazing baker. You could do anything you wanted."

"You don't understand," I say with a sigh. "People like me don't get out of our lives without a miracle."

"So be your own miracle."

His words linger between us.

Then Jessica is calling us back together and the disembodied voice tells us to find our marks.

"Now, Peyton," she begins, "as the double winner of the Landmark Challenge, you have earned a huge advantage. For this round, you may have not one but two crew members help you and Hakulani move your tower from the prep to the stand in front of the judges. And you can take away a crew member from another team, if you choose."

"Oh yeah," Hakulani says, but I just grin as big as my mouth will allow. Our structure is by far the tallest, but it's also the lightest, as far as I can tell.

"Do you want to use it?" Jessica asks.

I glance over at Dani and Lola. Both of them look nervous, and they should be. Dani has been horrible to me since we arrived, so she shouldn't be surprised that this is coming. I turn back to Jessica.

"We are absolutely going to use the extra set of hands," I say with a laugh, and Hakulani and I high-five.

"I thought so," Jessica says. "What about the second advantage?"

I look up at Hakulani. "What do you think?"

"It's your call." He shrugs. "But just make sure you're doing it for the right reasons."

I look back at Dani, and I know what I need to do.

"I'm not going to use the second advantage," I tell Jessica, who looks surprised, along with everyone else.

"You're not?" Lola asks.

"If I'm going to win, I want to make sure it's a fair fight. So, no, I'm not going to use it."

"All right," Jessica says. "Then it's time to present your towers."

Hakulani and I are the last to present our display, so while Paulie and Malik are being judged, I have time to think about what Hakulani said.

He's right about how much emphasis I'm putting on the scholarship and winning the competition. I hear Caitlin's voice telling me that even if I got kicked off, I would have fans and other chefs eager to potentially take me under their wing, but I don't know how much stock I can put into anything Caitlin says after seeing what she tried to do with all of us. That said, I can't stop wondering if there's another way for me to become a pastry chef that doesn't start with winning. Then my daydream is interrupted by a deafening crash, and I look over to see Dani and Lola looking down at the floor as their chocolate fondue fountain spreads across the floor. It's like stumbling upon a gruesome crime scene, and over at the judges' table, all three judges are standing, horrified.

"It slipped," Lola says quietly. "I couldn't adjust my grip and it slipped." She looks at Dani, who is still in shock. "I'm so sorry."

Dani shakes her head, but I can tell that she is trying not to cry, because she keeps blinking and looking anywhere but at the chocolate spreading across the floor. "It wasn't your fault," she says, defeated. "I felt it sliding and I tried to compensate. I think I overdid it."

"Cut," the disembodied voice calls. "Let's get this cleaned up."

In an instant, I'm next to Lola and Dani, pulling them into a group hug. Paulie is right beside me saying something comforting to Dani. They may not like each other very much, but this isn't how you want anyone to go out of the competition.

"It's going to be okay," I tell Lola.

She laughs, but there's no humor in the sound. "It's really not."

We stay like that for a moment more until the PAs tell us to move, and then we all sit and watch as the professionals come in and clean up the mess. They try to salvage what they can, but in the end, there's nothing they can save of the once towering flow of chocolate.

To no one's surprise, Dani and Lola are eliminated, and even though Hakulani and I win, it's a bittersweet victory.

As we say our goodbyes, I whisper to Lola, "I am sorry."

She winks at me and smiles, but there are tears in her eyes. "You haven't seen the last of me. This was just the beginning."

I pull her in for a hug and swallow back my tears because I know the cameras are still watching. I knew what this competition meant to her. I knew why she wanted to win—to prove herself just like the rest of us. And now it's over, and she seems almost relieved. As we step away from each other, Hakulani's words come back to me again. *Why do I think that the only thing I deserve is nothing?*

The ride back to the apartment is silent. Malik and

Paulie sit in the rows ahead of us, and Hakulani sits with his arm around my shoulder as he quietly hums one of his favorite songs from back home. If I'm going to believe I deserve more, I can't keep playing this role, especially when I know it's hurting other people.

I lean in close to Hakulani and cover my mic as I whisper in his ear, "We're in the final four."

"I know," he says.

"You know what that means, right?"

He nods. "It's time for Operation Just Friends. So we're breaking up?"

"Soon," I say with a sigh. "But it's been fun."

He nods, but doesn't say anything.

CHAPTER TWENTY-SEVEN

WE HADN'T EXPECTED A DOUBLE ELIMINATION when we left the apartment earlier today, but when we get back, everything from the master bedroom has been cleared away.

"Anyone want to switch rooms?" Malik says as we stare into the room.

"Pass," I say, stepping back into the hall. No one says anything, so I just mumble, "I'm going to make the tea."

"See you on the roof," Hakulani says. "I need to take a shower."

Paulie follows me into the kitchen. "That was cool what you did," he says. "I was actually surprised."

"What are you talking about?" I ask, grabbing the pitcher out of the cabinet and filling a pot to boil water in.

"Not using your advantage on Dani."

"Well, as you can see, I didn't need to use it."

"Yeah," he agrees. "But you didn't know they were going to drop their display."

"True, but my issue was with Dani. Lola didn't need to pay the price for what someone else did."

"I know. Which is why I thought it was cool."

I watch the pot, the bubbles beginning to form on the bottom but none breaking free to the surface. "Thanks."

"So," he begins, "this thing with you and Hakulani."

"What about it?" I ask.

He looks at his hands. "I just didn't realize you were into each other."

"We're having fun," I say.

He nods. "Okay."

Then Malik walks into the kitchen to get the glasses and saves me from having to say anything else.

"From six to four," he says. "That double elimination was rough."

"No kidding," Paulie says. He picks up the pitcher and heads to the freezer for ice.

Malik looks between Paulie and me and shakes his head. "I'm heading to the roof."

Paulie puts the pitcher half-full of ice down next to me. "Need anything else?"

"Nope, you should head upstairs with Malik. I'll bring it up."

"Okay," he says, turning away.

Alone in the kitchen, I take a deep breath. It's hard to believe we've only been here for a week and a half. The studio has kept us so busy that I'm looking forward to a restful weekend. Of course, we still have to get through the next challenge, but that can wait.

I hear Hakulani's footsteps coming down the hall. "Hey," he says, coming around the counter to stand next to me.

"Final four," I say.

"When?" he asks, giving me a knowing look.

I grab a piece of paper and write, "After the next Landmark Challenge. Before the elimination."

He nods in agreement.

I hand him the pitcher. "Make yourself useful."

"Yes ma'am," he says, leading the way.

Once we're upstairs, Hakulani fills a glass and hands it to me before filling one for himself and passing it on.

Once we all have a glass, Malik begins the toast. "To Lola and Dani."

I raise my glass. "It's no secret that Dani and I weren't friends. Still, I have to admit, the girl knows her way around a kitchen."

"And Lola," Paulie adds, "is going to reform the buffet. Ten bucks says she'll have a chain before we're twenty-five."

I laugh, but mostly because it's true.

Hakulani raises his glass. "I have no doubt the culinary world is going to welcome them both with open arms."

We spend the rest of the night around the firepit, reminiscing about everything we've done since we got here. I don't know what it is about being in the final four, but it screams time to reflect.

"Do you think you're a better chef than when you came here?" Malik asks.

I think about his question for a moment. "I think I've challenged myself to do things I wouldn't have thought of before coming here. They haven't always turned out the way I wanted them to, but I've learned a lot."

"I would agree with that," Paulie says. "But I think the people I've learned the most from are you guys. Like, we're supposed to be each other's competition, right? But yet everyone has been willing to share tips and secrets."

"Like how to make fancy French cookies with two old eggs," Hakulani says, raising his glass in my direction.

"Exactly," Paulie says, smiling. "I didn't know that."

"Okay," I say, "I'm going to bed. This lovefest is getting to be too much."

"It wouldn't be a lovefest if Dani were still here," Malik reminds me.

"True."

Everyone stands to follow me downstairs, but I stop them. "I didn't mean to break up the party."

Malik picks up the pitcher. "It makes sense to go to bed. Who knows what they're going to throw at us tomorrow."

"Good point," I say. "Okay. You may follow me."

When we get back to the kitchen, there is an envelope on the island.

"Was that here before?" Hakulani says.

"I was the last to leave the room and it wasn't there," I say. "The PA elves have struck again."

"Open it," Paulie says, nudging Malik.

Malik reaches for the envelope and pulls out a card with four prepaid credit cards, four subway tickets, and a map titled *Food Trucks of New York City*.

"It says, 'Take tomorrow off and explore the to-go foodie world on us. The camera crew will be ready to follow you around at noon. Have fun, but don't go crazy. Love, Jessica.'"

A slow smile spreads across my face. "Does that mean that we get the run of the town tomorrow?"

"No challenge?" Hakulani says. "Are they serious?"

"How much is on the cards?" Paulie asks, picking up the credit card on top and flipping it over. "This says one hundred dollars."

"We each get a hundred dollars to eat for one day."

"This is going to be a blast," Hakulani says. "And, with that, I'm going to bed."

"Need to rest up?" Paulie says.

"Absolutely."

We scatter without another word. As excited as I am, I don't know how long it takes me to fall asleep, but if I had to guess, I would say it could be measured in less than ten seconds.

The next morning, I wake up and stretch. Not having to get up early to get to the studio is a luxury, and one I'm not willing to give up so easily. I check the clock and realize that even though we don't have a challenge today, it's probably a good idea to get up and get ready.

After showering and throwing on some jeans and a top, I head to the living room, where the guys are playing pool again. "You guys are always playing. I bet you could walk into a bar and run a hustle."

All three turn to me with a look that says whatever I just said is ridiculous.

"Never mind."

A knock at the door lets us know that the camera crew is here, and just like that we are ready to roll.

"Who has the cards?" I ask, and Hakulani stands and hands a set to me.

"I'm so excited that I'm finally going to ride the subway."

There are two great things about an around-the-world food tour of street carts and food trucks. One, you don't have to agree with your friends on what to try next; and two, since you're walking the entire time, you burn off the food almost as fast as you consume it. Okay, yes, the drawback is that sometimes the spices from India and Thailand don't always play well with each other, but by the time we return to our designated meeting point, I'm moments away from falling into a food coma.

Another thing I learn is that there are a million different food trucks in the city. Some we find through the map; others just appear on our path like magic.

"How do you think they're going to spin this into a challenge?" Malik asks.

"No idea," Paulie says, slouching down in the seat. "But you know it's something about a food truck."

"Obviously," Malik says. "But I mean, what are they going to have us do?"

The conversation turns to possibilities, and I try to listen, but honestly, what I need now is a nap. Between the heat of the city and the superhuman amount of food I've just consumed, I have a hard time staying awake on the subway, until Hakulani stands and offers me his hand to stand up.

Then we lead the way onto the platform and up the stairs to the street.

As we approach the apartment building, the camera crew still in tow, I remember the first day I entered this building. It feels like a lifetime ago, even though it's only been a couple weeks. In other news, I've almost started to forget about the cameras, but not completely.

"Anyone up for a roof night?" Malik says.

I shake my head. "If I don't get off my feet and under my covers, I'm going to die."

"Okay, grandma," Paulie says.

"Joke's on you. My Grams never went to bed this early. Night."

Before falling asleep, I realize this show is turning me into a baby. All I do is eat, sleep, and feel like crying. And I'm okay with that tonight.

CHAPTER TWENTY-EIGHT

MORNING COMES TOO SOON, AND BEFORE I KNOW it, we are back in the studio with Jessica smiling at us.

The disembodied voice tells us to line up, and we move quickly.

Jessica smiles at us. "This is going to be a fun Landmark Challenge. Yesterday, you spent the day roaming the streets of New York looking for the best food trucks the city has to offer. I hope you took notes, because you're going to need them."

A chorus of affirmative greetings rings out, and she beams. "That's good because now you're going to take those flavors and combinations and work in teams of two to plan a menu for your own food truck."

We whoop and holler, but deep down I'm nervous. I mean, I love a good food truck as much as the next person, but we don't know the first thing about running one.

As if reading my mind, Jessica adds, "And to make sure you don't violate any health codes, I would like to introduce your coaches, Eddie and Oscar Brown, co-owners of Gourmet Grub to Go, New York's hottest food truck franchise."

"We stopped by your truck on Church and Fulton," Hakulani says quickly.

Eddie nods with approval but says nothing.

Jessica continues. "Hopefully you were all inspired by the amazing cuisine you can find all around the city because you are . . ."

I look at Hakulani. I'm pretty sure I know what she's going to say.

". . . going to run a food truck of your very own for one whole day. The winner of this Landmark Challenge will be determined by your total sales at the end of the day."

"No judges?" I say in surprise.

Jessica shakes her head. "Not unless you count the entire population of the city."

"I'd rather not," Paulie says.

"And since you worked so well together in the previous challenge, that's your team for today."

I look up at Hakulani and grin while Malik and Paulie do their special handshake.

"With the help of our guest chefs, you'll set the theme, the menu, and the prices. We'll provide the location and truck."

I try to look excited but have to force the smile on my face. As much as I loved eating my way through the city via food truck, I also remember the long lines and the hot, cramped kitchens.

Jessica continues. "You have one hour to come up with a concept so our design team can get to work on your truck graphics. Then you'll have three hours to come up with your menu and get your shopping list together."

"And then?" Malik asks.

Jessica smiles. "I'd get to work if I were you," she tells us as the clock begins to count down one hour.

Hakulani and I sprint to the back of the room, leaving Paulie and Malik behind. On my prep station there's a giant pad of paper and a package of colored markers. I spin the pad around and dump the markers out.

"Okay, concept. What are we thinking?" I ask, pulling the cap off the brown marker and getting ready to write. We look at each other, but no one says anything. It's like we have a collective brain freeze.

"We need something unique," Hakulani says. "When we were out yesterday, was there any type of food that you thought was missing?"

"Hot dogs?" I say with a straight face, and we both burst out laughing.

"There wasn't a Spam truck," Hakulani says. I can't tell if he's joking or not, so I write the idea down.

"I can honestly say there was not a Spam menu out there."

"I was kidding," he says. "We can't serve Spam. Maybe in Hawaii where it's more common, but I don't think it's going to have enough of a fan base in New York City."

"Probably not," I agree, before breaking out into a big grin. "But a Hawaiian food truck could be a hit."

Hakulani nods. "I think that would be awesome."

"It sounds like we might have a concept." I cross out "Spam" and write "Hawaiian food" on our pad of paper and gesture for our guest chef to join us. Jessica must notice because she follows Oscar as he makes his way over to us. I already see Eddie joking with Paulie and Malik.

"Do you guys need help with a concept?" he asks.

"I think we might have one," Hakulani says.

Oscar's lips purse slightly and he nods his head as we tell him about our idea.

"What kind of food would you serve?" he asks.

We look at each other. "I thought we just needed a concept to start," I say.

Oscar nods again. "True, but you have to make sure you have enough to make a menu. You need to keep it simple but still be competitive. I'm not saying you need the entire menu hammered down now, but enough to know you've got a good plan."

I look at Hakulani. "You're the resident expert. What would you recommend?"

"Maybe loco moco?"

"What's that?" I ask.

"A ground beef patty on a bed of sticky rice with brown gravy and either a sunny-side-up or fried egg on top."

"Okay," Oscar says. "That sounds like a solid dish that doesn't require a ton of ingredients, which is good when you're working in a small space, but that's a dish that is really only going to appeal to your more adventurous eaters. Since you're making rice, I would suggest thinking of some other toppers."

"We could do mochiko," Hakulani says. "It's our version of fried chicken."

"Good," Oscar says. "What else?

"Garlic shrimp?" I suggest. "Grilled or fried."

"Maybe you could upsell by offering fried rice instead of regular," Oscar suggests.

"And if they don't want it in a bowl, they could opt for tacos," I suggest. "We could add a slaw taco option, as well, for the vegetarians."

Oscar nods. "I think it sounds like a solid concept. Draw up the plans for the truck so they can get to work on it, and I'll be back to check on you when you're ready to work out your menu."

Then we spend the next forty-five minutes chatting, debating, and sketching out the dream version of what we want our truck to look like.

"Do you think they could attach a sign at the top that looks like multiple waves?" Hakulani asks, pointing at the top of my sketch.

"We can ask," I say, making a note and adding waves to the top of the truck. "Like this?"

He nods. "Yeah. By the way, what are we going to call it?"

"Island something," I suggest. "Like Island Breeze?"

"What about Ono Grindz?" Hakulani says. "It translates to 'delicious food.'"

"I think it's perfect." I lean down and fill in the space we left for the name on the side of the truck. "Our menu board can be a chalkboard square and I can do the lettering in the morning."

Oscar joins us and peeks over my shoulder. "Not bad," he says approvingly. "Hopefully they can get a turquoise truck."

"We listed yellow or black as other options." I point out.

"It's going to get really hot in a black truck," he says.

"Yeah, but it will really make the graphics pop," Hakulani counters.

"That's true," Oscar agrees. "Well, only one way to find out, so you better go turn that in."

I roll up the sheet and leave the guys to start brainstorming the menu and listing the different ingredients. On my way up to the judges' table I run into Paulie.

"How's it going?"

He shrugs. "Good. We're going for a man's man menu."

"Sounds very masculine."

"Better go," he says. "I need to make plans to kick your butt tomorrow."

"Like that's going to happen." I hip check him gently as I push by him.

When I get back to our station, Hakulani is starting on the shopping list.

"How's it going?"

"Well, we've got good news, and we've got not-so-great news," he says.

"Okay. What's the good news?" I say, looking over the recipes and ingredients.

"Oscar is going to be on the truck tomorrow helping us out," Hakulani says as he grabs a marker and adds another thing to the list.

"That's not good news," I say. "That's great news. So, what's the bad news?"

"To make the best fried rice, you need to use day-old rice."

"Oh," I say, then it sinks in. "Oh, no."

He nods. "Yep, and Oscar thinks we should each make the dishes at least once so that we're able to cover for each other tomorrow."

I sigh and run a hand over my face. "Do we have all the supplies?"

He looks at the well-stocked pantry and fridge. "Yeah, I think we're going to be okay. Jessica said if we get a list for today she can send one of the PAs out to get what we need."

"Well, put rice on that list."

"Fifty pounds?"

"That's a lot of rice."

"Better to have extra than not enough."

I nod. "Why not. Rice is pretty cheap."

Hakulani and I search the pantry for all the ingredients we need.

"We should probably get the shopping list pulled together for the PAs," I say, waving Oscar over.

He's more than happy to help us estimate how much food we need to order for tomorrow.

"Oscar, you are a lifesaver," I say. "I don't know if we would have been able to figure that out on our own."

"I think we still need something sweet," I say, stirring the brown gravy for the loco moco.

A grin spreads over Hakulani's face as he grabs the supply list just as a PA is about to pick it up.

"One sec," he says, scribbling something down. "There you go," he says, handing the list back to her.

"Um, Hakulani," I say, looking him directly in the eye, "you want to clue me in?"

He grins. "There's only one Hawaiian treat for a hot summer afternoon. Shaved ice."

"Like a snow cone?" I ask.

Hakulani shoots me a glare that could melt one of his shaved ice cups. "You'll see. Once you've had a real shaved ice, snow cones will be like eating gravel." He looks over our station and then calls over his shoulder, "Hey, Oscar, you ready to have your taste buds blown? Because Ono Grindz is open and we are ready to serve."

CHAPTER TWENTY-NINE

AFTER WE FINISH IN THE KITCHEN, THE FOUR OF us, along with Oscar, Eddie, and Jessica, head off to check out the trucks we're going to be using tomorrow. As our bus pulls up to the location, I tap Hakulani on the arm and point excitedly out the window. "They got a turquoise one," I say. "If they can put a wave on the top, it's going to look so cool."

Next to our truck is a black one with orange, yellow, and red flames painted on it.

Paulie leans forward. "I told you it was badass."

I look closer. "Is that a grill mounted on the back?"

Malik laughs. "Yup."

Hakulani looks at them. "Are you doing ribs?"

"And pasta," Paulie says, looking offended. "We're calling it, 'Stick to Your Ribs.'" He makes an arch with his hands to emphasize each word.

Jessica laughs as the bus pulls to a stop. "Let's go see your trucks."

The guys race off the bus, jostling to be the first on the ground. When Hakulani sees I'm not behind them, he waits for me to catch up.

"Are you excited?" I ask, thinking back to his conversation with his girlfriend. I lean closer to him so Oscar doesn't hear me. "I thought you hated the idea of working on a food truck."

"I don't know. I guess there are worse things a person could do. You get to make your own hours, your menu."

"That's true," I agree.

Oscar unlocks the back of the truck and motions for us to step up. Everything is shiny and new, from the smooth grill-top to the pristine cutting boards. "This is amazing," I say.

"I promise you, not all trucks look this nice—especially after a couple months on the street."

Hakulani stands, completely stunned, while I check out the cabinets and the small fridge. "Too bad we don't have the food yet," I say. "We could start prepping."

Jessica pops her head in. "Are you guys already talking about getting to work?" she asks.

Hakulani nods. "No food."

She nods. "And the design team still needs to finish the outside."

"That sucks," Hakulani says.

"Plus side," Jessica says, "we found the shaved ice machine you wanted."

"That will make things go much easier," he says, turning to me. "There's a little trick to making the perfect dome, but this machine will help make it a lot easier, since neither of us have done it before."

"Will someone be able to bring the ice tomorrow? We'll need several blocks."

She nods. "I think you'll find everything you need when you arrive."

"Don't forget the rice," Hakulani reminds her.

"We've got it covered," she assures him.

Paulie and Malik pop their heads in. "Looks a lot like ours," Malik says.

"Inside, they're twins," Eddie says. He stands back and looks between the two trucks. "But you couldn't tell from the outside."

"Now that you've seen where you're going to work tomorrow, we should probably head back to the apartment. You've got an early morning tomorrow," Jessica says.

"How early?" I ask, knowing I don't want to hear the answer.

"Five-thirty," Oscar says, taking a step back.

"In the morning?" I ask, sure that he must be messing with me.

"Hey, be glad the network has filming permits and we can park the truck for you, or it would be even earlier."

"And you would have at least three or four parking tickets, too," Eddie chimes in.

"Fine. But I won't be cheerful," I assure Oscar.

"Noted."

We load back onto the bus for the drive back to the apartment. The driver makes a detour so Jessica can show us where our trucks will be parked the next day.

The next morning, the bus drops us off around the corner from where our food trucks are supposed to be parked. "Why did Jessica have the driver let us off here?" I ask through a yawn.

"So we can get your reaction to the finished designs," she says, coming around the corner. The woman needs a bell around her neck so I know where she is.

Eddie and Oscar are with her. "Not to mention you need the time to stock your truck and get used to it. This isn't like your stations back at the studio. You need to go inside and decide who is going to do what and practice moving around in there with each other." Oscar grins. "Working in a truck like this is a little like a dance."

"Exactly. Now, let's go see your trucks."

The truck closest to the corner is Stick to Your Ribs.

"I feel like you need a leather jacket and a Harley to eat here," I say. "Checking out the menu, I'm impressed with what they've come up with."

I nervously look at Hakulani, but he shakes his head. "Not even a little worried. We're going to crush them."

Next to the black truck is our baby, complete with the

wave on top. Jessica motions for us to come over. "The design team wanted to give you a little wow factor, so if you stand over here . . ." she says, motioning for us to come over. When I do, I feel the slightest mist of cool water.

"No way," I say. "There's a mister up there?"

She nods. "And hidden speakers that will play all the Hawaiian music you want."

"Hey," Paulie says. "We don't have music."

I spin around on him. "You have an outdoor grill," I remind him.

"Yes, and I really need to get it started so I can have something to serve."

Paulie heads for his truck. "Gotta get started on Grannie's gravy." He gives us a hang ten sign before disappearing up the steps.

"Let's get started," Oscar says, stepping out of our way so we have more room to check out the kitchen, move a few things, and start figuring out how to divide up the responsibilities.

"What happens when we run out of a dish?" I ask out the window to Oscar. "There's no way to run and make more."

"When you run out, you run out," he shrugs. "You'll have a lot of white rice, which is a big component of most of your dishes."

With that bit of advice and a quick glance at the truck, we begin reviewing the menu and come up with a plan for prepping everything once the food arrives.

"Now might be a good time for me to write out the menu on the front of the truck, too," I say, grabbing some chalk stashed in a drawer. When I get outside, I pull out the price list I came up with when Oscar was helping us with our supply list.

Oscar watches as I write out the menu and says, "You'll need to make sure you cover your food costs and labor at least. Otherwise, you could be in for a surprise at the end of the day."

"Are any of them under- or overpriced?" I ask, stepping back to check my work.

Oscar moves to stand next to me. "I would charge for the add-ons for the shaved ice, but other than that, it looks pretty good. Because you used chalk, you can always adjust the prices if something isn't selling. Call it a special and mark it down; the goal is to sell out of everything by the end of the day."

Half an hour later, there's a knock on the truck door, and when Hakulani swings it open, a PA instantly begins placing boxes of produce on the floor. Without hesitating, Oscar and I form an assembly line and begin to pile the supplies onto the counters as Hakulani starts to unpack them. It takes almost an hour, but we manage to find a place for everything.

"Is there a fan?" I ask, lifting my hair up and fanning the back of my neck. After unloading everything and turning on the stove and the fryers so we can start cooking, it is starting to get hot in the truck—and it's not even seven o'clock yet.

"Just the one in the front of the truck," Oscar says, before pointing to the warming oven. "You know how to work one of these?"

I nod. "Water in the bottom and turn it on?"

"Yep."

After turning on the warmers, I swing behind Hakulani as he begins to mix up the batter for the breaded shrimp, while Oscar squeezes against the counter where he is chopping cabbage for the slaw. "Someone needs to be the point," I say. "I don't know what to do next."

Suddenly Hakulani stops mixing. "Where's the rice?" Hakulani and I say at the same time.

We were so busy getting everything unpacked and set up that we forgot to check to make sure our day-old rice was here.

"Did they bring it from the studio?" I ask. "I told them before we left last night to make sure it got brought over. It was on the list."

"I don't see it," Hakulani says.

I lean out of the truck and scan the street. "Where's a PA when you need one?" I mutter. Half a block away is a camera crew, and I jump out of the truck and race toward them.

They see me coming and immediately grab their cameras.

"Do you know where the PAs are?" I ask, slightly winded.

The sound guy nods before muttering something into his walkie.

"Be right there," the speaker crackles.

A minute later, the PA who had dropped off our food appears. "What do you need, Peyton?"

I'm kind of surprised she even knows my name. Normally the PAs just bark at us and usher us from one place to another, so I figured they just knew us as a collective. "We stayed at the studio last night making a bunch of white rice to use today. I left instructions for it to be brought here this morning."

At the words *left instructions*, the PA's eyebrows raise slightly. I guess they don't like having the tables being turned on them.

"I'll check on it," she says, but she doesn't reach for her phone. She looks at me for a moment more, and when I don't walk away, she asks, "Was there something else?"

"Um, yeah, could you check on it now? Maybe I can come with you to get it?"

Her eye twitches like she wants to roll her eyes at me, but to her credit, she refrains. "Just let me check on it, okay?" She pulls her phone out and turns her back toward me. Did I interrupt her bubble tea break or something?

She is talking in a hushed tone, but I think I hear her ask, "When can you get here?" And it might have been followed by, "She's not going away until I tell her something," but I can't be sure.

After she hangs up the PA pauses for a moment before spinning around and flashing me a wide smile. "It's still in the cooler at the network. They're getting it right now, and it should be here in half an hour."

"Thank you," I say curtly. The show employs a lot of production assistants, and some of them are way more chill than others; she's somewhere in the middle.

As I jog back to our truck, I manage to avoid running into Paulie as he steps down onto the sidewalk. He catches me and swings me around like we'd been rehearsing the move all our lives.

"Hey," I say.

"Hey yourself."

There is a quiet moment when he looks at me and I feel my cheeks grow warm before he lets me go. I look at the truck to give myself a second to cool off. "It smells so good," I say. "I wish we would have thought to grill outside. When we're cooking, the inside of that truck is a bazillion degrees."

"That is hot," he says.

"No fraternizing with the enemy," Malik calls out.

I give him a wave. "Get back to the grill."

"I better go," Paulie says, turning back toward the truck, but not without giving me a quick smile.

"We've got tough competition next door," I announce when I get back to the kitchen. "The smell is going to bring people in like crazy."

Hakulani flips a switch and the sound of Hawaiian music

and surf begins to play through the outdoor speakers. "And then we will distract them with visions of a white sand beach." He puts his hand out for me to take. "Dance with me."

"We need to prep," I argue, my earlier confidence fading with each second that the challenge grows closer.

"We can prep in a minute," he says, tugging me by the hand and leading me down to the sidewalk.

"I'm going to teach you the hula step."

"That's what it's called?" I ask.

He shakes his head. "It's actually called Kalakaua. Now, start by swaying your hips from side to side."

"Are we really doing this? On the sidewalk in New York City?"

"I'll teach you one step and one arm movement. You never know what you might have to do to drum up business."

I look for any sign that he's joking, but there's none. "Fine."

"All right, now we're going to start with our right foot. You're going to step forward, sway your hips, step back together. Tap your foot."

I do as he instructs, feeling about as elegant as a baby giraffe.

"Good. Now repeat with your left foot." We repeat the step over and over. "Make sure you sway with each step."

I try to do what he says and am rewarded with applause from Paulie and Malik.

"I can't," I say, pulling away when Hakulani reaches for me.

"Thank you. But I'm probably better at watching dance than doing it."

"You worry too much," he says.

"What?"

"About what other people think of you. You worry about that a lot."

I start to argue that he's wrong, but I don't get a chance.

"Okay, okay, back to work," Oscar says out of the window. "Did you find the rice?"

"It'll be here in thirty minutes or less."

As I walk back toward the truck, Hakulani grabs my hand. "I'm sorry. I shouldn't have made you do that, and I really shouldn't have said what I said."

"It's fine," I say.

He gives me a hard look. "You don't mean that."

"Maybe not yet, but I will soon. Let's just get to work."

He nods. "Right."

As soon as we get inside, Hakulani and I busy ourselves with preparations.

"Rice is here," a voice calls out from the back. Jessica directs a PA to load it in. "Where do you want it?"

Hakulani moves some bowls I just washed out of the way. "Here. I need to get it started. Thanks, Jessica."

She nods.

Other than the sound of the wooden spoon against the flat

top grill and knives on the cutting board, the truck is quiet. With all the activity and appliances going, it starts to really warm up. Oscar jokes that we should be glad we didn't get the black truck and assures us that this is normal. I push open the windows at the front of the truck for extra ventilation. I would personally like to sit under the mister, but Hakulani reminds me that it's for paying customers.

As we work together to get the dishes prepared, every step we make becomes a part of some improvised dance. Shifting here, stretching there, doing everything we can to stay out of each other's way as we prepare to open at eleven. In a short time, the tension between us dissipates and I start smiling.

Just before we're supposed to start taking orders, I glance out the window and see the line outside the truck. And not just any line. A line all the way down the sidewalk and around the corner. I would brag about it, but the line next door at the other truck is about the same length.

"There's a hungry crowd out here," I say, turning back with a look of panic in my eyes.

"Are we ready?" Oscar asks.

We all look at each other.

"Yeah," I say. "I think we are."

"Then get ready to rock and roll," Oscar says.

I give Hakulani and Oscar each a high five and then grab the order pad to take the first order.

"Loco moco with sticky rice and mochiko with fried," I call over my shoulder as I rip off the ticket and place it on the order strip by Oscar, who starts filling paper boats with rice. I grab two cups and quickly fill them with shaved ice, then pour green apple syrup over one, spritzing it with sour spray, and flavor one with tiger's blood, a combination of strawberry and watermelon with just a hint of coconut and blue raspberry topped with sweetened condensed milk. After that moment, everything seems to pass as a blur of tickets, rice, shaved ice, and money exchanging hands.

At some point during the day, I remember Jessica stopping by to see how we were doing, but the lines were so long and I was so focused on making sure that I kept an eye on the fryer, that I barely had time to say anything. By the time we sell out of everything, I feel like I can say: I make a mean Hawaiian shaved ice.

"That was intense," I say, looking at Oscar while we wipe down the inside of the truck. "You do this every day?"

"Six days a week. We take Sunday off unless we're working a festival or private event."

"What about nights?" I ask. "I bet you could make a killing when the clubs close."

"Sure," he says with a shrug and a laugh, "but then I would have to claim the truck as my permanent residence. Running a food truck is a lot of fun. It's a lot of work, too. You have to find the balance in your life. Work too much, you ignore friends and family, and then you wake up and no one's around but your staff."

Hakulani nods. "I get that. I don't know what I would do if I had to give up surfing because I was running some big kitchen somewhere."

I hand everyone a shaved ice as we continue to wipe down the truck, preparing it for the next person who'll get a chance to own a piece of their dream.

CHAPTER THIRTY

I CLOSE THE DOOR, LOCKING IT BEFORE HAND-ing the keys over to Oscar. "Thank you so much," I say, smiling at him. "I had more fun cooking today than I have in a while."

"Yeah," Hakulani adds. "I know it was a competition, but it didn't feel like it."

"You two are a good team," Oscar says, pushing the key into his pocket. "Who knows. Someday you might give us a run for our money."

"Don't count on it," I say. "It was fun, but getting up that early every morning? No thank you."

Hakulani puts out his hand to shake Oscar's as a PA arrives to corral us to the sidewalk, where Jessica is waiting to announce the winners.

"Good afternoon," Jessica says to everyone as the cameras set up around us. "Our filming permit is about to expire, so we're going to have to make this quick."

"What?" Malik says. "You mean you *won't* be putting us through painful suspenseful pauses?"

"If I didn't do that, you would think I didn't care."

"Yeah," I say, "but why are they so long?"

"It's a rite of passage. My host did it to me, and now I do it to you. And if you're lucky, the network will ask you to come back and host, and then you can do it to a future round of aspiring chefs."

"That's not a rite of passage," Paulie says. "That's hazing, and forty-four states have laws against it."

The camera guy clears his throat and spins the camera toward Jessica.

"Just for that, I might make you wait. And wait. And wait," she says, staring into the camera. I'm not sure if she's talking to us or the camera guy, but the red light turns on before anyone has a chance to ask for clarification.

"Congratulations," Jessica says. "You survived a hectic day running a food truck. Unlike our previous challenges, the winner of this competition will be determined by your sales totals and your tip jars."

Hakulani and I grin at each other. Sure, Paulie and Malik had a good turnout, but we actually ran out of food. And while I didn't have a lot of time to watch the tip jar, it was pretty full by the end of the day.

"All of your profit and tips will be combined and donated to

Feeding America, a nonprofit organization that supports food banks, soup kitchens, shelters, and other community organizations," Jessica says, her face bright and excited.

We all clap and cheer.

Oscar and Eddie move in to stand on either side of her, each carrying an envelope. The cheering grows louder as our mentors take their places.

Jessica grins and waits for us to settle down. "I was going to say let's give a hand to Oscar and Eddie, but I think you just did." Turning to Eddie, she says, "I believe you have the final profit for Malik and Paulie."

He nods and holds it up. "First, I want to say working with these young men was a lot of fun. They both work hard and have great ideas. I would trust either of them with my truck."

Paulie laughs and claps his hands together. "Let me know when you need a vacation."

I smile but keep my eyes on the envelope.

Eddie opens the flap and pulls out the card inside. "Not bad," he says before spinning it around. "One thousand eighty-six dollars and forty-five cents."

Paulie and Malik slap hands.

"Yes!" Malik says.

Paulie shoots a grin at us. "Beat that," he says.

"No problem," Hakulani says, but he's lacking his normal confidence.

"That's a lot of money for Feeding America," Jessica says. "Great job." She turns to Oscar. "And what about your team?"

Oscar looks at us and nods his head. "I want to echo my brother. Working with these aspiring chefs reminded me why I love what I do. Watching them brainstorm the menu and concept was a lot of fun. But," he says, holding up the envelope and shaking it slightly, "the proof is in the pudding."

As he lifts the envelope flap and slides the card out, my stomach flip-flops. I really want to win this competition, but Malik and Paulie made a lot of money. I don't know if we even came close.

"Four hundred thirty-two dollars and fifty cents," Oscar says, and my heart drops.

No way did we make so little.

"I'm sorry," Oscar says, hope reviving in my chest. "That would be one thousand four hundred thirty-two dollars and fifty cents."

I jump up as Hakulani turns to pick me up in a hug, and the top of my head connects with his chin. Which makes both of us laugh.

Jessica giggles and waits for us to settle down. "Congratulations, you have won the challenge and the all-important advantage during the next challenge."

Hakulani side hugs me. "This is awesome."

"Right," I say. "I really needed a win."

To their credit, Paulie and Malik come over to congratulate us.

"Nice job," Paulie says, giving me a hug.

"Thanks. You guys were serious competition."

Jessica interjects. "You both did a great job, and you raised over twenty-five hundred dollars for Feeding America."

Everyone applauds and cheers again.

"But your next competition is a very important elimination. After that, we will be down to the final three."

Her words hit us all hard, and all the joy of winning the competition is sucked out of the room.

I adore all these guys and don't want anyone to leave, but this is a competition, and someone has to go. These thoughts occupy my mind as I return to my dressing room to drop off my chef's uniform and change into my clothes. When I exit, Hakulani is waiting for me, and we fall in step with each other as we make our way to the bus. As we move down the hall, he reaches out and takes my hand. It's something he's been doing all week, but today it feels wrong.

"You okay?" he asks as we wait for the elevator. It dawns on me that we are alone, without cameras, for the first time since the confessional room.

I nod, but I'm not okay. "Hakulani, we need to talk about our deal," I say.

He looks straight ahead. "Okay."

I can't read his expression, but I'm not sure he's going to like what I've got to say. "We got each other to the final four, but we really shouldn't drag it out any longer."

"You're right," he says.

I nod. "Anyways, we've been faux dating for a week. That's a third of the competition, so when you think of it like that, it's been a long time."

"And you're sure it's today? There's no time for us to have second thoughts and change our minds."

"No, I'm not sure; but it's the right thing."

"Okay. So, tonight?"

I nod as the elevator opens. He leads me in before dropping my hand to push the button. He doesn't reach for it again. "For this to work, we're going to have to make a good show for the cameras."

"Yep."

I lean against the wall. "But I don't want it to be ugly. I want us to still be friends on and off the show, without people talking."

He nods.

"We'll order food in, take it to the roof, start talking about what we want to do with our lives, and come to the realization that we just want different things. And while this has been fun—"

"It's time for the fun to come to an end?"

"Exactly."

"It has been fun," he says. "Getting to know you. The real you," he adds pointedly.

"I can say the same about you," I answer.

As the doors open, he takes my hand. "For old times' sake?"

"Why not."

We climb aboard the bus and sit down next to each other.

"It's weird," I say, letting go of his hand and looking up at the roof.

"What is?"

"Soon there will only be three."

"You and me and one of these other dudes," he says with a grin. "You can't get rid of me that easily."

The drive back to the apartment is quiet. Everyone is lost in their own thoughts. For me, it's how lucky I am to have made it this far. And that with Dani being gone, I can finally enjoy being in the apartment. I don't have to worry about her digs.

Traffic is unusually light as we head home, and it doesn't take long for us to get there. As the elevator ascends, Malik says, "I think I'm going to order something for dinner and crash early."

"Same," Paulie says. "Not all of us have an advantage. Going to need all the energy I can get for tomorrow."

"Where do you want to order from?" I ask.

Paulie looks thoughtful. "What about the deli next door?"

I laugh. "You know, even though we've had a chance to eat—and make—some amazing food, a deli sandwich sounds perfect."

"Right," Paulie says. "I could go for a pastrami and corned beef."

The doors open and I step out first. "Race you to the menu." I don't wait for him to respond as I run down the hall to the kitchen.

"Cheater," Paulie says as he follows, Hakulani and Malik right behind him.

I pull out the menu, and after we study it, it's decided that we're going to get a sandwich platter with enough slices of corned beef, pastrami, and brisket to feed us and have left-overs for tomorrow.

"Don't forget the steak fries," I say as I head to my room and the bathroom for a quick shower. Hakulani and I might be about to break up, but that doesn't mean I want to look like I just finished working in a food truck when we do.

I jump in the shower and let the water wash away all the sweat and smells of the day. Working on the truck was a lot of fun, but I have rice in places I can't even explain. Once I'm clean and dressed, I head back to the kitchen, where a PA is unloading our order.

"You didn't have to do that," I say as she lays out the meat on several plates.

"It's the job," she says, and I think it's the first time I've had what could possibly pass as a conversation with a PA since running into the door on day one.

"Well, thank you," I say. "You guys have been awesome taking care of us over the last few weeks."

She nods. "You're welcome. Looks like you're all set."

"Thanks again."

She nods and disappears down the hall and onto the elevator.

"Food!" I call out, and I can hear the guys moving in their rooms. A moment later, they swarm the island, loading their bread up with meats and cheese and veggies.

"Thanks for setting this up," Malik says.

"Wasn't me," I say, stepping in to grab some brisket. "One of the PA elves was in here setting up."

"You mean you actually saw one of them?" Paulie asks. "Do they look like the studio PAs?"

"You mean like college students? Yes. Just like that. It's uncanny."

Hakulani piles some steak fries on his plate and heads up to the roof.

"You better go," Paulie says. He's sounds like he's joking, but the words land flat.

He doesn't wait for me to answer before he heads back to his room.

"I know Dani was the bringer of drama," Malik says, laughing mostly to himself. "But you have these two boys fighting over you, and they don't even know it."

"It's not like that."

"It's exactly like that," he says and follows Paulie down the hall.

"If you only knew," I mutter as I squirt ketchup on my fries and head up to the roof.

Hakulani already has the firepit on, creating the perfect mood for our breakup. I have to hand it to him. He has a way of making us look good without a lot of work on my part.

I set my plate down. "Hey," I say, and I'm startled by how nervous I am. While I haven't gotten used to the cameras being around, they don't normally make me nervous anymore. But tonight is different.

"Hey," Hakulani says back, and his voice is low and gravelly. He tries to cover by reaching for his drink and taking a gulp.

"This was a great idea," I say, holding up my sandwich. "I don't think I've ever put this much meat on a sandwich before."

If this is how our breakup is going to go, we're in a lot of trouble.

"Can you believe we've got less than a week left?" I ask, trying to get the ball rolling.

He nods. "It's actually been on my mind a lot," he says, not looking me in the eye.

Red flags begin to signal that this feels like I'm being set up to be the dumpee. I calm myself before answering.

"Because we're so close to the end?"

He nods. "And so close to going home. One way or another."

I take a bite and chew thoughtfully. I swallow, take a sip of water, and ask, "If you win, hypothetically—because obviously I plan on winning—"

He laughs and his smile is more natural now. "I'm not so sure about that, but go on."

"If you win, where are you going to study?"

He takes his time answering. "Well, I don't know if I could handle living on the mainland forever. But at least LA is kinda close to home."

I pause, my sandwich halfway up to my mouth. "You wouldn't stay in New York?"

He shakes his head. "It's nice enough," he says, "in the summer. But I don't know if you noticed. The Hudson River isn't exactly the ideal place to surf. And the winters? I don't know if I could handle it."

"But all the food," I say, trying to make a case for New York.

He laughs. "They have restaurants in LA, you know. Like, a lot of them." He pauses for a second. "What about you?"

"You mean when I win?"

He nods, picking up a steak fry.

"I think I'll stay here. I mean, there's a campus in Miami, but that's not my scene."

"And New York City is?"

"I think it could be."

"You're from the South," he says, like he's reminding me. "You know this hot weather isn't going to last forever."

"Yeah, but winter doesn't last forever either, right?"

"Two days of winter and I would be on a plane home. I might be the wrong person to ask."

We sit in silence, letting the first real conversation we've had settle down around us.

"Have you thought about going to school in California?"

"Too many earthquakes."

"Florida has more hurricanes than California has earthquakes."

"Yeah, but you can see a hurricane coming and decide if you want to leave or hunker down. Earthquakes just pop up and surprise you."

"So no California," he says, sadness slipping into his voice.

I look down at my sandwich and make a point of pushing it away. "And no New York for you."

"No." Hakulani sets his plate on the floor next to him. "So what does that mean?"

I'm so glad he doesn't just dump me right now.

"I don't know. I mean, no matter what happens, we're going to be on opposite sides of the country."

"And busy trying to break into the business," he adds.

"And broke," I remind him.

"That goes without saying," he says with a hollow laugh.

"So," I say, the word hanging in the air. Even though I thought I wanted this to be a mutual breakup, I also don't know how to end it.

"How about this," Hakulani says, sounding a little more cheerful. "Instead of taking whatever this is any further, we end on a high note with the Landmark Challenge win, and we walk into the next competition as friends."

"Good friends," I say in agreement.

We finish our food in silence, soaking in the night sky as the cameras mark the moment our fake relationship evolved into a true friendship.

CHAPTER THIRTY-ONE

ONE OF THE DRAWBACKS OF BEING THE LAST GIRL standing is that I'm the *only girl*. While the boys are playing pool and hanging out, I could really use a chance to talk to someone about feelings and boys—and feelings about boys. But instead I sneak into the kitchen for a lunch consisting of two apples, a cheese sandwich, and a bottle of water before going back to my room. Maybe I should be spending time with the guys, who, from the sound of it, are still playing pool, but there's something nice about taking it easy—especially since our next competition starts tonight.

After my breakup with Hakulani last night, I came back to my room to find two garment bags waiting for me on my bed, but I was too wiped out to even look at them. I just picked them up and put them in the closet so I could curl up in bed for a while. Now, I walk to the closet and check out what's inside. I pull out one labeled with today's date and the number "1," and the other bag has tomorrow's date and the number "2." I lay bag number one on my bed and unzip it; inside I find a classic yellow A-line dress with a full skirt.

I can't lie. I feel like a princess. Right up until I slip on the heels and get the feeling like I'm walking on stilts. Still, looking at my reflection, I do not look like poor girl from Florida. Sweeping my hair up off my neck and trying to pull it into a pretty updo or fancy ponytail, I really wish Inaaya were here—she would know what to do with it. Whatever the next challenge is, it must be fancy. Remembering we get to keep the clothes from the show, I try to think where I could wear something like this back home, and I draw a blank.

I leave my room and head down the hall, lifting my skirt up a little so I don't trip on the hem.

"Wow," Paulie says when he sees me. "You look incredible."

"Thank you," I say, looking at the guys, who are all dressed in black suits. Looks like I'm not the only one whose wardrobe has gotten an upgrade.

"Not too bad yourself," I reply, reaching over to straighten his tie.

Word about Hakulani and me must have gotten around because he seems to be in a better mood. Maybe Hakulani was right about him, but I internally shake my head and try to focus on the competition. I'm too close to the end of the show to get distracted and involved with someone else. Plus, I can't even imagine how Caitlin will spin me in a second romance.

For the first time, Jessica shows up at the apartment. "Are you guys ready for a trip to Broadway?" she asks. "Because I am."

"Broadway?" Malik asks, standing up. "We're going to a show." He looks down at his outfit. "That makes more sense."

"Not just one show," Jessica says. "But two. One tonight and one tomorrow afternoon."

"Which ones?" Paulie asks.

Jessica shrugs. "I guess you'll find out when you get there."

He doesn't have to say anything else. We head straight to the elevators and down to the waiting bus.

Except when we reach the street, there's no bus. Instead, there's a stretch limo waiting for us.

"A limo?" I say, my eyes wide with disbelief. Now I really feel like a princess. "I've never been in a limo before."

"It's your lucky day," Paulie says as the driver opens the door. "Ladies first."

I slip in, sliding across the smooth leather until I'm next to the window.

Hakulani comes in next, making sure to sit as far away from me as the car will allow. Last night, after the breakup, we wanted to make sure we didn't give the network any more footage than we already had. Even though we're both aware that they can cut the scenes together however they want. But for tonight, we're friendly, but at a distance.

Paulie steps in, sitting next to Hakulani. Malik sits down next to me. He glances at me and whispers, "My first time in a limo, too."

I grin. "The perks are almost worth the fear of getting cut."

"I know, right?"

The limo weaves through traffic until it pulls up in front of the Richard Rodgers Theatre, home of my repeat playlist three years running, *Hamilton*. I reach over the back of the seat, gripping Malik by the shoulder.

"They better not be messing with us," I say, bouncing in my seat. My voice is so light and quiet, I sound like a little girl. I don't even care, because if I had a bucket list, this would be at the top.

He pulls his shoulder away and gives me a look that tells me to chill out.

"Sorry," I say. "But it's *Hamilton*."

He looks at the others before leaning closer. "I feel the same way. I've watched all the Ham4Ham online."

"Then why aren't you more excited?" I ask as the driver gets out of the car and walks around to Malik's side.

"Because I look good in this suit, and bouncing around like a giddy fool messes with the look." He points to the camera placed along the light bar.

"Right. I should have known they would be filming us in here, too."

He nods. "You can get away with it because you're a girl, and girls always jump up and down and clap."

"We do not."

He cocks his head to the side and gives me a hard look.

"Okay, maybe *sometimes*, but this time, the moment really demands excitement."

The door swings open and the driver holds it for Malik to exit. When he's out, he turns back and offers his hand to me. "My lady," he says, giving a slight bow.

I laugh as I accept it and step out, careful not to trip on the curb. "Thank you, kind sir."

Instead of dropping my hand, he tucks it in the crook of his elbow.

"I'll act as your buffer tonight," he says, giving a nod behind us as Hakulani and Paulie follow.

"Thank you."

I only met Malik a few weeks ago, and I realize that it actually bothers me a bit that we're down to the last week and I'm only just now getting to spend more time with him. Then again, I've been with Hakulani a lot this last week, and so I can imagine why someone wouldn't want to be the third wheel. Plus, he's been alone since Adam left, so I'm sure that was hard when the rest of us still had our roommates.

In front of the sign advertising the show, Jessica is waiting for us.

"Do you think she gets paid really well for the hosting gig?" I ask Malik just before we step out.

"Huh? Probably. Why? You thinking about going for the hosting gig for the next season?"

I make a face. "No! Good lord, no. She seems to like doing it, that's all."

Out on the sidewalk, we're pushed into a small space next to Jessica. People walk by us, giving a quick look at the camera crew, but once they realize they don't know who we are, they just keep walking.

Just as we're about to start filming, a young woman walks up to Jessica and asks for her autograph. She seems genuinely surprised but signs the woman's notebook and poses for a picture before waving as the woman walks away.

"That could be you someday," Paulie whispers, stepping into line next to me.

"Or you," I say. "Can you imagine just minding your own business and a fan comes up to ask for your autograph?"

He shakes his head. "I can't even imagine having fans."

"Right? So weird."

Jessica turns back to us, her face slightly flush. "Okay, let's get started."

"Hey, Jessica," Hakulani says. "How come you never gave us your autograph?"

"You never asked," she says. "Don't worry. It won't be long before I'm asking for yours."

Paulie and I look at each other. *So weird*, we mouth to each other.

The red light turns on and Jessica begins her intro.

"It's Broadway, baby," she says, her smile sparkling. "For the next challenge, you are going to look for inspiration from one of New York's most famous streets."

I can't contain my excitement, and I hop up a little as I start clapping. So much for playing it cool—if Dani were here, she would be having a field day.

"Someone's excited," Jessica says with a laugh. "And you all should be. This weekend you are going to see two of Broadway's hottest shows. Tonight you'll be seeing *Hamilton*, and tomorrow you get to see the matinee performance of *Waitress*."

I clap and try to refrain from cheering, but I can't stop a soft "woo!" from escaping my lips. Of all the cool things we've done so far, this is hands down the coolest.

Jessica hands us our tickets.

"Front mezzanine, row A?" Paulie says with a whistle. "These are some of the best seats in the house."

Jessica leads us up to a side entrance where a stagehand checks a list and lets us in. "We need to get some shots of you in your seats for the show," she explains. "So you're going to get seated a little early tonight."

She leads us up some stairs to the entrance to the lower mezzanine. "Here we are."

The usher greets us cheerfully and leads us to our seats. I latch on to the railing to steady myself and glance up, first seeing the camera filming our arrival, but my eyes slide past the crew to the stage. "Wow," I say, stopping so suddenly that Malik staggers to avoid running into me.

I look over my shoulder. "Sorry," I say quickly and begin walking forward.

"These seats are great," Hakulani says, leaning over the rail of the mezzanine and looking down. "You can see everything." He sits back, trying to find a comfortable pose. "The chairs are another thing altogether."

Malik and I laugh as he shifts.

"I guess the theater wasn't expecting a Hawaiian culinary star to show up," I tease.

"Well, I guess I'll deal with it," he answers with a wide smile.

I start reading the playbill, scanning the bios of the cast and crew. I'm vaguely aware of the crowd beginning to fill in around me.

"I'm glad we got to come in early," I say. "I'm just not sure why."

The lights flash, warning the theatergoers that the show is about to begin, and the camera crew begins to pack up and head out.

"You're leaving?" Malik asks.

"Can't film in the theater," the boom operator says. "House rules."

"I highly support those rules," I say, sitting back in my seat. As the opening notes float throughout the theater, I allow myself to be transported to the early days of New York City and the beginning of the United States. During intermission, Malik and I trade opinions on the times and the themes that are still relevant today—and not once did I think about the competition. The second act is as good as the first, only more heartbreaking. At the curtain call, I stand and cheer, along with the rest of the audience.

Back on the street, none of us can contain our excitement.

"It was so good," I say for probably the hundredth time. "I love how so many of the cast had double roles, and they completely transformed from one act to the next."

"Like the actor who played Peggy and Maria?" Hakulani says in agreement. "I almost didn't recognize her."

And that's how the conversation goes the entire way back to the apartment. Each of us recounting our favorite scenes or lines and, of course, there was singing. I don't even care if they use the footage from tonight.

If we're supposed to design something around one of the shows we see this weekend, I can't imagine that *Waitress* is going to inspire me more than this show.

CHAPTER THIRTY-TWO

TURNS OUT, I WAS WRONG ABOUT THE EFFECT
Waitress could have on me. The show is about a woman in a small town who makes amazing pies and is trapped in a loveless marriage with a man who's wasting his life. As the house lights go up, I don't move. For this show, we're sitting in the front row. With no one between us and the stage, it was like I was watching my possible future play out in front of me. Okay, yes, the show ends on a hopeful note, but it's still exactly what I fear will happen to me.

"Are you crying?" Paulie asks. When I don't answer, he leans forward. "You *are* crying."

"I don't want the cameras to see me," I say, looking down the row at the PA motioning for us to come with him. Malik and Hakulani stand and move down the row. "I don't want them to film me like this."

Paulie takes one more glance at the PA and then grabs my hand. "Come on," he says as he drags me in the other direction, weaving between the other theatergoers.

"Where are we going?" I ask, surprise replacing my mixed bag of emotions.

"Just keep up." We follow the crowd to the far end of the lobby, allowing ourselves to be carried away by the mass of bodies. When we exit the Brooks Atkinson Theatre, instead of heading to the waiting limo, Paulie leads me down the block and around the corner to Broadway. From there, he grabs my hand and leads me down the stairs to the subway.

"Where are we going?" I ask.

"Somewhere the cameras can't follow," he says. "Do you still have your card for the subway?"

I stop for a second and motion to my outfit. "No pockets."

"Right. It's nothing. I have enough on mine for both of us." He swipes his pass, and then hands it to me to use. Once we're through the turnstile, he pulls me along as he races to catch the train before it leaves.

Breathless, I lean against the pole in the middle of the train as the doors shut. Paulie lunges into the car, his body pressing up against mine.

"You okay?" he asks, pulling back. "I didn't mean to crush you."

"I'm fine," I say, shifting my body to grab the pole as we begin to move.

"Are you *really* okay?" he presses.

"Not now," I say, looking out the windows as the lights blur by. With each stop, people get on and get off, moving around me, but I don't say anything.

"What's with you and Hakulani?" Paulie says gently.

"Nothing," I sigh.

"Were you using your relationship to get a little extra screen time or something?"

There is a bit of an edge in his voice, and I feel like this is a trap or a trick question. "No—"

"Because he said you were."

I groan inwardly: definitely a trap.

"Okay," I say, rubbing my hands over my face. "Are you going to let me talk or not?"

"Are you going to tell me the truth?"

Our voices are getting a little louder as both of our tempers start to rise. Being in the line of fire of Paulie's quick responses sucks. "The truth is complicated."

He shakes his head slowly and turns forward. "The truth shouldn't be complicated. By definition, it's supposed to be straightforward."

"Sure, in a perfect world," I say, waving my hand around the car, "but this isn't a perfect world. It's not even the *real* one."

He scoffs at me. "At least we can agree on that."

The train rolls to a stop and the doors hiss open. A few people get out and come on, and Paulie and I just watch them—each of us lost in our own thoughts.

"Okay," I say softly, once the train starts moving again. "Hakulani and I weren't really in a relationship—not exactly. We were both in a tough spot and we found a way to help each other get a little further in the competition. But in the end, neither of us wanted to get to the finals by lying, so we ended it." I look at my hands folded in my lap and then over to him. "Honestly, I'm surprised he even told you that we were in a relationship."

Paulie looks down, his face a little sheepish. "He didn't tell me that exactly."

"What did he tell you?"

"That you guys were hanging out together—in a G-rated relationship kind of way."

"And?"

"That it was over."

"And?"

He doesn't answer right away, but then he sighs and says, "And that was all I heard because I might have walked out of the room and slammed the door in his face."

I sit back. "That seems a bit dramatic, don't you think?"

"No, I don't." He shifts in his seat, twisting to face me.

"Why not?"

"Oh, come on, Peyton."

I can hear Hakulani in the back of my mind, but I silence him. If Paulie does like me, he is going to have to say it—I'm tired of playing games.

"No. What, Paulie?"

"Because I *like* you, okay? And I was hoping, after the show, that we could hang out or whatever."

"Why didn't you say something?"

He looks at me like I've just sprouted a second head. "Because of the show. And the scholarship."

I open my mouth to say something, but then close it. On day one, I thought that Paulie was supposed to be the player of the group, but I realize now that I've seriously misjudged him. In fact, he might have been the most kind and thoughtful person on the show after Inaaya.

"What was the tough spot?" Paulie asks, his voice quiet.

"I can't," I say, shaking my head. "Not right now, okay?"

He watches me for a second and then nods. "Okay."

We sit in a more relaxed silence for a few stops, watching the train gain and lose passengers. I look at each person and try to imagine what their life is like—where are they going tonight? Are they in love with someone? What are their dreams and hopes? Then Paulie's voice breaks me from my reverie.

"This is our stop," Paulie says, taking my hand and standing close to me as we wait for the doors to open. Unlike the tunnels in Manhattan, we step out onto a platform high above the street. "Come on," he says, pulling me to the stairs.

"How far is it?" I ask, allowing him to pull me along.

He doesn't say anything as we cross the street. "We're

here," he says, nodding toward the red-and-white checkered sign.

"Vinnie's Pizza and Grinders? Why this place?"

"Just go in," he says with a laugh. "You aren't the only one with secrets." He leads me through the front door; a bell jingles as we walk in.

"Sorry, folks," a voice from the back calls. "We're closing in a couple minutes."

"Uncle Vinnie," Paulie calls out. "Surely you can stay open for family."

A head pops through the kitchen door. "Paulie?" he says. "I thought you were off being a hotshot TV star."

"I am," Paulie says. "But even the best food in the world can't compare with one of your pies."

"You are a liar," he says, "which makes you the best nephew I have."

"Gee, thanks, Uncle Vinnie," a second voice calls out.

Paulie stretches his neck like he can see behind the wall. "Is that Cyrus?"

Uncle Vinnie comes out into the dining area, followed by a guy who could be a dead ringer for Paulie.

"Yes, it is," Paulie says as the two hug.

"Man, I thought I wasn't going to see you."

"When do you leave for Chicago?"

"Wednesday."

"And they still have you working here?"

Cyrus gives Paulie a knowing smile. "You can't stay at Uncle Vinnie's without throwing some dough around."

Vinnie gives Paulie a big hug before turning to me. "You gonna introduce your girl?"

Paulie groans. "I'm so sorry, Peyton," he says before introducing me to his family.

"Don't take any of his crap," Cyrus offers as he shakes my hand.

Vinnie, on the other hand, forgoes the formality and gives me a big hug like we've known each other forever.

"Uncle V," Paulie says. "You can't just hug total strangers."

"When you're in my place, you're family."

"I'm not sure that's how the rest of the world sees it," Paulie counters. "I know you guys are closing up, but I was wondering if we could hang here for a little while."

Vinnie gives Paulie a hard stare. "Why?"

"We just need a place to get away from the show."

"Are you on the show, too?" Cyrus asks me.

I nod.

"Very cool. I hope you're teaching my cousin a thing or two."

"Actually, he's taught me a lot," I say.

"That's my nephew."

"She's exaggerating," Paulie says before turning to Vinnie. "So can we hang for a little bit?"

"As long as you prep some dough for tomorrow. It'll keep your hands busy so your hands don't get too busy, if you know what I mean."

Paulie's face turns a deep shade of red before, luckily, Cyrus saves the day.

"I think we can trust the honorable Paulie, don't you think Uncle V?" he asks as he leads Vinnie to the back and out the door. Before he leaves, he adds, "But as the person who has to prep tomorrow, I would greatly encourage you to stretch the dough." And then they're gone.

"I'm so sorry about my uncle," Paulie says, and he's so embarrassed I can't help but laugh.

"It's fine. I mean, a little over the top compared with what I'm used to, but it was cool to meet some of your family."

"Yeah. Cyrus lives in Chicago. He's just here for part of the summer."

"Must be nice to get to see him."

"It is, but that's not why we're here," Paulie says, turning to look me in the eye. "What happened back at the theater?"

I point at the counter. "Can I sit there? It's a long story."

"Sure. Just don't tell my uncle," he says, grinning.

I smile. And then I tell him. About my dad. About the deal with Hakulani to try to stay in the competition. About Caitlin and how she manipulated me to get better ratings, and how the musical we had just seen was the manifestation of everything I fear for my future.

"I had no idea," Paulie says as he picks up a ball of dough and starts pressing it out with the tips of his fingers. "I didn't realize all that was going on."

"Caitlin never talked to you about storylines?"

Paulie shakes his head. "She only talks to me during the challenges sometimes."

"Huh," I say. "I wonder why."

"What are you going to do now?" he asks.

I hop down off the counter, almost falling as my shoes catch a patch of flour and slip a little. Paulie catches me before I can embarrass myself too much. He holds me for a second or two more before letting me go.

He clears his throat. "You okay?"

I nod, but my head is swooning. Spending time with Haku-lani was fun and easy, but as much as he makes me blush, Paulie makes me feel safe.

"What were we talking about?" I ask.

"What you're going to do now that you and Hakulani have ended your charade and everything," he reminds me.

"I don't know. Finish the contest. See what happens next. But right now, I think I'm going to learn how to throw pizza dough in the air."

Paulie laughs. "You think you can learn how to throw in a night?"

"How hard can it be?" I ask. "You learned."

"Wow, you're going to come at me like that? In my uncle's shop?"

I roll my shoulders, never breaking eye contact with him. "Would you please teach me how to throw pizza in the air?"

"Do you need to catch it?"

"That would be preferable."

He grabs a dough ball and puts it down in front of me. "Wash your hands."

When my hands are clean, I compare the size of our dough. "How come yours is bigger?" I ask.

"Baby steps," he says before showing me how to prep the dough.

My first attempt ends with us waiting for the dough to drop from the ceiling. It doesn't take long, but it's long enough for Paulie to mock me for my earlier comments. The second attempt is a little better. The third attempt lands on Paulie's head like a cake covered in fondant.

"I just can't allow you to injure any more dough balls," he says as I poke a hole in the dough for his eyes, nose, and mouth. He promptly removes it from his head and shoots it in the trash like a basketball.

"Hey," I said. "I was using that."

"For everyone's safety, I think this lesson is over."

"Not cool," I say, taking a small handful of flour and tossing it at him.

"Hey," he shouts, and the seriousness in his voice takes me by surprise. "Watch the clothes."

I'm so focused on trying to tell if he's joking or serious that I don't see the spray of flour until it hits me on the side of the face.

"Are you kidding me?" This time I don't hold back and let him have a full blast of flour full on in the face.

"Oh. It's like that?" he asks, flour floating in the air with every word.

I try to say I'm sorry, but I'm laughing too hard, so all I can do is back away.

He raises his eyebrows, or at least I think he raises his eyebrows. It's kind of hard to tell with the flour clinging to his features, which just makes me laugh harder. Without looking away, he picks up a bowl of flour and starts toward me, holding it with both hands so it hangs over my head. I sober quickly once I realize that he is serious and start pleading for mercy. I keep backing up and squirming to find a way out as Paulie toys with me, an evil smile on his face like he can't wait to give me my just reward. Then, just as he's about to dump it, I reach up and tip it back toward him. The metal bowl clangs to the ground, and the look of shock on his face is too much for me to handle. I bend over at the waist, tears turning the flour on my skin to paste.

"I give up," he says.

"Yes! I win. I win," I say, dancing around him. I should have remembered that my shoes and flour don't mix, because a minute later I'm falling again. And just like before, Paulie catches me.

"You okay?" he asks.

I am very aware of his arms holding me up. I get my footing back and stand, my head inches from his chest. Looking up, our eyes lock. My breath is the only thing I can hear in that moment. That is, until he says, "I think I'd like to kiss you now."

I nod slowly. "I think I'd like that."

And then he does.

His warm lips meet mine and the rest of the world fades away. I feel myself lean against him, my hand resting above his heart and I swear it's beating in time with mine. The kiss lasts just a few seconds. It would have been longer except Paulie pulls away suddenly and spins me around so that his back is facing the glass window.

"How did they find us?" he hisses, and I peek over his shoulder to find the red light from hell.

CHAPTER THIRTY-THREE

WHEN PAULIE FINALLY OPENS THE DOOR, IT'S NOT just a camera crew, but Caitlin, too. I expect her to lay into us for taking off, but she's so happy she managed to catch me kissing someone on film that she laughs it off.

"How did you find us?" Paulie asks.

"Do you really think we would let you run off in the city without a way to track you?" she asks.

Paulie pats himself. "Did you put a tracker on us?" he demands.

"In your shoes," she says. "Don't worry. We've only used them when you were unsupervised. Now, if you don't mind, let's get this cleaned up and get on the road." She pulls out her phone and makes a call. "A cleaning crew will be here soon. You might want to let your uncle know, in case he wants to supervise."

Paulie picks up the cordless phone and punches in a speed dial.

"How did you know that?" I ask.

"You think Cy is the only one who has put in hours here? For everyone in the family, it's practically required to spend a summer slinging pie." After talking to his uncle, Paulie hangs up. "He'll be here in a few minutes," he says.

"We'll wait on the bus," Caitlin says, walking to the door and holding it open for us.

The thought of stepping up on the bus turns my stomach. Hakulani and I just ended our fake relationship, but that doesn't mean he's going to be okay with this sudden turn of events with Paulie.

My worry is wasted. Hakulani gives us a slow golf clap as we walk down the aisle. Malik just grins at me, but I know he's going to want details.

Paulie and I sit in silence as we wait for his uncle. "Be back," he says.

I move to watch the exchange through the window. It doesn't take long and ends with his uncle giving Paulie a big hug.

I move back to our seats as he steps back into the bus. When he sits, I ask, "Was he mad?"

"Nah," Paulie says. "He just asked if you were worth it."

"You're kidding?"

"Nope. My uncle's a romantic."

"What did you tell him?"

"The camera crew got it all on tape. Guess you'll have to wait to find out."

I lightly punch him in the arm. "Rude."

He looks at me with wide eyes. "Me? I'm not going around kissing a guy one second and then punching him the next."

"Shut up," I say, crossing my arms over my chest.

Paulie takes my hand, interlocking our fingers together, but says nothing. In fact, he doesn't say anything else until he walks me down the hall of the apartment, stopping at my door.

Turning toward me, he looks into my eyes and I see gold specs in the center of his dark brown ones.

"Goodnight," he says, his voice low and husky.

"Goodnight," I repeat, very aware that my palms are starting to sweat.

Paulie puts his hand on the side of my cheek and leans in, gently kissing me on the lips before pulling back. "See you in the morning."

I nod, but don't say anything. He sidesteps me and heads for his room.

When I shut the door behind me, I feel a pang of sadness. I would give anything to have Inaaya here so I can process what just happened and to have someone who will get excited with me. Heck, even Lola or Dani would be okay by me. I smile as I gather my things for a shower. With every step I take, flour falls off me, leaving a faint white dust everywhere. Okay, maybe not Dani.

The next morning, when we load up in the bus, Hakulani gives me a huge I-told-you-so grin before he climbs in, and then

Paulie follows, coming to sit right next to me. He leans over and quietly tells me what happened after we said goodnight. Apparently, after he left me in the hallway, Paulie and Hakulani sat down and hashed things out, however guys do that stuff.

The drive to the studio seems like the shortest one yet somehow, and the next thing I know, we are getting ready to get off. Hakulani and Paulie have already left, but Malik, unable to resist any longer, stops me before I get off. "So, you and Paulie?" he asks, giving me a grin. "It's about time."

"Shut up," I say, but I'm smiling back at him.

He holds up his hands in surrender. "Hey, I made this call during week one. I mean, Hakulani's good-looking and all, but Paulie is the right one for you."

"I'm glad you think so."

Jessica meets us in the studio, and she doesn't look happy.

"What's wrong?" I ask her as we get closer.

She smiles, trying to fool us, but she fails. "We're going to get started in a few minutes," she says, her tone clipped. "Go ahead and line up."

When we're lined up and the camera begins rolling, Jessica takes a deep breath and pastes her smile on her face. "Over the weekend you were all treated to two Broadway shows, and I hope you had a great time."

"Best weekend ever," Paulie says, and I look down to hide my silly grin.

Jessica's smile falters. "I'm glad you think so. But today's twist is that the challenge is a surprise elimination round."

My stomach drops. This close to the end?

But Jessica isn't done. "And it's not just an elimination, but—" She pauses letting the anticipation build. "—It's another *double* elimination."

My smile evaporates. "You're not kidding?" I ask before I can stop myself. "Another double?"

I look at the others and see that they are as shocked as I am.

"*Always* expect a twist," Paulie says.

Jessica gives us a minute to settle down before continuing, the multiple cameras panning to catch each expression. "For today's challenge, you will be creating a layered cake based on one of the Broadway shows you saw over the weekend. You'll have six hours to complete the challenge."

As upset as I am about the double elimination, the fact that it's a baking challenge means that I have a chance of making it to the finals. For a moment my nerves are replaced with excited butterflies—*the finals*.

"All right, the beginning of the semifinal challenge and your six-hour time starts . . . Now! Good luck," Jessica says and we move to our kitchens, still stunned from the announcement.

Yesterday, I thought it would be hard to pick the show to use for inspiration, but in this moment, the choice is obvious. I gather three pie pans and six deep round cake pans, as well as another mixer. Then I start sketching out my idea as well as listing all the ingredients and any special things I'll need to make sure this dish is a success. I run to the pantry, grabbing as much as I can before the others get in here and start taking what I need.

Jessica, seeing all the extra supplies I'm getting, comes by my station with the cameras in tow. "Hey, Peyton."

"Hi. Wild twist, right?"

"You have no idea," she said. "But I'm more interested in what's going on over here."

Jessica really is a good host.

"I am planning on making pie dough and three different cake batters."

Jessica looks at me in confusion. "I get the cake batters, but why are you making pie dough?"

I grin at her, but I keep my eyes on the measuring cup. "You'll see. It's something I've always wanted to try but never have."

Her voice betrays her surprise. "You've *never* made this before?"

"Nope."

"And you're going to *try* it during the semifinal round?"

"It's a little crazy."

"It's a lot crazy," Malik interjects from his station. "I like it."

Jessica smiles at him before turning back to me. "I see you

have key limes, which we all know I love, but you also have strawberries, marshmallows, and whipping cream. Honestly, Peyton, I have no idea what you're doing."

"Go big or go home, right?"

"I guess. Just keep an eye on your time. The cake has to be ready in six hours, including decorating."

"Got it."

As I ice my cake and prepare to place the fondant decorations on, I feel more myself than I have since I got here. More who I want to be. When I stand in front of the judges and present my cake, I don't think I've ever been prouder of a creation.

"What is it?" Angelica asks.

"A piecaken," I say. "Think of it as turducken, but with cakes and pies." I realize I am risking offending Angelica's sensitive palate, but if that happens, so be it. She's been telling me to think outside of the box, and it doesn't get more creative or inventive than a piecaken.

Billy looks confused. "But where's the pie?"

I laugh and the PAs bring out a tray with three pieces of each layer. "The pie is baked and then baked again inside the cake. The decoration is inspired by the musical *Waitress*."

"Why did you pick *Waitress*?" Jessica asks. "I thought you were uber excited about *Hamilton*."

"Oh, I was," I assure her. "In fact, when *Waitress* ended, I thought there was no way I was going to use it as my inspiration."

I turn to face the judges. "The main character was so much like me, it was scary. I watched my greatest fear play out on the stage. When it was over, I hated it."

"What changed your mind?" Billy asks.

I think for a minute before answering. "The more I thought about Jenna, the main character, the more I realized she was stronger than I was giving her credit for. She took her situation in life and found the courage to change it. Not to a fairy-tale ending, but to the best one she could make happen. There was so much more to her than I could see."

"Like this piecaken?" Billy asks.

I laugh. "Exactly."

"Tell us about it," he prompts.

"Sure. The first layer is key lime pie in a vanilla bean cake."

Billy looks up. "Your famous key lime pie."

"Not famous yet, but I'm working on it," I tease, and he laughs.

"Next is a lemon pie in a strawberry cream cake, and the third is a chocolate cake with a sugar cream pie center."

"The combinations are pretty simple, don't you think?" Angelica says, but this time I'm prepared for her.

"Some people might think they are simple. The combinations I selected stand up well on their own, but when you pair them together, the textures mingling in each bite, they create a culinary experience that is completely original."

"I couldn't agree more," A. J. says, licking the back of his fork.

I watch as Angelica takes several bites of each layer. To my surprise, she looks at me and says, "It's not bad."

My mouth gapes open. That has to be the nicest thing Angelica has ever said to me. And, yes, the bar is pretty low when you figure the first day we met she threatened to send me home, but today, I'm going to take her "not bad" and own it.

After everyone else presents their cakes—all of them had a variation on *Hamilton*—we're sent back to the waiting room while the judges make their decision.

No one says anything as we wait. I know I left everything out on the floor, but as I look around the room, I can't help but wonder if it was enough. Did I meet the expectations of the judges?

I can tell everyone is as nervous as I am. Hakulani is tugging on his puka necklace, and Paulie is reading the emergency evacuation instructions that are taped to the wall while bouncing on the balls of his feet. And Malik is lying back against the couch, his eyes closed, but I know he's not as chill as he likes people to think.

"They're ready," the PA says, and we walk, in silent single file, back to the set.

Jessica smiles at us. Maybe a little too brightly, and we try to mimic her for the sake of the camera.

"This is it," she says. "The two remaining contestants will

square off tomorrow in the finale." She pauses and I take a deep breath, knowing her perfected pauses are going to feel like forever. "The first person advancing to the finale is . . ."

Come on, Jessica, just tell us already.

But the pause continues, and I look at Malik and Paulie, who are standing by my side. I wrap my arms around their waists and feel Hakulani's long arm reach behind Malik, his hand coming to rest at the nape of my neck.

Everything gets quiet as we wait. And then Malik's expression changes instantly when Jessica calls his name.

"Me?" he says, obviously stunned. "For real?"

I give him a congratulatory hug as Hakulani slaps him on the back. "You deserve it," he says.

Paulie echoes his congratulations.

As Malik takes his place next to Jessica, the only thing I can hear is the beating of my heart. I prepare myself to not hear my name. I chant a plea that I won't cry over and over. It's during that time I completely miss Jessica announcing that I'm advancing to the finale, too. It's not until Paulie lifts me up and swings me around that it becomes real.

There's no time for me to say everything I need to before Hakulani and Paulie are rushed out of the the kitchen by the PAs, but I catch Paulie's gaze just before the swinging door closes.

And I totally cry.

CHAPTER THIRTY-FOUR

THE APARTMENT IS EERILY QUIET WHEN WE GET BACK.

"Do you want to have a slumber party on the roof?" I ask Malik in the elevator.

"Sure," Malik says, standing in the doorway of the master bedroom.

"What are you doing?" I ask, giving him a hard look.

"It still smells like Dani."

I laugh, leaning around him to sniff. "It really does. I have to find out what she wore because it has staying power."

"Either that or she's haunting you from the outside world. Meet you on the roof in ten," Malik says.

"Raise a glass?" I say, holding an imaginary cup in the air.

"Raise a glass."

I head back to my room and grab everything I need for a quick shower. Nine minutes later, I'm in comfy PJs and heading up the stairwell. By the time I get to the roof, Malik has already claimed the comfortable couch by the fire.

"Dang it," I say, flopping down in the one across from him. "How did you get the tea done so fast?"

"Made it before we left," he says. "Just in case."

"Can you believe they switched everything up?" I ask. "It's weird."

He sits up and pours a glass. "All I know is we are still here."

"I'll drink to that," I say, taking the tea he offers me.

When his is full, he lifts it in the air. "To the two loves of Peyton Sinclaire."

"Shut up," I say. "It's not like that."

"Oh really," he says, laughing. "Just promise me that when this is all over and the cameras go away, you're gonna tell me what it *is* like."

"I will. Swear."

He nods. "I was really glad it was the four of us at the end."

"What, you didn't want Dani to stick with you to the end?" I say, teasing.

He shrugs. "I don't know. She was pretty cool to me. I don't know what it was about you, but she could be ruthless."

"Yeah, I know, I was there."

"Funny thing was, when you weren't in the room, she was chill as hell."

"Really?" I say, confused. "I just assumed she was talking about me behind my back."

"Nope. Only to your face."

"That is weird."

I lie back and stare up at the sky. "Did you really think you would make it this far?"

"Yes," Malik says.

"Really?" I ask, turning to look at him.

He looks me dead in the eye and shakes his head at the same time he says, *"Yes."*

I laugh, the exhaustion of this experience audible. "Yeah. Same."

"So, is this how it's going to be all night? Is your strategy to keep me up so I'm too tired to kick your butt tomorrow?"

"No, but it's a good idea."

Silence settles between us as we listen to the buzz of New York City at night.

"Hey, what happened yesterday?" Malik asks.

"What do you mean?"

"Well, one minute you're right behind us, and the next minute you and Paulie are nowhere to be found. Then Jessica had to call Caitlin, and she was pissed."

"She didn't seem that way when we saw her."

"Of course not. You gave her a fairy-tale first kiss that's going to make every guy puke and every girl develop a false idea of what a kiss should be like."

"And here I thought my key lime pie was my legacy."

"What really happened?" he presses.

"I don't know. But something in that show really struck a nerve, you know? That waitress could easily have been me in ten years, and I felt like the world was spinning out of control. Paulie helped me get away from the cameras."

"I get that," Malik says. There is a pause as we both relax and let our minds wander. "So what's next for you?"

"I have no idea."

"Well, you know I will always have a couch for you for whenever you want to visit."

"Oh, you think you're going to win tomorrow?"

"Maybe. Doesn't matter if I don't. I'm not planning on ever going back to Alabama—there's no place for me there."

"What about your family?"

"I think I'm more of a city boy," he says.

"If you don't win, you're just going to . . . what?"

"Get a job, find a place to live. Not as nice as this, obviously, but something. I'll figure it out."

I lie down on my back, my eyes still taking in the night sky. A few minutes later I hear Malik's breathing slip into a quiet, peaceful rhythm, so I head back down to the bedrooms and grab blankets and pillows. When I return, I drape one of the blankets over Malik and settle in for the night.

From beside me, I hear Malik mumble, "I called it, Florida. First day. You and me to the end."

"You never told me that," I say.

"Well, I thought it."

"Looks like you thought right. And in less than twenty-four hours, it will be all over."

"You nervous?" he asks.

"No," I say, shaking my head yes.

"Me neither."

After a few minutes, I hear his soft breathing and wait for sleep to finally win out.

CHAPTER THIRTY-FIVE

WALKING INTO MY DRESSING ROOM THE NEXT morning is a startling and tear-jerking experience. The first thing I see is the unmanned camera planted in the corner. The second thing I notice is the crisp white chef's jacket hanging on a shepherd's hook. The third thing I see is the walls, normally unadorned, now sporting a series of photographs from the past few weeks.

"Oh my gosh," I whisper, looking at each image. However, the girl who is the focus of each picture is someone I barely recognize. I remember feeling nervous and in over my head, but the girl in these pictures, sporting a turquoise jacket, doesn't look like that. Her head is held high and her smile exudes confidence. I move, frame by frame, studying every one of them for any hint of insecurity. There's even one picture of Angelica taking a bite of my piecaken, and her face is one that can only be described as delighted. Why couldn't I see that then?

Slipping my arms into the white jacket that has replaced

my turquoise one for the finale, I take a deep breath and close my eyes. A quick rap on the door lets me know that it's time to head to the set. I take one more moment to enjoy the calm before I embrace the storm of emotions and frantic energy of the kitchen, then I turn and leave my dressing room. When I enter the hallway, no one is there. In fact, I don't see another person until I reach the double doors leading to the set and see Malik standing there.

Malik gives me a quick nod before turning his attention back to the swinging door.

The PA pulls open the door and gestures for us to enter.

A few minutes later, the set lights up and Jessica looks straight into the camera and says, "Today, weeks of hard work will be put to the test as our finalists compete to find out who is the Top Teen Chef.

"Let's take a look back on their road from home cooking to the battle of their culinary life."

The lights dim and our final packages play on the screen at the back of the room. I watch the season flash in front of us and groan to myself as the shots of my disastrous first competition play out. Malik doesn't hold back and actually laughs, which seems to be okay with the producers because there is not an order from the disembodied voice that tells us to be quiet. As the film fades to black, I wipe away a tear that has managed to escape.

"So here we are," Jessica says, looking warmly at us both.

"Final two, baby," Malik says.

A voice booms through the studio. "Not so fast."

Malik and I look at Jessica in confusion. This is the finals. Surely they wouldn't put a twist in during the finals? I look around for any clue of what's about to happen.

Jessica smiles at us. "There might have been one thing we didn't mention. A little side competition, if you will. Little did you know that, behind the scenes, our past contestants have been taking classes in another part of the city, and one of them has earned a second chance redemption."

"Are you kidding?" Malik asks.

I can't even speak.

Angelica motions for us to look toward the swinging doors. "And the redemption contestant is . . ."

"Please be Paulie," I mutter under my breath.

The doors swing open.

"I'm back."

Dani.

"Son of a—" I say, before someone cuts off my mic.

"Cut," the disembodied voice says. The entire set erupts to make room for Dani's kitchen station but my eyes are trained on Jessica.

I'm so focused that I don't see Dani heading toward me. She grabs my elbow and spins me around.

"Hey," I say, trying to shake her off.

"We need to talk," she says, reaching up under my jacket and ripping the mic jack out of the battery pack.

"No, *we* don't need to talk," I say, tugging my arm but unable to get her off me. "You're hands are like vise grips," I complain.

"Just shut up and don't draw attention to us," she says, pushing the door to the waiting room open and leading me toward the bathroom.

"What the hell, Dani?" I say, finally able to free myself. "You've been horrible to me ever since we got here and now you make this surprise return and drag me off like you know where a dead body is and you need me to help you bury it."

"I owe you an apology," she says, her eyes locking onto mine.

I did not expect that.

"Excuse me?" I say. "You owe me what?"

"I treated you so bad, and I am so sorry."

"I don't understand."

She sinks down into one of the nearby seats. "I thought you knew."

I'm still clueless about what she's talking about. "Knew what?"

"That we were supposed to be rivals on the show."

"Rivals?" I ask, still not getting it.

"Yeah, you know, spoiled socialite with a famous chef for a father versus the trailer park Barbie."

"Oh," I say, starting to comprehend.

"Caitlin said you knew and were on board."

I laugh. "Caitlin says a lot of things."

"Peyton, you have to believe me. I would never have said any of those things if I thought for a second you believed I meant them."

"Well, assuming this is all true, I have to hand it to you. You played your role perfectly. But I'm curious, how did you figure out I was out of the loop?"

"You didn't use your advantage against me."

"I didn't use it against Lola," I correct her.

She nods. "I get that. But if you were really gunning for me, you would have used it anyway. When you didn't, I started putting the pieces together."

"So was there really a secret competition?" I ask.

She shakes her head. "When I got cut, Caitlin told me to stick around. That she wanted to resurrect my spot. I told her I had plans with my dad and couldn't do anything after today."

"Which is why she decided on a double elimination for the last challenge."

Dani's eyes widen. "Are you serious?"

I nod. "Oh yeah. Hakulani and Paulie both went home yesterday."

"I didn't know. I swear. I bet she brought me back thinking that it would cause some sort of drama."

"What do we do?"

She shakes her head. "There's not much we can do. Part of our contract was signing a nondisclosure agreement that says we can't bad-mouth the show, the network, or anyone associated with the show or the network."

"Oh course it does. But I was talking about today," I say, wiping my hands on my jacket.

"I don't know. Do we play along or get real?" Dani looks up at me, waiting for me to come up with some kind of answer.

I shrug. "I really don't know."

"If Caitlin finds out I told you, neither of us stands a chance to win. And I'm fine with that, but I heard you telling someone that you really needed this scholarship, and I don't want to wreck it for you."

"Then I guess we keep up the charade," I say. "For one more day."

"There's one more thing," she says, looking nervous again. "Caitlin made me a deal last night, and I wanted to tell you about it."

"What kind of deal?"

"The kind where I win the finale."

I lean against the wall because I'm not sure I can handle whatever she's going to say next. "What's in it for her?"

"Ratings," Dani answers. "Dad said she pitched this show on the premise she could pull off the entire show in less than three weeks. She told the network it was going to bridge the gap for those teen foodies who also want drama and conflict."

"And then she made sure there was both."

Dani nods. "Pretty much. Also, there's an automatic advantage."

"Really? And does this have something to do with your winning the show?" I ask.

"You are correct."

"So what is it?"

"The whole cast is coming back."

"Are you serious?"

The hope and excitement in my voice must have been too obvious, because then Dani huffs out a sigh and says quickly, "Focus. Any minute now they're going to realize your mic isn't working. If they haven't already."

"Sorry."

"The deal is, each finalist can select one of the eliminated cast members to be our sous chef. If I pick Paulie, Caitlin promised she would make sure I won."

"Because Paulie and I are . . . I don't know what we are, but we are something."

"Yeah."

I look at her. "Thank you. I really appreciate you telling me."

"I couldn't stand it if you thought that was the real me."

I half laugh, half sigh. "I'm not sure any of us were ever able to be the real version of ourselves."

"Good thing we have our lives to figure it out." She reaches under my jacket to plug my mic back in. "For what it's worth, I hope you win," she says before reconnecting me.

CHAPTER
THIRTY-SIX

WE RETURN TO THE SET AND STALK AWAY FROM
each other. When Dani walks near Caitlin, she mutters something, and whatever it is, Caitlin smiles with satisfaction.

"What's that all about?" Malik asks.

I look up at the cameras before answering. "Who knows?
But she better stay away from me."

"Yeah," Malik says slowly, looking from Dani to me and
then back. "Doesn't matter, Peyton. We beat her once, and we
can do it again."

"Yeah, we can. Time to get ready to crush her."

The disembodied voice calls us all to the front where Jessica is waiting to do her introduction one more time.

She smiles into the camera and says, "Welcome back to
what is already shaping up to be a surprising finale to *Top Teen
Chef.* We have three finalists who are ready to do everything
they can to win the title and the culinary scholarship that goes
with it. But," she says, holding up one finger and shaking it

slightly toward the camera, "before they do that, there's one more twist we want to throw at them."

I steal a glance at Dani, who is looking straight ahead.

"Your advantage is just outside the doors."

We all turn our heads toward the swinging doors, waiting for the too-long pause to end. When it does, the doors swing open and in walk all the eliminated contestants.

Even though I know it's coming, my eyes widen, and I clasp my hands over my mouth in surprise and excitement as Adam, Inaaya, Lola, and Hakulani enter. Paulie is the last to enter the set, and I can't stop the stupid happy grin from taking over my face.

We turn back as Jessica resumes talking. "Each of you will have the chance to select a sous chef to assist you in this last, crucial challenge."

I swear I am going to pass out if they make us do an extended pause.

Jessica pulls out the bag she used during our pairs elimination and I notice Dani flinch with recognition. "Inside this bag are three tiles with numbers on them. Reach into the bag to find out the order in which you will choose your sous chef. She approaches Dani, offering the bag to her.

Dani reaches in, feeling around for a moment before pulling out the number "1."

"Lucky draw," Jessica says, moving to me.

I reach in and pull out the second choice tile, leaving Malik with the third choice.

Jessica hands off the bag to a PA and returns to her spot. "Dani, you drew the number one choice, so who are you going to select as your sous chef?"

I'm not ready to say that I've forgiven Dani. I mean, she came clean with everything that happened before, but words still have consequences. However, I know how cunning and ruthless Caitlin can be, so I don't want Dani to take on Caitlin and feel like no one has her back.

She looks up, her jaw tense. "I would like Lola as my sous chef."

I let out a long breath and steal a glance at Caitlin to see her reaction. All she does is shake her head ever so slightly when Dani looks at her, but Dani doesn't hide her response. She shrugs her shoulder and gives Lola a big hug as she joins Dani, and then they walk to their station.

When Jessica asks who I pick as my sous chef, I don't worry about the pause. I immediately answer, "Paulie!" which gets a laugh from the rest of the cast, so I guess the secret is out.

Paulie smiles wide as he makes his way over to me, and we turn to face the cameras again as Malik selects Adam as his second in command.

"For those remaining cast members who won't be cooking today, we have seats for you on the set so you can see everything," Jessica says, raising her arm to indicate that everyone else should have a seat.

"Today," Jessica says, after everyone is settled, "the rules are simple: Make us something divine. Take everything you have learned and put it on a plate. You have three hours to complete this task, and then you'll have to face the judges." Jessica gives us all one final look, and then says, "And your time begins now."

And with that, the final elimination challenge begins.

"So," Paulie says, "what are we going to make?"

"When I think back about this experience, winning will be the highlight of it, of course," I say with a straight face.

"Obviously," Paulie assures me.

"But the thing that I will take with me beyond that opportunity is you guys—my friends."

"Friends that you ultimately have to crush for your own success, but . . ." Paulie teases.

I place both hands over my heart. "You get me. That is so precious."

"So what about your friends?" he prods.

"You guys helped me grow. It seems like we've been together for so much longer than just a few weeks, so I want to throw a party," I tell him. "A rooftop dinner party for eight."

"I like it."

"Here's the plan," I say, grabbing a pad of paper and pencil. Paulie watches over my shoulder.

After watching me for a few moments, Paulie says, "Peyton, I like your style."

I give him a smile, take a deep breath, then divide the list of supplies in two, before we race off to get our ingredients. After we return to our station, we are a whirlwind of chopping, straining, and stirring, occasionally bumping into each other as we complete each task. And every time, I blush before ducking my head and pretending to look for a mixing bowl or focusing intently on what I'm doing until my face cools off.

"You know the cameras are catching everything, right?" Malik whispers when we almost collide at the ice cream maker.

"I have no idea what you're talking about."

"Oh, okay," he says, mocking me.

"What are you making?" I ask, watching his purple concoction slowly fall out of the machine into the waiting bowl.

"Ube ice cream," he says, grabbing a spoon from a nearby cutlery caddy. "Try it."

"That is not only a gorgeous color, but the taste is mind-blowing," I say, trying to snag another bite, but Malik shoos me away. "Will you please teach me how to make it someday?"

"Maybe," he says. "If you stick around after I win."

"So, when you said we could take Dani, what you really meant was you were coming for both of us."

He grins. "Kinda surprised I had to spell it out for you."

"Nice," I say, pretending to glare at him.

"Good luck, Peyton," Malik says, before grabbing his bowl of ube ice cream and rushing to the blast chiller.

"Back at ya!"

When I get to my station, Paulie has several pots simmering. I breathe in. "I know I'm jinxing myself, but this all smells amazing."

"Well, the genius is in your menu."

"So win or lose . . ."

"It's all your fault."

"For the record, not the kind of support I need right now."

"Mental note made."

By the time Jessica announces there are five minutes left, Paulie and I are so in sync we don't even speak as we prepare the plates.

"This is great," he says.

"Let's just hope it's enough."

"Time," Jessica calls on cue as all six of us stand back, our hands in the air. Then a wave of relief washes through all of us, and we all laugh and let out huge sighs, swiping sweat—and maybe a tear or two—from our faces. Then the rest of the cast comes over, and for a brief minute we are together as a group, celebrating the end. No matter what, we've all cooked our asses off.

"Peyton," Jessica says once we all settle down and the rest of the cast has returned to their seats. "Would you please step forward and present your meal?"

I glance at Paulie and smile. Here goes nothing.

"You got this," he says, giving me a thumbs-up.

Stepping forward, I begin. "Being on this show has changed me in ways I could never have imagined. I have been challenged on so many levels. And when I think about the past few weeks, I know the one thing that will shine the brightest is the friendships that have come out of this experience. So, when selecting the menu for today, I wanted to celebrate that friendship by planning a dinner party.

"For the soup course, inspired by my friend Adam, who almost has me convinced that I could survive without meat, I present a cold melon and basil soup." After what Caitlin did to him, I figure the more that people say his name, the less likely it is that she can edit him out of the show completely. I look to Adam, who gives me a tiny golf clap and a big grin.

"Next we have a Tex-Mex shrimp wonton appetizer for my friend Lola, and the salad course is a chickpea salad, which is inspired by Inaaya, the best roommate ever."

I give the judges time to taste the first three courses and make their notes. There are no comments or bantering this time, just quiet chewing and the beating of my heart thundering in my ears. When Angelica motions for her plate to be taken, I introduce the main course.

"For the entrée, I have prepared a grilled flatiron steak topped with a mango and herb salsa, with a side of rosemary and thyme potatoes. This dish is inspired by Hakulani and Paulie, who, while very different, complement each other so well. And, of course, you can't eat all this food without some good old-fashioned sweet tea."

"That's me," Malik says, and the entire set erupts in laughter, myself included.

Unlike previous rounds, none of the judges ask any questions, and so I stand there while they eat. A. J. occasionally raises his eyes and nods his head, but as for the rest, they're playing things pretty close to the vest. I glance over my shoulder at Paulie, who is watching Angelica particularly closely. Finally, it is time for the final dish.

"For dessert, you have a chocolate cupcake with passion fruit cream filling. This is for Dani, who is also more complex than meets the eye."

The judges eat every bite of the little cake, even Angelica. Then they write a few notes, glance at each other, and begin their feedback.

"Peyton Sinclaire," A. J. says. "I wanted to say your full name because around the kitchen, we don't really use last names, but your name is one that people need to remember. I've been in the food business my entire adult life, and never before have I met such a talented pastry chef who is constantly ready to learn something new." He turns to the other judges. "I had the cast over to my new place last week, and Peyton spent the entire time with my head pastry creator, and he couldn't stop talking about her willingness to listen and take direction. He never talks about anyone I hire like that." A. J. turns back to me. "When you're ready, stop by and see me. When Rex sees someone with untapped potential, I'm smart enough to listen to him."

"Thank you, chef," I say, absolutely astonished. Did A. J. just offer me a job at Prima il Dolce? I glance over at the cast members sitting along the side of the set, and they're cheering silently for me. I try to catch my breath and stop the tears of joy as I listen to Billy's critique.

"When you first stepped foot in the kitchen, I wasn't sure what to make of you. You were timid and unsure with your dishes, and you were woefully undertrained. But like A. J. says, you take the notes we give you, and every week you've made progress. I think you have a bright future ahead of you, and I'm looking forward to see where you land."

Can too much praise make you pass out? Because I think I'm going to.

Of course, Angelica is the last to speak, and I brace myself for what, I'm sure, are going to be very brusque comments. "Peyton, I don't know what to say. I have watched you struggle to find your place in this competition, and I could list every flaw I've found with your cooking from day one . . ."

My heart sinks, and suddenly I feel like I'm going to pass out, but this time from shame.

"But tonight," she says, shaking her head, "this meal is perfection. We asked you to find your passion and infuse it into your cooking and that is exactly what you did today."

Did I hear that right? Is Angelica actually giving me a compliment? I can't hold back the waterworks, and I have to look away to wipe a tear from my eye. To my surprise, Angelica rises from her seat and comes down from the judges' table to give me a hug. It's so out of character that I'm concerned she might have been taken over by body snatchers.

"You have truly found who you are as a chef, and that is a gift," she says in my ear. "Don't squander it. Find a place where your passion is valued. It will be worth it."

I nod my head as she pulls away. In my wildest dreams, I never could have imagined that this moment could happen.

Standing next to Paulie, I feel his hand on the small of my back as he leans in and whispers, "You crushed it."

I don't say anything because I barely trust myself to speak.

Malik and Dani present their dishes, and then it's time for the judges to debate the winner. However, this time, instead of us leaving, they are the ones to exit the set.

The disembodied voice calls, "Cut," and Inaaya is beside me in an instant, pulling me into a hug.

"I've missed you so much," I say, half laughing, half crying.

"It's been less than a week."

I pull back from her and stare at her meaningfully. "I have so much to tell you."

One eyebrow arches up. "Oh, really?"

I smile and tell her, "Yeah, but later."

"You better," she says.

The rest of the cast comes out, offering congratulations and just generally basking in the reunion. And for the first time since we got here, everyone is getting along. The die has been cast, and we've all been a part of something bigger than ourselves, and it's kind of awesome.

We continue to mingle until the judges return. Then, in an instant, the set goes quiet and everyone returns to their marks without being told.

"The judges have made their decision," Jessica says. "Dani, please step forward."

Dani does as she's asked, with her head held high. She could have taken the easy way out. She could have done what Caitlin asked her to do, and there would have been nothing any of us could have done to stop her. But she was better than that, and I hope, when the show is over, we can start a real friendship.

"Dani, I'm sorry, but the judges have not selected you as the next Top Teen Chef."

Dani nods her head. "Thank you for the opportunity," she says, before walking over to where the rest of the cast is waiting for her, arms open to welcome her.

I reach down and grab Malik's hand. Final two. Just like he predicted.

I look up at Malik. "Who would have thought?" I say quietly.

"Malik and Peyton," Jessica begins. "I have watched you both take the notes you've been given and apply them, week after week, striving to be better. Your dishes tonight are a testament that you have not only taken advantage of your time here, but your time in the city as well, allowing it to become a part of you. The ability to pour your experiences into your food is the sign of a truly talented chef."

I feel a rush of pride, even though I'm pretty sure someone wrote all those nice things for her to say.

"But," Jessica says, "only one of you can win the title of Top Teen Chef and the scholarship that goes with it."

Billy steps forward. "Malik. Peyton. This is the moment you have been working toward since your first day on this stage. The winner is . . ."

Just. Say. It.

I glance at Malik, and I'm pretty sure he's holding his breath, which reminds me that I should probably breathe before I pass out. Any day now, Billy. If you take another second, my heart is probably going to stop.

"Malik."

Instinct takes over and I clap my hands and hug my very stunned friend. Yes, I am very much aware that I didn't win.

However, there will be plenty of time for me to feel upset later, because right now this moment belongs to Malik.

"I'm sorry," he says into my shoulder.

I laugh and give him a nudge. "No, don't be sorry. You won and you earned this." I push him toward Angelica, who is holding one of those huge checks with his name written on it.

The stage explodes with activity; the other contestants descend on him with congratulations and hugs.

While everyone's attention is on Malik for the moment, Paulie stands close by until I lean into him and he gives me a hug. "You okay?"

"Do you want my honest answer?"

I feel him nod and my throat feels like I swallowed fire.

"It really, really *sucks*."

CHAPTER THIRTY-SEVEN

THE DISHES CLINK TOGETHER AS I PICK THEM UP and carry them to the sink.

"Timer, Peyton," a voice bellows from the kitchen.

"Thank you," I say, pushing open the swinging door and heading out.

"It's hard to be the pastry talk of the town, isn't it?" A. J. says from the other side of the diner's counter.

"Be easier if your boss didn't keep booking weddings and other special events in his wildly successful den of decadence," I counter.

"You came to me, remember?" A. J. says with a laugh.

"It's fuzzy."

"Then let me remind you. It was about a week or two after the finale of *Top Teen Chef.* You walked up and gave me some sad story about trying to make it in the big city, but man, life is so hard, and you could really use a job. You said that you'd do anything—wash dishes, sweep the floor, anything. Ring any bells?"

"Well, I *am* getting a headache, so bells might be involved."

"Whatever," he says, swiping at the air in front of him with a laugh. "Anyway, you're still good for this weekend, right?"

"Oh course," I say, picking up a sack of flour to refill my supplies.

"There are a lot of people coming to see you. Food TV is doing a whole spread on the one-year anniversary of Prima il Dolce's opening."

I pull open the oven door and begin slinging pies onto the metal table behind me. "Yes, A. J., I will be there. Have I ever let you down?"

"No," he says with a laugh. "Even when I call you in on a big day because we've run out of pies—again."

"Hey, Peyton," one of the waitresses out on the floor calls out. "You got a fan out here."

I walk through the kitchen and into the diner. "Where?" I ask, wiping my hands on a towel and then folding it neatly into my apron.

"Table twelve," she says, pointing.

"I know where table twelve is," I say, teasing, before giving the little girl a big smile.

"Are you Peyton?" she asks shyly.

I kneel next to her. "I am."

She hides her face behind her hands and giggles.

"Go ahead," her dad says, giving her a slight nudge.

Then she takes her hands from her face, sits up straight, and holds out a napkin and pen in her hands. "Can I have your autograph?" As soon as the words are out of her mouth, she buries her head behind her dad, one eye peeking out.

"I dare you to leave here without it," I tease, taking the pen and napkin from her and scrawling the signature like I've done this a million times—which I guess I have by now.

Well, I've *practiced* my signature a million times. In the privacy of my Brooklyn apartment. That I share with Paulie and Malik. Who also make fun of me endlessly for leaving my signature lying around the apartment on scraps of paper and the corners of take-out menus.

"Here you go," I say, sliding the napkin back to her.

"Thank you," she says sweetly. "I was hoping you were going to win."

I look her in the eye and give her a gentle smile. "Me too."

"She recognized you right away," her mom says as I stand up.

"It's the hair," I laugh. "Enjoy your meal, and I hope I'll see you again sometime."

I weave through the busy diner and make my way back to my locker to change. Grabbing my backpack and garment bag, I head for the exit, stopping by A. J.'s office and popping my head around the door. "Hey, I'm heading to class now," I remind him. "And I've got a big test to study for, so I won't be in tomorrow, okay? I left more than enough pies on the cooler."

"Have fun in class," he says without looking up from his orders and paperwork.

"Thanks," I say, turning and heading out the back door near the bathrooms and making my way to the busy sidewalk.

After the show, I obviously didn't get the culinary scholarship to the American Culinary Institute, but that didn't stop me from applying to other schools. It takes thirty minutes to get from the diner to school, assuming the trains are running on time, so I should make it there in time today. I take a second to give my little fan a wave through the window and then head into the crowded streets of New York. As I wait for my train, I study the poster in one of the countless promotional frames scattered along the subway walls. Eight teens, all dressed in white chef's jackets, are standing in a line, looking directly at the camera.

The next season of *Top Teen Chef* is about to start, but I don't know whether I should be happy for them or I should send them a sympathy card. Maybe with Caitlin no longer working on the show, it won't be so bad for them.

Hearing the announcement for my train, I wade into the waiting crowd. I snag an open seat and pull out my tablet to watch the latest trends in confectionery. It's something to pass the time, and one of these days I'm going to find a new technique that Rex hasn't seen before. It's becoming my life's mission to keep learning and improving.

I walk the four blocks to campus and jog up three flights of stairs to the locker room.

Spinning the dial on my locker, I open the door and drop my backpack in before pulling out my white chef's jacket. I place the garment bag on the hook. As I slip my arm into the sleeve, someone's chin sets down on my shoulder, and then I hear:

"You're late."

"And yet I beat you here," I say, spinning around.

Paulie opens his locker and grabs his jacket. "You were baking pies at the diner this morning, weren't you?"

"How could you tell?" I ask.

"You smell like sugar and cinnamon, so it was either apple or peach today."

I laugh and close my locker, giving the lock a spin. "You're wrong."

Paulie gives me a look.

"It was *both*," I say, making a face.

He waits for me to pull my hair back before falling in step with me on our way to class. "You ready for this afternoon? Did you remember to grab your dress?"

"Yep." I groan.

"Are you sure you wouldn't rather go home and sleep?"

"I didn't know that was an option," I say. "But no, it'll be fun to walk down memory lane."

"We can remember how it all began," Paulie says, taking

my hand and kissing it gently before we head to our different classes. "Have fun in chocolatier class," he says, trying to get under my skin.

"Enjoy Rump Roast one-oh-one," I say back.

Two hours later, when class is out and we're on the train heading to Manhattan, I lean my head on Paulie's shoulder. He smells faintly of herbs. "Are you happy with the way things turned out?"

He looks up from the chart he is studying and down at me. "You mean when I didn't win the scholarship?"

"Yeah, but I was thinking more about how lucky you were to meet me."

He pretends to think about it before planting a kiss on the tip of my nose. "I can't think of a more perfect ending. Or beginning."

ACKNOWLEDGMENTS

Writing a book often feels like a solitary process to me. Until I sit down to write the acknowledgments, and the list of people I need to thank grows exponentially.

At the top of that list is Britny Brooks-Perilli, editor extraordinaire. Thank you so much for taking a chance on a book that found its way to you via Twitter. #MSWL works! I am so lucky to have you as a partner on this project. You were the perfect combination of taskmaster and cheerleader. But through everything, you never stopped believing in Peyton or me, and I can never thank you enough. If not for you, I am not sure this book would have made it across the finish line.

To Julie Matysik and everyone at Running Press, including Michael and Frances, thank you for all the behind-the-scenes work you did for *Whisk*. I especially want to thank Mike McConnell, whose eagle eyes made this book so much more than it would have been without him.

When I first learned *Whisk* was going to get an illustrated cover, I was excited and a bit nervous. But when I saw the sketches by Laura Pacheco, I was smitten! Thank you so much for taking my words and turning them into visual art. It is a dream come true and I will forever be a fan!

Whenever I am overcome with doubt and anxiety about my place in the literary world, I know my amazing agent will be there to push me to be the best version of myself. Thank you,

Liza Fleissig, for knowing when and how hard to push me and, more important, for never letting me give up on myself. These words do not do justice to how much of an impact you have had on my life, but they are the best I can do without turning into a bumbling mess. You are so much more than an agent to me. You are my friend, and I am blessed by this.

Over the last several years, I have been so lucky to spend time with librarians and teachers around the state of Indiana. You remind me daily that books and the words that are in them can make a difference in a student's life. Thank you for sharing my books with your students. I am so humbled by the support you have given me over the years.

While writing *Whisk*, I was blessed to be a part of an amazing critique group. It's because of the YA Cannibals that Peyton's story became a fuller version of the original. Laura Martin, Jody Mugele, Rob Kent, August Mugele, Ed Cho, and my agency sister, Lisa Fipps—thank you for your relentless feedback and your never-ending support. No matter where we go in the future, know that I am always here for each of you and I will shout about all your future success from any mountaintop you choose . . . but seriously, maybe pick a sledding hill. One where I can drive to the top. We all know, in the zombie apocalypse, I will be one of the first to go because of "cardio."

While I love all my YAC family equally, I need to call out Shannon Lee Alexander especially. Thank you for always being there when I need a friend to lean on or to vent to or just talk with about being a swim mom. Please know that I am always,

always here for you. If you try to run, it will only end in a cage match. And you know I have been planning for that my whole life, so it's just easier to be my friend.

To Sarah Cannon, Jessica Owens, Annie Sullivan, Gail Werner, Liz Osisek . . . my MWW friends have become my PAY sisters. I am so grateful for your support, not only in work but in life. While none of us are probably going to be TikTok famous, each of us is on our own journey and I would not want to travel with anyone else! Love you all, and I will chat with you on Friday . . . or is it Sunday? Someone send a link.

On the first day we met in person, I used you as a human shield to hide behind when I was about to fangirl over a certain author. I never imagined that you would become one of my favorite people in the world. Anna-Marie McLemore, you have inspired me, humbled me, and supported me since before our debuts, and I can never express to you what your friendship means to me. Be kind to yourself and know that you are more than enough.

I have been blessed to find a theater community that was willing to let a novice work the lightboard! To my KidsPlay and Crazy Lakes Acting Company family, I am always inspired by your commitment to the arts and your support of me! I cannot wait until I can dim the lights of the theater with you again!

Erin Vetters . . . I can't express enough how much you inspire me! Whenever I got tired of working on this project, I would draw from your strength and perseverance and rest in the idea that there is nothing we can't overcome to achieve what we want if we're willing to put in the work! I miss our walkie-talkie banter and look forward to the next production!

To Megan Coffin and Sarah Stutz. Thank you for letting me be your adopted senior mom this year. I know how appreciative you were for all the goodies. As my final gift to you, I wanted to let you know how much it meant for me to get to share in your very weird high school graduation experience. No matter where you go or what you do, I will always be cheering for you. Have faith in yourself and never stop reaching for your dreams. You are both amazing young women, and I am honored to know you.

I do not know if I would have survived the final months of finishing this book without the Secret Pool Party Sisters and Corey keeping me sane. Between Yahtzee over Zoom and, of course, the Friday night socially distanced face-to-face time next to the pool, the laughs, and the conversations that brought us closer, it is a bright spot of 2020! Thank you, Mary, Marie, Vicky, and Corey. You were the best bubble mates a girl could have!

Some people swing into our lives and then dash out, leaving a mark, but not a lasting one. Then there are the ones who dance into our lives and never leave. Becky, you have been a constant in my life for my entire adulthood . . . which I know is only like two or three years. Isn't it amazing how time stopped when we met? In all seriousness, I am so proud of how you have handled the curveballs that have been thrown at you over the last several years. Your perseverance is a testament to your strength. Thank you for always being there when I need you. Lazy river days are in our extremely near future.

Sometimes we need a friend who will tell us how it is and not apologize for it. Other times we need a friend who will get down in the mud puddle with us, even after working a twelve-hour shift. How lucky am I to find both of those qualities in you, Shannon F? Some would say I am incredibly lucky. I would say that I have been blessed. Thank you for being willing to not only go down the rabbit hole with me but also pull me back when I go too far.

It is sometimes in the most unexpected places that you find that person who is so much like you, it's kind of scary. For me, that would be the parents' waiting room at dance class. Amber, thank you so much for basically forcing me to let you volunteer in the school library. That one act sealed our fates. From coaching some outstanding BotB teams to the hours we spend on the phone flipping our hair, it is almost like we're the same person. Almost. Thank you for being my 99 percent friend. You mean more to me than I could ever express.

To my fierce sister, who always leaves me in awe. I love you so much and am always amazed at your commitment and determination to live your life on your terms. You might be a badass on the outside, but you still inherited some of Gram's grace. And to Luna and Xyla, Aunt Gigi can't wait to see you again.

I would be remiss not to mention my mother, without whom I would not be here today. Literally. I hope those days in labor have finally paid off. I love you so much and will always be grateful for your support. Thank you for helping me become the woman I am and being there when I need some redirection.

Everything in my life has brought me to where I am today, and I wouldn't change much . . . I might live closer.

Keegan and Cooper, what can I say to you that will convey how much you have changed my world? Keegan, as I watch you turning from child to young man, I want you to know that I love you so very much. Even when I wake you up before sunrise for swim practice. Know that there is nothing I would not do for you, even if it means making you do things you think you don't want to do. I am so excited that I get a ringside seat to watch you grow into the man you will be. Cooper, the world can be an overwhelming place. Trust me. I know. But I am so proud of the way you approach life. How you throw yourself into your love of the arts, how you are willing to try something even if it's hard, and how you always keep looking for the good in people. You are a loyal friend, and I am lucky to call you son. Never stop looking for the joy in life. Thank you both for letting me hug you a little longer than you might like, and for those nights of snuggling that are becoming rarer and rarer. I know my job as your mom is to raise you to be the best people you can be, and I am happy to do it, but you will always be my babies.

What do you write to tell the love of your life how much he means to you? Louis, you are my Paulie. You are the person that makes me believe I can be whatever I want to be. You make me better, and after all these many years, you still surprise me. You are the person who knows me like no one else and does not back away from the dark parts. I love you so much. Thank you for loving me back.